Praise for Jane's Previous Novels

Close Enough is a journey of heartbreak and celebration. Ms Vollbrecht has done it again. She has taken her newest novel, *Close Enough*, out of the realm of just another lesbian story and has woven a saga about real people, their joys and their sorrows, their searches for self through the twists and turns of this thing we call life. It is a page turner from the beginning to the end. This reader found herself unable to put it down. The characters are flesh and blood, so much so they become part of the reader's family. Their problems and set-backs demand the reader's full attention, and their happiness is cause for celebration and tears of joy. Congratulations to this author for a job well done.
~**Violet Jones**, on Amazon.com, July 2007.

If Jane Vollbrecht were a baseball player, her batting average would be close to 1000. *Close Enough* is another home run for readers.

Close Enough is a family saga that begins in 1942 and continues into the mid 1980s. Over a hundred people are mentioned in the book, but the major characters soon sort themselves out, the rest fade into the background, and readers are left with the key players whose lives are intricately connected. Vollbrecht has a knack for developing realistic characters no matter how brief their appearance, and she makes her main characters unforgettable.

Vollbrecht causes you to visualize all the important features of each decade as it pertains to the heroine of the book, Frannie Brewster. Although this is a multi-layered story, the primary quest is accompanying Frannie as she uses faith, determination, and the love of those closest to her to reach closure in the one area of her life that has never been resolved.

Why did Frannie's mother give her up for adoption? Will she ever find the answers after 42 years, 4 months, and 5 days of wondering? Or will she have to settle for answers that are merely close enough. You won't have to settle, however, in your search for good reading. *Close Enough* is as close to real life as it can get and still be fiction.

~**K. C. West**, co-author of *Superstition Shadows, Celtic Shadows,* and the soon-to-be-released *Greek Shadows*.

In Broad Daylight is a great story and so much deeper than the "run-of-the-mill" stuff that is out there. Older women lead vital lives with fascinating stories; I'm glad to see that sort of character in this book.
~**Brenda Adcock**, author of *Pipeline, Reiko's Garden, and Redress of Grievances*

Most books in this genre follow a general formula. First, two beautiful women meet; either one or both are wealthy. They fall in love. While or after falling in love, they deal with some kind of troubling situation, then they ride off into the proverbial sunset and live happily ever after. While that approach is enjoyable most of the time, *In Broad Daylight* is so much more creative and intriguing. It holds the reader's attention from cover to cover, delivering two full stories at once.
~**K. Johnson**, on Amazon.com, June 2007

In Broad Daylight is a story of dichotomies. Vollbrecht has written a genuine lesbian romance while providing a critique of that very genre. But beyond that veneer, she provides a profound examination of how our secrets lead to lives lived in darkness. Through this novel, she shows how we have reached the point where literature by and about lesbians can move beyond the darkness of the bedroom and into the light of everyday lives. In this book, Vollbrecht shows us that in unbinding the hidden parts of ourselves, we ultimately win the freedom to fully live in plain sight – in broad daylight.
~**K. L. C. Smith**, Toronto, Ontario

Bev:

Sing your song, all
the way
through the
Second Verse.

Thanks for your friendship
and support!

Jane Vollbrecht

Jane Vollbrecht
08/2010

Yellow Rose Books

Nederland, Texas

ISBN 978-1-932300-94-9
1-932300-94-5

First Printing 2008

9 8 7 6 5 4 3 2 1

Cover design by Donna Pawlowski

Published by:

Regal Crest Enterprises, LLC
4700 Highway 365, Suite A, PMB 210
Port Arthur, Texas 77642-8025

Find us on the World Wide Web at
http://www.regalcrest.biz

Printed in the United States of America

Acknowledgments

Each successive book further proves to me that it takes many people to bring a book into being. I would like to express my appreciation to at least some of the key players who helped with this one.

To Alicia Gutierrez, muchos gracias for your help with the dialogue in Chapter Ten.

To Mary and Trinka, I'm grateful to you for jumping in late in the process to help with the final version.

Brenda Adcock repeatedly assisted me in redirecting the storyline and also provided much needed guidance for me in crafting the characters. A mere "Thank you" is inadequate, but it's all I know to say.

Donna Pawlowski has my gratitude for designing the book's cover.

My deepest thanks to Ruta Rudzirs for her careful review of the final version of the manuscript. She greatly improved the book you hold in your hands (and saved me from a total meltdown.) Thank you, my friend.

I'd like to acknowledge assorted (unnamed) members of the medical profession—to those of you who do your jobs well, you amaze me; to those of you who seem to forget that you're treating people and not illnesses, please get a clue.

To the readers who have contacted me with their praise for my earlier books, please know that your encouragement is often the only thing that keeps me at the keyboard.

My siblings, Tony, Paul, and Kathy, continue to be my rock and my refuge in a world where predictability is difficult to come by. Thanks for letting me be your little sister.

And finally, to Cathy LeNoir, my publisher, thank you for your vision in creating Regal Crest Enterprises so that books like mine might have a home.

For Quentin and Soph's only daughter.
They're proud of you, and so am I.

...music heard so deeply
That it is not heard at all, but you are the music
While the music lasts.

T.S. Eliot, *The Dry Salvages, Stanza V*

Chapter
One

"DID YOU BRING your journal with you, Gail?"

"Yes. Not much new or different in it, though."

"Change is gradual, incremental." Doctor Marcella Wilburn adjusted her wire-rimmed glasses and tucked her hair behind her ears. "You won't notice much from one day to the next, but when you look back over the whole journey, you'll see you've come a long way." She uncrossed her legs and then crossed them again with the opposite leg on top.

For at least the hundredth time in six months, Gail Larsen wished she'd have had the good sense to find a different therapist. Problem was there weren't many to pick from in the hills of eastern Tennessee. If she were willing to go forty miles north to Knoxville or sixty miles south to Chattanooga, she'd have had a much larger pool to draw from, but lately, it was all she could do to persuade herself to drive to Sweetwater; she knew herself well enough to know she'd never make it to her appointments if they necessitated long drives to get there.

The psychologist glanced at her watch. "We've got about fifteen minutes left. Why don't you go to your first entry after your last visit here?" Doctor Wilburn suggested. "Pick a line and read it out loud."

"Wilburn pissed me off again today." Gail betrayed no emotion as she read. "I'm glad it's the insurance company's money and not mine."

Doctor Wilburn rearranged herself in her leather chair. It squeaked like a series of tiny farts. It had happened so often in her sessions with Doctor Wilburn that Gail had taken to thinking of it as the Wilburn Sonata in F-Flat.

"What did I do that angered you?"

"Who knows? All it says is I was annoyed." Gail gestured at the page in her journal. "Don't feel special. Two lines later, I say the same thing about the checker at the grocery store, and in the next paragraph, I blast the President and everyone who voted for him."

"It would seem that you're still struggling with some issues involving anger."

Please don't let her say 'and you know anger is often fear wearing a mask.'

"Anger is usually a safer way of manifesting a deeper emotion."

"So you've told me, Doctor."

"Do you think that might be the case?"

"If you're asking me if what I'm really feeling is fear, I'd have to say no—which is what I've told you every time you've asked me that in the past seven months."

"You're not having any problems with fear?"

"Isn't that what I just said? But ask me the same question a third time, and I can show you what anger looks like."

"Maybe you should read me something else from another page of your journal."

Gail flipped forward in her spiral notebook. "July sixth. Called Scranton. Mrs. Adler was an asshole, as usual."

"What else did you write that day?"

Gail read from the page, "I'm not some stranger who's asking questions for the hell of it. Would it kill her to tell me how Marissa is doing?"

"Did she tell you anything about what's going on with Marissa?"

"Does Howdy Doody live at the Vatican?"

"How did that make you feel?"

Fire flashed in Gail's eyes. "Didn't we have this conversation the last time I was here? How do you think it made me feel? This whole mess is my fault. If I had made us do living wills when we talked about it, none of this would be happening."

"But you didn't. And remember, Marissa could have taken the initiative to get her legal documents completed, so you're not really to blame."

"Might as well be. I'm paying the price."

"So is Marissa."

"Thanks for the reminder. I'd almost forgotten."

"Why do you think you should carry the responsibility for this?"

"Because there were lots of things I should have done differently, and now both Marissa and I are trapped in endless living hells." Gail laughed derisively. "Separate hells at that."

"Would it be any better if it were the same hell?"

"Yes!" Gail snapped. "No," she amended. "I don't know."

"What's your ideal picture of this situation?"

"That's a stupid question."

"You're entitled to your opinion, but I'd still like you to tell me what you'd change about this circumstance."

"Everything."

"So you'd change having met Marissa and falling in love with her?"

"No, of course not."

"But you said you'd change everything."

"I meant her having polio. The accident. Her parents taking her back to Pennsylvania. Her being kept alive by machines."

"You realize, though, that if you could change any single detail, every other detail would likewise be changed."

"What's wrong with wanting life to be good again?"

"Nothing. And I'd like to think that the time you're spending with me in these sessions will help you find your way back to feeling that life is good again."

"But it will be life without Marissa. How can life be good without her?"

"You tell me. What would it take?"

"All this chasing in circles isn't doing me any good, Doctor Wilburn. The short answer is I want what I can't have, so what's the use?"

"My short answer for you is to learn to want something else."

"Thanks for the advice." Gail looked toward the window, the view blocked by the thick sheers covering it. "Doctor Henry said I needed a note from you, or she won't refill my Zoloft prescription."

"How do you feel you're doing with your depression?"

I swear I'll slap her if she says 'anger turned inward on yourself is usually the cause of depression.'

"I ask because it could well be another measure of the base emotions you're grappling with."

"I get up out of bed every day. I feed the cats. I log on to my computer and edit whatever the office has sent me to work on. I eat at least one meal a day. I talk to friends. I'm fine."

"It doesn't sound as though there's all that much space between the ground and the sky in your world." Doctor Wilburn held her palms one above the other a few inches apart to demonstrate. "I'd like to hear a little more evidence of engagement in life."

Yeah, and I'd like to hear you confess to your parents how you wasted all the money they gave you for shrink college by scoring angel dust and ecstasy.

"Before we close for today, I want you to write a promise to yourself in your journal. Put down three things you'll do to stretch your routines and put you in contact with more of the world around you. Doing at least one of them and writing about it in your journal will be your homework for our next session. Let's see, we're only meeting once a month now instead of every week, so that will be..." The doctor scanned the calendar, "August fourteenth. While you're making those notes in your journal, I'll write a note for you to take to Doctor Henry so you can get your meds."

Doctor Wilburn reached for her pad of personalized vellum sheets on the table beside her. Her ultra suede skirt rubbed on the chair and brought forth another chorus of the Sonata in F-Flat. If Gail hadn't been so fed up with the doctor giving her the same worn-out, useless commentary about not being in touch with her real emotions, she'd have played her usual diversionary game of picturing the therapist in a concert hall, sitting in her chair, farting out the William Tell Overture.

Instead, Gail clicked her ballpoint pen and wrote hastily: One, find a new therapist. Two, find a doctor who will write more than a thirty-day prescription for antidepressants. Three, dump the new therapist.

SUMMER IN THE Great Smoky Mountains. Gail watched the clouds form lazy halos around the mountain tops and felt the warm breeze dance across her skin. Surely it was a kind and generous god who had created that topography and that climate and then put them together in one place. If only Gail still believed in any god whatsoever, let alone a kind and generous one.

She wheeled her Chevy S-10 out of the parking lot adjacent to Doctor Wilburn's office and started for home, eight miles out of Sweetwater on Tennessee Route 322. She punched the power button on the radio.

"Stay tuned. After these messages from our sponsors, I'll be playing our top three at three — the songs that were number one hits on this date for each of the last three years. Take a walk down memory lane for July sevent—" Gail hit the button before he could finish saying "teenth." She didn't need a reminder of the date.

Two years.

It had been two years since the bottom had fallen out of Gail's heart. In some ways, it felt as if she had never known life to be any other way, and yet sometimes when she woke up after a night of taunting dreams, before reality pushed its way to the forefront, she could still almost convince herself it was all an illusion and Marissa would be waiting for her in the kitchen.

Instead of following Route 322 to the house, she overshot the turn and headed up State Road 72. The brown information sign at the side of the road told her it was twelve miles to Tellico Dam.

What the hell. The day was already shot.

Even though it was mid-week, the perfect summer weather had lured a big crowd to the lake spilling into the valley behind the dam and between the mountain ridges. Gail parked her truck and buzzed the windows down. She listened to the laughter and snatches of conversation that wafted on the wind. She observed the boaters and the jet skiers and the swimmers for a while and then surrendered to the memories of 730 days earlier.

"HURRY UP, GAIL. You know the canoes will go fast on a day like this."

"I'm coming. I'm getting our lunch ready. Have you got the life jackets?"

"Everything except the lunch basket is in the car. The next sound you hear will be me pulling out of here without you."

Despite her bout of polio when she was ten, Marissa Adler was an active, enthusiastic outdoorswoman. Much of the time, she wore leg braces to provide greater stability and strength for her twisted legs. She was capable of walking without the braces, and often chose to do so if she only had to traverse a short distance or if the braces interfered with what she wanted to do.

Even with support, her legs always tired quickly, and the braces were too cumbersome to allow her to hike anything except the most benign footpaths, but she could paddle a canoe with the best of them. Her first love was kayaking, but she found the exertion required to roll a kayak upright if she was dunked was too taxing for her weakened legs and compromised lungs.

In the summer months, Gail and Marissa spent part of almost every Sunday in a rental canoe at Tellico Lake. After a couple of hours rocking on the waves, they'd enjoy a picnic under the towering pines and then drive back to their home in Sweetwater.

Gail had met Marissa fourteen years earlier when she took one of Marissa's classes – Twentieth Century Female Authors – at the University of Tennessee in Chattanooga. Gail and Liz, her last lover (one in a long string), had parted company several months earlier. Gail hoped some mental stimulation might help break her out of her loneliness and boredom.

Gail had left Plainfield, Minnesota, right out of high school and wandered from one coast to the other (including a brief stab at college in Colorado) for the better part of six years trying to figure out what she wanted to be when she grew up. In a perfect world, she'd have gone back to Minnesota to pursue the woman she'd dreamed of since sophomore year of high school, but it wasn't a perfect world. Doubts in the deepest part of her soul kept her from following that dream. Instead, she had floated from one part of the country to another and tried everything from being a court reporter to performing yard maintenance to selling ad space for a newspaper.

Sandy, a woman she met in Maine, convinced her that the two of them should hike the Appalachian Trail, south end to north. Two days after leaving the trail head in Georgia, Gail knew she'd had as much of that brand of fun as she could stand and dumped Sandy and the hike less than twenty-five miles into the trek. For no particular reason, other than it was one of the nearest places that might have employment opportunities, she had moved to Chattanooga.

Two weeks into the class, Gail invited Marissa to have coffee after class, and two months later, they moved in together. Four years into the relationship, they began looking for land on which to build their retirement dream home. But when they found an ideal one-level cabin that fairly begged for them to claim it as their own, they left the city and moved to the woods. It meant Marissa had to commute an hour each way between their cabin and the University, but the serenity of their home was worth the sacrifice.

Shortly after moving to Chattanooga, Gail had found work as an editor for a weekly advertising publication. By the time she and Marissa moved to the cabin in the hills outside Sweetwater, Gail had been hired as an editor for Outrageous Press, a feminist publishing house based in Philadelphia. Through the wonders of telecommuting, Gail could work from home to edit the manuscripts assigned to her, and home could be anywhere.

"HEY! PAY ATTENTION to what you're doing, jerk!" The shout Gail heard from outside her truck brought her back to the present. Gail shifted her focus to follow the voice that had broken into her reverie. The wake from a powerboat had sent a family scurrying from the edge of the lake, dragging their blankets and bags with them. "Dope!" the man shouted as he shook his fist at the vanishing craft. "You're not the only one out here, you know."

GAIL FELT THE lump rise in her throat as the rest of her memories came flooding back. Marissa had good upper body strength, but her legs were more liability than asset, especially without her leg braces. It was a short walk from the handicapped parking spaces to the water's edge at Tellico Lake, so Marissa never brought her leg braces along when they went canoeing. Besides, she couldn't wear them comfortably while in the canoe. Marissa was religious about having her life jacket on when she was out on the water. That Sunday morning two years ago had been no exception. She had strapped herself into her vest while Gail loaded the canoe with their backpacks filled with water bottles, sunscreen, extra tee shirts, and bug spray.

They had been out for about an hour when Marissa said her shoulders were starting to burn from too much sun and she wanted to slip into a long-sleeved shirt. They guided the canoe to a quiet spot protected by one of the many land points jutting into the lake. They dropped their paddles onto the floor of the canoe and drifted while Marissa pulled her shirt from the backpack and shucked her life vest so she could slip the shirt over her head. At that precise moment, a low-slung racing boat, its nose high in the air from the force of its inboard motor gunned to full throttle, roared around the point, headed straight for them. Gail screamed for all she was worth, and at the last possible second, the driver of the powerboat heard her above the deafening roar of the engine. He cranked hard to his left and missed the canoe with nothing more than three feet to spare.

But the undulating water rolled toward them with a tsunami-like force, and the canoe flipped before either woman could react. In every one of the thousands of replays Gail watched in her mind's eye, she saw one of the paddles pop free and smack Marissa on the side of the head seconds before she was pitched into the lake.

Gail was thrown free of the canoe, and with her life vest firmly wrapped around her upper body, the buoyancy of the hollow fiberfill kept her afloat. Marissa, however, was trapped under the canoe—stunned from the paddle blow to her head, legs limp and useless, and left without her life jacket, which was bobbing farther away from the accident scene and headed toward shore, some four or five hundred yards off.

Gail kicked and flailed, trying to get near the canoe, but the life vest hindered her progress. It took a few minutes for the powerboat's driver to maneuver the craft back to the location of the mishap. He cut the engine, and the two men leapt into the lake to try to undo the damage. One of them helped Gail get to the speedboat and climb in.

"She's under the canoe. You've got to help her. She has polio."

If Gail said it once, she said it fifty times.

It was no easy task to right the overturned canoe. When the canoe flipped, Marissa's body had lodged with her midsection draped over the center bar of the canoe, trapping both her upper and lower torso underwater. The two men managed to get the canoe upright. Gail could see Marissa was limp as a rag doll. Her body flopped onto the floor of the canoe like so much dead weight.

The men half pushed, half dragged the canoe over to the big boat and hastily tied a rope to it so they could pull it to shore. A small crowd had heard the commotion and had gathered to meet the boat as pulled up to the landing. An ambulance, sirens blaring, raced up as Gail stepped off the boat onto the dock. Someone had called 911. Gail stared in horror as emergency medical technicians worked on Marissa.

"Is she dead?" Gail asked the EMT who had completed CPR and had his fingers on Marissa's wrist.

"No, but it doesn't look good. Respiration is shallow. Pupils are dilated and unresponsive." He flashed a light into Marissa's eyes again. "How long was she in the water?"

"I...I don't know," Gail stammered.

"Maybe four or five minutes," one of the bystanders said. "It seemed like a long time."

"Is there next of kin? Someone we should notify?" the other EMT asked as they lifted the gurney to its wheels.

"No. Only me. I'm her next of kin here."

"We're taking her to Knoxville General. You can ride with us if you want to."

"I've got a car. I'll follow you." Gail yanked the keys to Marissa's

Taurus out of the zipped pocket of her cargo shorts. She was always in charge of the keys, regardless of whose vehicle they used.

"You'll get a ticket if you go the speed we'll be going. When you get there, go to the emergency desk. They'll tell you how to find her." The EMTs loaded the stretcher into the back of the ambulance. One climbed in with Marissa and the other slammed the rear doors. "What's her name?" he asked as he sprinted for the driver's door.

"Marissa Adler," Gail said. "She's a professor at UTC," Gail added, as if it made any difference.

The ambulance spewed gravel as it pulled out and raced for the main road. Gail hurried to the car and leapt into the front seat. As she turned the key in the ignition, it occurred to her she'd never driven Marissa's car. As was true of all of Marissa's vehicles, it was equipped with hand controls to compensate for her partially-paralyzed legs.

Gail couldn't help but wonder if learning to use hand controls instead of foot pedals would prove to be the very least of the adjustments she'd be making in the hours and years to come.

SUNDAY NIGHT. MONDAY morning. Time stretched on endlessly, brutally.

Gail sat in the ICU waiting room or paced the adjacent corridors. All of the doctors and most of the nurses treated her as though she were an inconvenience. She didn't have a durable power of attorney for Marissa's health care, Marissa didn't have a living will, and as soon as the hospital staff learned that Gail was "just a friend," they relegated her to the role of curious onlooker.

Louise, one of the night nurses, was more sympathetic than the others and permitted Gail a brief visit to Marissa's bedside. As best she could through the maze of tubes and monitors, Gail held Marissa's hand and laced her fingers in her hair. "I love you, Ris. Please don't die. I'm right here. I'll always be here for you," she whispered into Marissa's ear.

Late Monday morning, one of the neurologists who had been treating Marissa deigned to talk with Gail.

"I really should only be discussing this with Ms. Adler's family, but since you're the only person immediately available, I'll bend the rules a little." The doctor pursed his lips. "Ms. Adler is in a persistent vegetative state. She suffered severe brain damage from being underwater and deprived of oxygen for so long. The EEG we did this morning shows that there is virtually no electrical activity in her brain."

"There's got to be something you can do, Doctor —" Gail strained to read his name badge "Ayinala. She's so young."

"I'm sorry. In my experience, this type of damage is irreversible. We're able to keep her comfortable, but because her lungs were already damaged from the polio, I suspect that very soon she will start to have difficulty with fluid retention in the chest cavity, and she's also likely to suffer congestive heart failure."

"But—"

The doctor held up his hand. "Please, you told me that Ms. Adler has family out of state. Because this was an emergency and you were able to provide us with information about Ms. Adler's insurance coverage, we didn't press the issue, but I really must insist that from now on, I only discuss her case with her relatives. If you want to help your friend, you need to get someone here as quickly as possible who can speak for her and make decisions on her behalf."

Before Gail could speak again, the doctor turned and strode down the hall. She went to the nurses' station and spoke to the shift supervisor.

"Please. She's my dearest friend. I only want to talk to her for a minute before I leave. I've got to go home to Sweetwater and make a call to her mother to tell her what's happened."

Something in Gail's demeanor swayed the nurse. "All right, you can go in, but be quick. A minute or two is all I can allow."

Despite her breaking heart, the shock of the news the doctor had delivered left Gail dry-eyed. She stood by Marissa's bed and gazed at the woman who had been her lover, companion, life mate, soul mate, confidant, and true best friend for fourteen years. How could it be that they'd never lie together in their bed, holding hands and talking about all of the issues, major and minor, that made up their shared life?

"Ris, I have to leave you for a little while, but I'll be back later today. Wherever you are right now, wherever you go, remember that I love you with all my heart." Gail bent down and kissed Marissa's forehead.

Gail made the drive from Knoxville to Sweetwater in Marissa's Taurus. She found an odd pleasure in using the hand controls—as if Marissa were somehow there with her.

Back at the cabin, Cubbie and Annette, the cats Marissa had named for her favorite Mouseketeers, let Gail know they were glad to have at least one of their humans home. She replenished their bowls of dry food and refilled their water fountain.

Gail wandered from room to room. The bathroom smelled of the almond and cherry bark shampoo that Marissa favored. Marissa's leg braces leaned against the buffet in the dining room where she had left them Sunday morning. The end tables in the living room were stacked with Marissa's literature texts and course materials. She was teaching a summer session and always did her lesson prep while sitting on the sofa. Both their coffee mugs were still in the kitchen sink, and the wrapper from the Mrs. Fields cookies she had packed in their picnic lunch lay on the kitchen counter.

Gail went to their bedroom. The bed was in disarray. They had made love before they left to go canoeing Sunday morning, and they both knew they'd make love again when they got back, so what would be the point in straightening sheets that would only get messed up again? Marissa's clothes lay on the dresser top, hung on the back of the chair, draped over the doorknob. Everywhere she looked, all Gail saw was evidence of the woman who had filled every part of her existence. A woman who, so the doctor had said, would never again laugh at Gail's corny jokes or sigh in relief as Gail rubbed her gnarled calf muscles — the woman who would never again awaken her with a kiss on the back of her neck. Time and again, they had talked about how some day a doctor or researcher might come up with a way to dramatically improve her polio-stricken legs. When that happened, the first thing they'd do was go dancing. Revising the list of songs they'd pick to dance to was one of their favorite fantasies. One of the tunes from their most current collection sprang into Gail's consciousness. The pain of that remembrance seared through her, making her weak and dizzy.

Despair washed over Gail much as the waves from the powerboat on Tellico Lake had done the day before. The energy to phone Marissa's mother in Scranton was more than she could muster. She collapsed on the bed and hugged Marissa's pillow to her chest.

The tears turned to sobs, the sobs to wails, and the wails to a keening lament so wrenching that the mountains surrounding the house rent the skies and pealed down wave after wave of rolling thunder, reverberating their compassion.

"IT'S BEEN THREE days since I've seen her." Gail's voice wavered as she spoke quietly to Louise, the night nurse. "Please."

"I'm sorry." Louise didn't lift her head. "If it were my decision, I'd let you go in, but now that Marissa's mother is here, I have to follow her wishes. She told me she'd report me to the administrator if she finds out I've let you see her daughter. It's out of my hands." Louise busied herself making notes on the charts in front of her.

Monday night Gail had summoned all her strength and called Marissa's parents to tell them about the accident. Mrs. Adler had flown to Knoxville the following day. Since her arrival, she had barred Gail from so much as standing in the doorway to Marissa's room.

Shortly after Mrs. Adler arrived, she confronted Gail in the waiting room. "Go home, Gail. There's no reason for you to be here."

"I belong with Marissa. I need to be here if her condition changes, or if choices need to be made for her care."

"Marissa's father and I have decided to bring her home to Pennsylvania. As soon as the doctors tell us she's stabilized enough to make the trip, we'll have her airlifted to a care facility at home."

"Marissa's home is here in Tennessee with me."

"You may have deluded yourself into thinking that was the case, but I can assure you, that part of Marissa's life is over."

"You're not going to keep her on life support, are you?"

"It's really none of your concern. Her father and I will do what we think is right."

"Marissa would never want to be strapped to a bed with a feeding tube and a respirator keeping her like...like...like she is now." Gail had gestured toward Marissa's room.

"She's our daughter. We'll make the decisions she can no longer make for herself."

"But Mrs. Adler..."

Marissa's mother cut off Gail's protest. "The only thing we need from you is for you to load Marissa's car with whatever you can fit into it. I know she has some photo albums with pictures from her childhood. We'd like those back. We want her diplomas, her financial records, her clothing, jewelry, and so forth. Her father will make arrangements with you to fly down in a few weeks and pick up the car after you've packed it."

Gail was too stunned to speak.

"Marissa told us that you and she bought the house together, so I don't suppose we'll have any legal recourse regarding that. We're not going to demand the furniture and appliances, although I'm sure we're entitled to have them. Given everything we need to do to arrange for Marissa's care, it's simply too much bother to deal with all that right now. Consider yourself a very fortunate woman in that you're being spared a court fight. But rest assured, Gail, you've taken advantage of our daughter and her generosity for the last time." With an arrogant huff, Mrs. Adler left the waiting room.

Following that conversation, Gail had raced back to the house in Sweetwater and rummaged through every paper in Marissa's desk and file cabinet, hoping against hope she had left at least a handwritten note about her wishes. Mrs. Adler was right about the cabin. It was jointly titled with rights of survivorship, so no matter what happened to Marissa, the Adlers couldn't take her home from her.

Many times she and Marissa had talked about needing to see a lawyer to tend to other paperwork, such as living wills and durable powers-of-attorney for medical issues, in case anything should happen to one of them, but that's as far as it had gotten — talk. They had agreed on two main matters: neither of them wanted any heroic measures, and a death with dignity was important to them. Fat lot of good it did now. Marissa could no longer state her wishes, and no one on the face of the earth cared that Gail should be the one to speak for her.

Gail toyed with the idea of faking a living will and forging Marissa's signature, but when she realized the document would have to be witnessed and notarized, she knew she was out of options. With nothing to establish her rightful place as Marissa's attorney-in-fact, Gail had no choice but to let Marissa's mother act as her de facto legal representative and dictate what would happen.

Gail had gone back to the hospital and waited—and waited—
needing desperately to be near Marissa and to touch her at least once
more. But Mrs. Adler was adamant. Gail was not to be permitted within
fifty feet of Marissa. Gail had overheard Mrs. Adler and the neurologist
talking. The next morning, Marissa would be loaded in an ambulance,
taken to the airport, and flown to Scranton. Gail tried to persuade the
nurse one more time.

"I really don't want to get you in any trouble, but this is my last
chance to see Marissa, maybe my last chance ever. If you happened to
step away from the desk and turn your back for a minute, you wouldn't
see me slip into her room."

"I'm not supposed to let you be here in the waiting room. It's
family members only up here in ICU."

"She is my family, Louise. We've lived together for fourteen years.
We've spent every holiday together. I know more about her and what
she'd want than her mother could ever dream of knowing. She hasn't
seen her parents in almost three years. Her mother wouldn't be here
now if we'd done living wills. Here, look at this." Gail pulled a slim
wallet from her hip pocket and extracted a photo from inside it. "This is
the two of us and our cats in our house last Christmas. You can't tell me
this isn't a family picture." The nurse took the snapshot from Gail's
hand.

"All right. I heard Mrs. Adler say she was going to make some
phone calls from her hotel room. But you can only go in for a minute,
and then you've got to get out of here. I don't think Marissa's mother is
the sort of woman who likes to have her instructions ignored."

Gail squeezed Louise's forearm, retrieved her snapshot, then
hurried to Marissa's room. She was shocked at how much worse
Marissa looked. Her skin was sallow and papery, her eyes transfixed
and empty. Her chest was sunken and her lungs rattled as the respirator
forced air into them. Her fingers and toes were curled in tight knots, the
nails discolored to a bluish-green tint.

"Hi, darling. It's me," Gail breathed as she leaned close to Marissa's
face. "I don't know if you can hear me or not, but I have to tell you
something. You'll be leaving Tennessee soon. I know it's not what either
of us wants, but there's nothing I can do to stop it. Your mom is taking
you to Pennsylvania tomorrow, and she's said I can't come to see you,
so this might be good-bye." Gail tasted her tears as they rolled down
her cheeks and onto her lips. "I'll never stop loving you, Ris. You've
given me the absolute best life I ever could have dreamed of. Cubbie
and Annette miss you already. I told them I'd tell you 'bye from them,
too."

Gail heard a stirring at the door behind her. "Really, you've got to
go..." Louise urged. Gail waved a hand to acknowledge the reminder.

"Marissa Ruth Adler," Gail's voice broke as she spoke the name,
"find peace, find joy, find eternity. And please be waiting for me when

it's my time to come join you." Gail laid her lips on Marissa's face for what she feared was the last time, the tubes preventing her from feeling Marissa's mouth against her own. "I love you, Ris."

The humming and hissing of the pumps and machines was Marissa's only reply as Gail stepped out of the hospital room and into the void that constituted the remainder of her life.

Chapter
Two

THE LOW-SLUNG sun was throwing long streams of orange light across Tellico Lake as Gail shook the last of the lingering memories from two years earlier out of her consciousness. She glanced down at the notebook beside her on the bench seat of the truck. She picked it up and opened it to the page where, at Doctor Wilburn's direction, she'd written the three promises to herself.

"July 17," she wrote. "I did something I swore I'd never do. I'm sitting at Tellico Lake. I can see the dock where the EMTs treated Marissa the day of the accident. Dr. W. said I should do things to make me stretch and experience more of life. Right now, this feels more like dying than living, but at least I did it. It's been two years. Marissa's parents still refuse to talk to me when I call. If it weren't for Amy, I wouldn't even know Marissa is still alive — if you can call it that. Amy says she's tried to convince her parents to take Marissa off all the life-support machines, but they won't do it. She's only Marissa's little sister, after all. It's the cruelest thing I've ever heard of. I wonder if I'll ever stop missing her? I wonder if I'll ever love anyone else?"

Gail closed the notebook and started the truck. She drove slowly out of the parking area and let her eyes linger on the sunset vista over the lake. The rays played off the low clouds on the horizon, making shafts of shimmering light. "Your favorite kind of sunset, Marissa," Gail whispered. "A God sky — you know the kind — the ones they always use for funeral home advertisements." She smiled as she remembered how Marissa would imitate a preacher's voice to command her to look at one of the wonders of God's firmament.

It was dark by the time Gail pulled up in front of the cabin. She felt something unfamiliar underfoot as she crossed the kitchen to switch on the lights. The cats, displeased at having been left alone again, had knocked the spice rack off the counter top and scattered a dozen kinds of herbs all over the kitchen floor. Several of the little pottery jugs had broken, adding clay shards to the potpourri.

"Brats," Gail scolded as she cleaned up the mess. "You know the road runs from this house back to the animal shelter, too." Cubbie and Annette wove in and out of Gail's legs as she swept around the chairs and the table legs. "Lucky for you they're closed for the night."

Gail stowed the broom, scooped some dry food into the cats' bowls, and poured herself a glass of iced tea. As she entered the living room, she noticed the light blinking on her answering machine. She hit the play button. "Gail, it's Penny. Call me." The second message kicked in. "Hi, Gail. I know you had a doctor's appointment this afternoon, so I'm not surprised I missed you. I've got a really terrific assignment I want to talk to you about. It's sort of a rush job, and you'd be perfect for it. If you get in before six, call me at the office. If it's later, call me on my cell. I'll be up late, so don't worry about the time, but give me a buzz, okay?" Lydia LaGrange, managing editor of Outrageous Press at the home office in Philadelphia, usually communicated only via e-mail. Something unusual must be in the works if she'd actually dialed the phone.

Gail checked the clock on the shelf above the television. She decided she'd call Penny, grab a bite to eat, then call Lydia.

"Hi. I got your message. Are you sick? Your voice sounded funny on the machine." Penny and Gail had been best friends back in high school in Plainfield, Minnesota. Their friendship these days consisted of birthday cards (usually belated) and a few phone calls a year.

"No, I'm not sick, but my dad is. The nursing home called me at work this morning. He's had a huge stroke. This one might be the end of the line."

"I'm sorry. Is there anything I can do?"

"No, I don't think so. You barely caught me. I've got everything packed and loaded, and as soon as I put the dogs in the car, I'm on my way up there to be with Dad."

"Okay. Be safe on the road. At least you won't have to worry about snow between Minneapolis and Plainfield."

"One of the few good things we can say about the summers in Minnesota."

"I'll be thinking about you and your dad, too. Call me and let me know how you're both doing."

"I will."

She didn't envy Penny the ordeal awaiting her. Gail had already gone through similar situations with both of her parents. Watching a loved one die an inch at a time was never easy. Thoughts of Marissa crowded the edge of her consciousness, but she shunted them aside and forced herself back to the kitchen.

Gail put together a green salad with lots of fresh vegetables heaped on top. She cut herself some wedges of cheese and grabbed half a bagel from the pantry. After refilling her iced tea glass, she plopped herself on the sofa and turned on the TV with the remote. It droned in the background while she ate. Ten minutes later, she turned the TV off and had the phone in hand again.

"Lydia? Gail Larson. Am I catching you at a bad time?"

"No, not at all. I take it you got my message."

"Um hum."

"Good. Listen, what are you doing the next three or four weeks?"

"I'm almost done with the manuscript from one of your new authors — the one with the strange last name I always have to look up to remember. The schedule says I'm supposed to have it back to her by July thirty-first. And then I've got the short story anthology you wanted me to get started on."

"Okay. Good. I can reassign both of those to one of our other editors. I've got a golden opportunity for you."

"Yeah?"

"What would you say about a chance to work with Connie Martin?"

"The reigning royalty of alternative feminist literature?"

"That would be the one."

"I thought you always assigned her books to Rhonda Helmstad."

"Generally, yes, but here's the situation. We found out yesterday Connie is going to receive an award from the Southern Women's Writers' Association. The banquet will be held in Atlanta in mid-October. Between now and then, we want to do a special promo edition of her newest novel. Rhonda can't edit it. In fact, she and her partner are leaving day after tomorrow for a six-week vacation in Australia and New Zealand. They can't change plans without forking over their non-refundable down payments."

"Isn't that an awfully ambitious timeline for Connie's book?"

"Sort of, but if you and Connie can get the manuscript ready to go, I've lined up a printer in Atlanta, and he promises me he can take care of this. All I want is enough copies to hand out at the banquet and for Connie to use at the book signings she'll do at the two gay bookstores down in Atlanta. Because the printer won't have to ship them anywhere, he tells me he can turn it around in time to meet our schedule."

"But won't you have to print it again to meet the distribution needs? Connie Martin sells thousands of copies of every book she writes."

"Sure, but think of it, Gail. The immediate publicity of offering a new Connie Martin book the day after she's been honored by a mainstream writers' group is going to push sales through the roof. And if we've already got the typeset manuscript sitting on go, Outrageous can flood the market in a couple of weeks."

"I've never done a book for someone as well-known as Connie."

"So? You've edited dozens of other books for me. It's the same process, regardless of the author. Besides, Connie's manuscripts are so clean, there's almost no editing to do. I really need you. C'mon, whaddya say?"

Gail didn't give herself time to let all of her doubts surface. "Sure. Why not? Send it on."

"That's the catch."

"What's the catch?"

"We won't be doing this the usual way of sending files back and forth electronically. I want you to go to Atlanta and work on site with Connie."

"You're kidding."

"Not for a minute. Big publishing houses do it all the time — writer and editor meet face-to-face and hash out any problem areas on the spot. But remember, we don't have the luxury of extra flexibility in the schedule."

"But files fly through cyberspace in a heartbeat. What do you gain by having me in Atlanta with Connie?

"Trust me. I know the synergy of live interaction. We want this novel to be an absolute smash hit. Connie already has most of the book written in first draft. I know you and Connie will have a real chemistry. The two of you working side by side will give the book precisely the extra zing it needs. Connie has already agreed to the arrangement. She's expecting you in Atlanta Friday, which gives you tomorrow and Thursday to get organized and make the drive."

"But I can't leave my cats."

"Not a problem. I had my assistant book you at an extended-stay, pet-friendly motel. She can give you the address and phone number. I'm sure it will work out fine for you. Oh, and if I didn't mention it, Outrageous will pay all your expenses while you're in Atlanta, and instead of the usual flat fee for editing the manuscript, you'll get a percentage of the first year's sales."

"I—"

"I've got another call coming in, so I've got to run. I'm sure you'll do a great job. A month from now, you'll be thanking me for setting you up on this assignment. Call me after you've checked in at the motel in Atlanta."

Gail stared at the receiver in her hand. Atlanta for a face-to-face editing job on a Connie Martin novel with Connie Martin? A small smile played across her face as she considered it. That should certainly qualify as an activity Doctor Wilburn would count as an expansion of her horizons.

"HI. YOU MUST be Gail. I'm Connie Martin."

Gail had only been at the Magnolia Suites Temporary Quarters for an hour. Cubbie was hiding in the tub in the master bedroom bath and Annette was still crouching in the far corner of the cat carrier. The noises coming from the cage made it very clear she was not pleased at having been transported across state lines for lord knew what purposes. When the knock at the door came, Gail assumed it would be someone from the management office bringing her the silverware, plates, and cookware they had promised to deliver to stock her kitchenette. The woman standing there was carrying a laptop computer and a tote bag stuffed with papers and books.

"Excuse me?"

"Lydia LaGrange called a while ago to say you'd phoned to tell her you were here. I thought I'd come right over so we could get acquainted and maybe get some work done this afternoon."

Gail swept a glance around the main room of her suite and wondered for the tenth time in as many minutes why she'd ever consented to participate in this rush editing job. The cats' beds, litter pans, canned food, dry food, favorite toys, and beddy bye blanket were in a jumble on the floor by the love seat. Her own suitcases, garment bags, and computer sat in an adjacent heap. Add to it the groceries, cases of bottled water, and coolers of veggies she'd brought with her from Sweetwater, and it looked like the staging area for a poorly organized wagon train. Yes, she had called Lydia as soon as she came through the door, but her plan was to tell her she'd made a mistake in assigning this project to Gail. In typical Lydia fashion, she had rushed off to another call before Gail could tell her she was going to drag everything back to her truck and boogey for the mountains of Tennessee.

"I guess you haven't had time to get settled yet." Connie followed Gail's gaze.

How perceptive...

"No. And frankly —"

"The two of us can whip this place into shape in no time." Connie strode into the room. "Let's see. You'll want to deal with your own clothes and toiletries. Why don't I take care of the food and other kitchen things?" She grabbed a bag of groceries and one of the coolers and headed for the kitchen, visible through the archway at the rear of the room. "I noticed the pet carriers. Too small for anything except small dogs."

"I brought my cats."

"Gee, I hope my allergies don't kick in."

Gee, I hope you won't mind when I kick your conceited ass out the door.

Gail was still standing at the half-open door when Connie returned from the kitchen. "I'll get the rest of these groceries put away while you get started on those suitcases." She nodded toward Gail's belongings, then picked up two bags by their handles with one hand and took a carton of water bottles with the other. "I noticed you don't have any meat products. That's good. I'm mostly a vegetarian, too."

Before Gail could tell her she simply hadn't brought any meat along and that she would certainly be buying some at the local supermarket, Connie once again vanished with her load into the kitchen.

"Hey, shake a leg, editor. I've only got one more trip to the kitchen, and you haven't so much as moved a suitcase yet." Gail closed the door but seemed rooted to the spot.

Does this woman mainline caffeine?

"Hot isn't it?" Connie asked as she stepped to the thermostat and dropped the setting a few degrees. "I love Atlanta, but the summers are a total bitch." She picked up the laptop and tote bag she had abandoned by the love seat when she began her ferrying to the kitchen. "Where shall we set up to work? In here?"

"Actually—"

"No, wait. Lydia told me she'd gotten you an executive suite. There'll be another room we can use as our office." Connie eyed the two closed doors off the right side of the main room. "I'll plug in my computer while you stash your gear in the bedroom."

Before Gail could stop her, Connie opened the door to the master bedroom. Cubbie, curious and quick to recover when he thought there might be company he could wrangle treats or play time out of, bolted into the main room of the suite. The sudden movement startled Connie. She jumped, dropped her computer and tote bag, and caught her foot in the shoulder strap of the carrying case. She tried to catch herself, but she was moving so swiftly she lost her balance. Gail lunged from across the room, but got there too late to keep Connie from falling to the floor. Connie knocked her head against the door jamb as she landed. Her glasses flew off her face and dropped beside her.

"I am so sorry." Gail knelt beside Connie. "Are you all right?" She retrieved Connie's glasses and slipped them in the pocket of her shorts.

"I think so, but I whacked myself a good one on the way down."

"Here, let me help you up." Gail offered her hand to Connie. "Guess I won't win any awards for first impressions."

Connie took Gail's hand and got to her feet. She closed her right eye tightly and canted her head. "Just call me 'Grace.'" She rubbed her temple gingerly. "You told me you had your cats with you. I should have expected them to show up."

"Come over here and sit down." Gail led the way to the love seat and pushed her garment bag and other things out of the way. "Let me see if there's any ice."

Connie eased onto the cushions. Gail pulled Connie's glasses out her pocket and set them on the end table.

"There is. I saw it when I was putting things in the refrigerator."

Gail went to the kitchen and made a makeshift ice bag out of a zip top bag and a dishtowel. "This might keep it from bruising too badly." She handed the bag to Connie. "Does your head hurt? How about some aspirin?"

"Do you have any Tylenol? Aspirin always upsets my stomach."

Gail rummaged in her stash of pill bottles in the smallest of her suitcases and poured three capsules into Connie's palm. "I'll get you a glass of water."

"A bottle of water, please. I don't want a glass."

With ice bag in place and analgesics administered, Gail had exhausted her repertoire of first aid for bumped heads. She sat mutely on one of the stuffed chairs facing Connie, who was leaning her head against the high back of the love seat. Gail could see Cubbie circling the pet carrier. Soon he had half his body in it trying to convince his sister it was safe to come out and help him explore their new digs.

Gail took advantage of the silence to assess the author in front of her. Connie had at least a dozen books in publication under the Outrageous Press logo. She had been their best selling writer every year for a decade. Though Gail had never edited a Connie Martin book, she had read most of Connie's offerings once they were in print. Some might accuse Connie of formulaic prose. Girl finds girl, girl loses girl, conflict, resolution, reunion, vine covered cottage, fade to black. But she had a loyal following of readers who faithfully bought everything she cranked out. So what if it wasn't great literature? She wove stories that held one's interest from cover to cover, and what was wrong with a little hot lesbian sex along the way?

Outrageous Press (well, Lydia LaGrange, really) left it to the author's discretion as to whether or not her picture was included in the thumbnail biographical sketch inside the back cover of each of its books. Gail was sure she'd never seen Connie's picture included in any of her books. Having met Connie, Gail was both puzzled and bemused.

The brass-balls approach Connie had demonstrated from the instant she walked through the door would have led Gail to expect she'd be first in line for as much publicity and exposure as she could garner, but the goddess of irony had scored a major coup when she put Connie Martin together. The pit bull personality was housed in a Pekinese body.

At best, Connie stood five one. She didn't do herself any favors by wearing her hair loose and long, hanging halfway down her back. It made her already short stature seem all the more diminutive. It was a pretty color—deep brown with lots of highlights hinting at a deep red auburn, but a shorter cut would have been far more flattering. Her full, pie-shaped face was accentuated by the round, black-rimmed eyeglasses she wore. The lenses in her glasses were tinted—probably a photosensitive coating—but they added a touch of Mafioso to her demeanor. Gail had gotten a glimpse of Connie's true eye color—a nice shade of soft brown—when her glasses went sailing as she fell. Contacts or clear lenses in her glasses (and different frames) would be a much better choice to let the impish quality of Connie's intriguing eyes shine out. Connie wasn't really fat, Gail decided, but she certainly looked like a woman whose most vigorous exercise consisted of slapping computer keys.

Soft. Soft and motherly. Who'd have ever pictured Connie Martin — the woman who makes most of lesbian America moist between the legs — looking like Little Miss Suburbia? No wonder she doesn't have her picture in her books. Sales would drop by half if her readers knew she's a Betty Crocker look-alike in need of a makeover.

Connie lifted her head from its resting place. "You know, Gail, I've just had a thought." She pulled her hand from the side of her face and let the ice pack drop to her lap. "I've been having trouble with one of the scenes in this novel we're working on, but maybe I've figured out how to fix it. I hope my computer didn't get screwed up when I dropped it a while ago."

Connie got up from the love seat, snatched her computer from the floor where it had been since her fall, and charged into the room the Magnolia Suites referred to as "the businessman's refuge." (Obviously, Magnolia's corporate office was rife with sexist fools.)

"Come on, Gail. I can use your help with this."

Betty Crocker? Betty Crocker on amphetamines, maybe.

"I KNOW THIS is the first time I've edited any of your work, but I thought Outrageous Press had a standing policy against anything in its books that smacks of abuse against women." Gail was holding a page from Connie's manuscript.

"Never say 'smack' when referring to abuse."

Gail offered a half-chuckle. "But it is the policy, right?"

"Right, but I didn't write anything that goes against the policy."

"You've suggested your leading character has shown up at the door to a woman's motel room with a black eye given to her by her lover. How is that not abuse?"

"I don't describe the situation where she got the black eye. I leave it for the readers to infer, if they choose to. You know as well as I do some hard-assed women lurk out there. They were beaten up by fathers, or in some cases mothers, who thought they could whip the lesbian tendencies out of them. Abuse is multi-generational."

"I don't disagree. All I'm saying is the guidelines I have from Outrageous Press tell me to rework scenes like this so it doesn't appear we're advocating violence in any way."

"Who's advocating? I'm using a subtle possibility as a vehicle to advance the plot."

"What is it you want to convey?"

"My leading lady is in a dead-end relationship, and I want to give her potential new love interest, who is in town for a business meeting at their mutual place of employment, an excuse for making physical contact with her."

"Okay, so why couldn't you come at it from a slightly different angle?" Gail hurried on before Connie could interrupt. "How about your protagonist hates going to women's softball games, but her current lover always drags her along. At the game on the afternoon in question, she gets hit with a wicked foul ball and develops a shiner. That evening, she goes by the hotel where her potential love interest is staying to pick her up and take her to the dinner meeting they're supposed to attend. You get to the same place in your story, but you avoid anything remotely suggesting your heroine is tied up with a wife beater."

Connie considered Gail's proposed alternative. "Huh. That might work. I'd probably have to jockey the timeframes a little. I mean, it's not likely she'd be going to a game on the same day she has a business meeting, but she could go to the game on say, a Sunday night, work from home on Monday to get ready for the meeting, and then go by the hotel, as you recommended."

"Right," Gail said. "The new love interest sees the black eye, asks what happened, then offers to help camouflage it with super duper liquid foundation and face powder. She could say something about having done some make-up work for a summer stock theatre or something."

"Good. I like it. And while new love interest is gently dabbing heavy duty cover-up lotion to our heroine's face, touch leads to caress, caress leads to knowing look, knowing look leads to impulsive kiss of fiery passion." Connie's fingers were flying over the keyboard as she spoke. "Damn, you're good. Lydia told me I'd love working with you." More clicking of keys as Connie deleted text and incorporated the changes.

Gail sat and watched while Connie worked.

"There. That takes care of that." Connie hit the save key.

"Can I ask you something?" Gail asked.

"What is it, oh worthy editor?"

"Did you always know you'd write lesbian romance novels? I mean, was it what you pictured yourself doing?"

Connie laughed like she was watching the final episode of *Last Comic Standing*. "Not by a damned sight. My plan was to get wealthy off the fruit of other women's wombs. I was going to be an OB-GYN."

"What happened?"

"About the fiftieth time I passed out when looking at blood or body parts in my early biology classes, I figured out I wasn't doctor material. The real kicker is I never believed I had a knack for writing until I started therapy to try to deal with my depression from not being able to get to med school. My shrink made me keep a journal. One of the things I had to do was write letters to myself about why I was still a good person and what I could do with my life instead. She's the one who suggested I turn some of those letters into short stories. When they started getting picked up by some of the women's magazines and then by Outrageous Press, I figured, what the hell? It beats fainting a half dozen times a day."

"At least you kept part of the dream alive. You're still making your fortune off the juicy fruits of other women's wombs."

Connie's face was unreadable. "Speaking of which, I guess I'd better get back to this," she pointed at the computer screen, "if we're going to have this hummer ready to go to print when Lydia wants it."

"Remember that line. It might make a good title for another book someday — When Lydia Wants It — the story of a woman with an endless capacity for love."

"Or something that substitutes for love."

"Can I ask you something else?"

"What?"

"How do you decide how many love scenes to put in your books?"

"If it were strictly up to me, there would be exactly zero in every one I write."

"No joke?"

"Nope. In my estimation, leaving the steamy entanglements to readers' imaginations is far more effective."

"But all of your books are full of hot bedroom gymnastics. It's almost always mentioned in the reviews I've seen."

"What can I say? Lydia LaGrange — and most other managing editors, I'd bet — are convinced sex translates into better sales. I guess she's right. Since I've started adding words such as 'wet, throbbing, panting, stroking, lick, probe, and take me now' to my books, I'm getting bigger royalty checks."

"But your story lines have gotten stronger, too, and your characters are more complex and more memorable."

"Probably not an objective assessment, since you're on Outrageous Press's payroll."

"True, I get regular paychecks from Outrageous, but no one is paying me to read your books. I do it because they're a great way to pass a few hours on a lonely evening."

"Thanks for the endorsement. I'm always glad to meet a satisfied reader." Gail found Connie's smile disarmingly shy and noted how Connie turned her face to keep from blushing in reaction to Gail's intense gaze.

Gail caught sight of the angry welt on the cheekbone, right below Connie's eye where she'd banged it on the doorframe two days earlier. "How's your eye feeling by now? It still looks a little puffy."

"Tender, but staying busy has helped me forget about it."

"Some more ice might take the swelling out of it. I'll be right back."

Gail exited the businessman's refuge and returned shortly with an ice pack.

"Here. Take a five minute break." Gail laid the towel with the zip top bag of ice against Connie's face. Connie reached up to hold the towel, but accidentally caught Gail's hand between her own and the cloth. Heat flared through both their hands and threatened to melt the ice.

"I don't usually —"

Whatever Gail intended to say to finish the thought was smothered and lost in Connie's kiss.

"DON'T YOU DARE put this in one of your sleazy romance novels." Gail exhaled slowly as Connie nuzzled her neck.

"No danger. I only write fiction. Besides, no one would believe this." Connie propped herself up, leaned over Gail's shoulder, and kissed her lips. "I might, however, have to spread the word about how excellent editors make terrific lovers."

"How does Rhonda Helmstad's partner feel about that?"

"I wouldn't know. Rhonda Helmstad is merely a very good editor. You're the best I've ever had."

"We have worked together on exactly three chapters and spent less than three days together. You might be a little premature in calling me the best editor you've ever had."

"Who's talking about editing?" Connie rolled over on top of Gail's body and lay full-length, face to face with Gail. "How did you ever learn to do that incredible balancing act while keeping me dancing on the edge of what felt like an hour-long orgasm?"

"Beginner's luck," Gail lied. She had no desire to explain to Connie about how much of her technique as a lover was due to adaptations necessitated by Marissa's physical limitations from polio.

"Want to perfect your style?" Connie propelled her pubic bones against Gail's. "I'd love to go for two in a row."

Gail's rational mind wanted to say no, but she hadn't felt the warmth of another woman's skin next to hers in more than two years. So what if she didn't even like Connie Martin? So what if she was bossy and egocentric and not particularly attractive? She was there, she was aroused (and arousing), and it felt so good.

"Tell me what you want," Gail said.

"I want you to make me believe what I write in my books isn't simply the wishful ruminations of a sexually frustrated author." Connie repositioned herself around Gail's upper leg and began to rock rhythmically. "Touch me in all the ways I need to be touched. Say my name and tell me you want me."

"You're my first lover, Connie," Gail whispered. "You have to show me what to do." She paused ever so briefly. "Connie. Connie."

The playacting let both women forget their inhibitions. They embodied the manifestation of every action verb Connie had ever used to describe the love scenes in her books and gave themselves over to complete physical abandon.

"I've never done this before." Gail moaned softly, not sure if she meant the words she spoke, or if it was still part of the role she was playing.

"I have, but only in my dreams," Connie replied.

After her sixth orgasm (but who was counting?), Gail was sated. "Enough," she said as she laid her palm on Connie's chest. She could feel Connie's heart still beating quickly. "How about you?" Excitement and exhaustion had turned every muscle in Gail's body to mush.

Several times, she was sure she had used up every drop of desire from some lost place deep inside, but a moment's contact or a muffled word would bring her back to the near edge of wanting, and Connie always obliged.

"Wonderfully satisfied. This was better action than I've ever gotten, including alone in my bedroom with all my special toys."

Gail cuddled up close to Connie, ready for some afterglow conversation and then to drift off to blissful sleep. Connie's right arm was around her shoulder — something of a snug fit since Connie's short arm barely reached around Gail's five-foot-seven frame.

"That was great," Connie sighed. She started drumming her fingers on Gail's shoulder blade. "Nothing like some Olympic-sized orgasms to work up an appetite. Do you want to eat here or should we go out for something?"

Food was the farthest thing from Gail's mind. Maybe if she didn't say anything, Connie would forget about it and they could fall asleep.

"There's a place with great fusion cuisine a little ways from here. Or we could go to the vegetarian place in Buckhead, but traffic will be a jug fuck between here and there. Some of the chains have good salad bars — probably our best bet so we don't lose too much time."

"Time for what?" Gail asked. Obviously, silence wasn't going to work.

"I am totally primed for ripping through at least another six chapters tonight. I don't want to waste creative energy waiting to get dinner." Connie rolled out from under Gail's head, which was still resting on Connie's shoulder, and was up and on her feet before Gail could respond. "Maybe you could run out and pick something up for us while I do a quick read through on the next part of the book." Connie jammed her stubby arms into her button-front, short-sleeved blouse as she spoke. "Then when you get back, you can edit what I've done while you eat." Connie finished dressing.

Connie left the bedroom and headed for the adjoining businessman's refuge. A minute later, Gail heard the clicking of the keys on Connie's laptop.

Maybe she could grab the cats, slip out the door, climb in her truck, and break every speed limit getting back to Sweetwater.

Gail dressed quickly and closed the door to the bedroom as she stepped into the main room of the suite. Cubbie and Annette were curled together on their favorite blanket, which had never made it farther than the floor by the love seat where she had dropped it a hundred years earlier. Hunger had apparently gotten the best of them. A bag of dry cat food was tipped over and spilled onto the kitchen floor. Cubbie picked his head up and gave Gail a look which seemed to call her many of the names she was silently calling herself.

"Hey, Gail!" Connie called from the next room. "Bring some dessert, too. Something chocolate."

"IF I DON'T get some sleep soon, I'll die."

"We're almost done. I need to polish these last four or five chapters and then you can have them. If we both make one more pass through the manuscript, we can wrap a ribbon around it and call it done." Connie barely looked up from her computer as she spoke.

"My brain quit working at least two hours ago. I'm so tired I'm useless as a proofreader. I probably wouldn't catch a paragraph full of nothing but a series of vowels and punctuation marks." Gail yawned and let her head flop back against the chair.

"If you're too tired to work, go grab a nap. I want to make sure I've caught every place where the text has to be fixed because of those changes we made last night."

Gail pushed back from the desk and dragged herself to the bedroom. Her nineteen days in Atlanta had been an endless blur of editing Connie's book in the businessman's refuge and fending off (not always successfully) Connie's physical advances in the bedroom. Following their first amorous romp, Connie invited herself to stay with Gail at the Magnolia Suites. She occasionally made trips to her house to pick up fresh clothing.

For Gail, days and nights were all jumbled together. Sometimes, they'd work on the manuscript until three in the morning, and then crash into bed, both so weary they wouldn't bother undressing. Most nights, they slept the sleep of the dead, but once in a while, one of them would accidentally brush an arm or leg against the other's body, and the hormones would gush. They'd roll and grope and pant and scream and writhe and kiss. Gail often prevailed in her attempts to bring things to a stop short of full-fledged lovemaking, but so much as kissing Connie was cheating on Marissa. There were moments — many moments — when she loathed Connie Martin — but never as deeply as she abhorred herself for being unfaithful. With or without abortive intimacies, Gail's fatigue always eventually induced sleep. But when she'd awaken and remember what she'd done, or almost done, she'd hate herself all the more.

For the first week, each time they finished one of their frantic physical frolics, Gail would promise herself it was the last one, but she had proved herself a liar so many times she had to stop saying it in hopes of keeping at least a little self-respect. Of course, her self-respect was in short supply anyway, since Marissa Adler was still lying in a deep coma in Scranton, Pennsylvania. How could she ever justify cheating on Marissa? What if one day she miraculously came out of the coma? What could Gail possibly say to excuse herself for what she was doing with Connie Martin?

Gail yanked her sneakers off and crashed onto the disheveled bed. It must have been at least thirty-six hours since she'd last put her head down. Atlanta in early August was a perpetual steam bath. The air conditioner ran nonstop, but the bedroom was still sweltering. Gail sat up and tugged off her tee shirt, shorts, and underwear.

She didn't know if she'd slept a minute or a month when she felt Connie sidle in beside her.

"Hi," Connie said as she kissed Gail's cheek. "You realize you're completely naked, don't you?"

"It's so hot in here," Gail answered groggily. "Did you finish the book?"

"I couldn't remember what we said we were going to do about the last scene with the ex-lover. I was hoping you'd be awake so I could ask you." Connie's lips found Gail's. "But it can wait."

"How do you survive on so little sleep? You're always still working when I go to bed, and you're always up before I am. I need to get a supply of whatever drugs you're taking." Gail rolled on her side, facing Connie.

"Writing a book keeps me energized. Once we send it to the printer for typesetting, I'll go underground for weeks on end. Besides, this time, I've got Venus helping the cause." Connie moved her mouth over Gail's breast.

Gail put her hands on Connie's shoulders and pushed her away. "Connie, don't. Please."

"We can make it quick, if you want."

"I don't think it's right for us to be involved."

"You didn't put up much of a fight other times."

"I know I didn't, but I should have. I'd be okay with talking, or holding hands, or listening to music, or maybe some kissing, but I don't want to go beyond that, all right?"

"Why settle for crumbs when you can have the whole cake?"

"Those aren't crumbs to me. They're some of the nicest parts about being with someone."

"Spoken like a woman who believes in happily ever after."

"Is there something wrong with happily ever after?"

"Nothing, except it's not very realistic for older women like me." Connie flopped on her back and lay woodenly beside Gail. "Pretty, popular women are allowed to dream of happily ever after. I'm not."

"Every one of your books ends with some version of happily ever after."

"And that's why they're called fiction—something made up—not real." Connie swung her legs over the side of the bed. "Maybe I'll go back and take another shot at those last thirty pages."

"What made you such a cynic?"

"Fifty-five years of living."

"And nothing in those fifty-five years was ever good and happy?"

"For a little while, maybe, but nothing ever lasted."

"It doesn't mean whatever comes next won't last."

"Why buck the odds? I've dug through enough boxes of horse manure to know there aren't any ponies hidden in them."

"Do you want to talk about it?" Gail asked.

"I've spent way too many hours and far too many dollars paying alleged professionals for the privilege of spilling my innermost feelings. No offense, but I don't think your armchair psychology will be what turns the tide for me." Connie stood up.

"I meant talk to me as a friend, someone you trust and apparently might have deeper feelings for."

"Same difference," Connie retorted.

"Hardly."

"Shows what you know."

"There's a big difference between talking things over with me and being in therapy." Gail rose from the bed and began to dress.

"Not always."

Gail sat back down and leaned back against the headboard to consider what Connie had said. "You slept with your therapist, didn't you?"

"So what?"

"That's unethical."

"Not if I consented." Connie folded her arms across her chest and stared at Gail.

"Even if you consented. What kind of therapist thinks it's okay to have sex with a patient?"

"In this case, a very handsome one with an ass so tight he could crack walnuts between his cheeks."

"He?"

"Sure. Why rule out fifty percent of the population?"

Gail opened her mouth to speak, but nothing came out. Connie dropped back onto the bed and sat beside her.

"I suppose you've never wandered to the other side of the line."

"I dated a guy for a while when I went to college for a semester in Colorado, but I was faking it every step of the way. Every time he kissed me, I needed a giant economy-sized bottle of Listerine." Gail dragged her fingers through her hair. "So, do you consider yourself bisexual?"

"I don't really like labels."

"Do you still sleep with men?"

"No, my stint with Doug—that was the therapist's name—pretty well cured me of pursuing that route."

"What happened?"

"I'd been seeing him for six or eight months. We'd been in a sexual relationship for five months or more. I was already writing for Outrageous, and my third book came out while I was seeing Doug. I figured, hell, he knows me—knows who I am and what my issues are—so, I gave him an autographed copy of my new book."

"And?"

"And the next week, he had his office manager call to cancel my appointment."

"What did he say the next time you saw him?"

"There was no next time. Every time I called to schedule a session, he'd have someone call to cancel it. I finally got the message."

"But you said he knew you were a lesbian."

"He came from the school of thought that preached one good fuck would straighten me right out."

"Did it?"

"You know, for a little while, I thought it might. I had feelings for the guy. He was funny, sensitive, generous. He was almost the equivalent of the perfect woman, but with a strange appendage."

"Since then?"

"Since then, I've stayed with the estrogen crowd."

"I've read the bio sketches in your books. You never mention a partner."

"Although the book is fiction, the expectation is you don't lie in the acknowledgements or the items printed on the book jackets."

"Don't you want to share your life with someone?"

Connie reached over and took Gail's hand. "I thought I was."

Gail felt her stomach somersault. Where would she find the strength to tell Connie about Marissa? It wasn't that she cared so much about what Connie might think of her for having cheated on a partner in a coma, but more what she'd think of herself for not having been honest about her situation.

"And if you'll get your lazy buns out of this bed, partner, we can get the rest of the book shined up before the sun comes over the horizon." Connie was up and gone before Gail could utter a word.

I will be so glad to get back to Sweetwater. The sooner this damn book is done, the sooner I'm done with Connie Martin forever.

"YOU'VE MADE YOUR point, Connie, but I still disagree." Gail pointed to a paragraph on the page in her hand. "I think it's a huge mistake having your main character lie to her boss in this scene. It's totally out of keeping with everything you've tried to establish about her up to this point. I could see her having a confrontation with him, possibly resigning if he won't grant her the time off she needs to deal with her lover's health problems, but if she lies to him here, the rest of the book is nothing but a house of cards. It all comes crashing down."

"It's my book," Connie said through clenched teeth. "She's my character. She does what I tell her to do, not what you think she ought to do because of some misguided notions about truth, justice, and the American way."

"But look ahead to Chapter Seventeen." Gail grabbed another sheaf of papers. "See? Right here she's on a rampage with her mother about the misleading things the mother has told the neighbors about the lover's illness. What's her motivation? Where's her arc? If she's lying, what right does she have to point fingers at her mother for doing the same thing she's done? This would have her telling lies about the same person and the same circumstance. It weakens your story, Connie. It would be simple to fix it."

Connie shook her head vigorously. "Nope, I'm not changing it."

"Will you at least consider talking it over with Lydia? She's got a good eye for these kinds of things."

"Let's drop it for the time being, okay? We need to finish the line edits in the last four chapters." Connie shoved the controversial page aside.

"Please promise me you'll think about it. Flag it in the manuscript and ask Lydia for her opinion. If she wants you to change it, a two sentence rewrite would take care of it."

Connie was mute.

"Or not. Your book, your choice."

They labored on to the final page.

Chapter
Three

GAIL SWUNG BY the post office on her way through Sweetwater to collect the month's worth of mail held for her while she was in Atlanta. All of her bills were paid by direct debit from her checking account, so it wasn't likely there'd be anything urgent in the stack the clerk handed her. All she wanted to do was get home, unpack, and reclaim a normal routine. Thirty-four days at Connie Martin's beck and call had left her sapped and disillusioned. Sitting on the sofa with a cat in her lap while she thumbed through magazines and catalogs was as close to exertion as she planned to get for at least a week.

The sight of the cabin as she pulled into the yard brought moisture to her eyes. If she could have wrapped her arms around the structure and hugged it, she'd have done so. She let down the windows on the truck and breathed in the thick, woodsy smell. Cubbie and Annette stirred in their carriers as if they, too, recognized the scent of home.

"Come on, guys. I bet you'd appreciate a trip to the litter box," she said to the cats as she kicked the truck door shut. "Come to think of it, so would I."

They all relieved their bladders, and then the cats accompanied Gail as she went room to room opening windows. She touched pieces of furniture and the edges of picture frames on the walls as if to assure herself she was really, truly home. She made several trips from the truck to the house to bring in all of the things she had hauled to Atlanta. If she didn't deal with putting things away immediately, everything would lie in a pile just inside the door. She willed herself to put a load of laundry in the washer and to empty the food coolers. After cramming the cat carriers in the hall closet and putting kitty supplies in the cupboard in the utility room, she took her small suitcase to the bathroom and unloaded cosmetics into the medicine chest and the vanity, then emptied the other suitcases and stashed them under the daybed in the second bedroom. Tasks done, she grabbed a Coke and collapsed on the sofa with the bundle of mail.

Credit card offers. Sale flyers. Requests for donations to obscure but worthy causes. *Newsweek*. *Reader's Digest*. Catalogs galore.

A real letter from a real person.

The return address said it was from Amy, Marissa's sister. Several years earlier, Amy had come to visit Marissa and Gail. The two days she'd spent with them at Sweetwater Cabin had been just enough for Gail and Amy to form a perfunctory friendship. After the accident at Tellico Lake, Gail had contacted Amy to ask that she keep her informed about Marissa's condition. Three or four times in the two years since then, Amy had sent a quick note to tell Gail Marissa was still hooked to machines that breathed for her, still being fed by a tube, still clinging to something approximating life. Gail wasn't sure she had strength enough to think about Marissa just then. Maybe she'd lay the letter aside and read it tomorrow.

No, better to do it now. Otherwise, she'd lie awake all night dreading having to read it in the morning.

Gail tore the edge off the envelope. A buff colored, half-sized folded sheet of lightweight cardstock slid onto her lap. The twenty-third psalm was printed on the back side. Gail felt her heart constrict. She turned the document over. The front bore a picture of streaming rays of sunlight pouring from billowy clouds. A few words were superimposed over the sunbeams.

Marissa Ruth Adler. November 13, 1953. July 30, 2007.

Gail willed her fingers to open the folded sheet. Born in Scranton, Pennsylvania. Parents. Siblings. Education. Work history. Awards and honors. Church where the service was held. Place of interment—a town with a name Gail would have found amusing in other circumstances. Pallbearers. Clergy. Music. Funeral home in charge of arrangements.

Not surprisingly, there was no mention of Gail Larson in the funeral pamphlet. Hell, it had been more than two years since she had been in the same room with Marissa. Gail didn't give a damn about not getting a passing nod about her role in Marissa's life, but she was royally pissed that her parents had had her buried. Everyone knew Marissa wanted to be cremated and have her ashes scattered at Tellico Lake.

And the music was all wrong. Marissa didn't want droning church music. She wanted Judy Collins's version of "Amazing Grace" and a jazz rendition of "Just a Closer Walk with Thee." Couldn't her parents have gotten at least one piece of the service right?

Who was Reverend Shelburg? Stupid fool probably never met Marissa—the real Marissa before she was in a coma. As if he could do a decent eulogy for her. Besides, Marissa wanted a celebration of her life where her friends from the University would talk about all the good things they remembered about her, not this canned production where the minister inserted the deceased's name and spouted religious drivel.

Gail opened and closed the pamphlet repeatedly and turned it over in her hands as though doing it enough times might somehow make the right words miraculously appear.

Dead.

Marissa was dead. Shouldn't she be crying? Shouldn't she feel something? Shouldn't she do something?

It was almost as though she could hear Marissa's voice. *"Some day, when my legs get better, we're going dancing."*

Gail moved across the room and scanned the rows of CDs on the wall unit. She found the one she wanted.

The opening strains from "Amazing Grace" echoed in the room. The digitally remastered soundtrack of Judy Blue Eye's voice resonated, full and rich. Gail crossed to the mantle and picked up the photograph of Marissa. Marissa's hazel eyes blazed as clear and inviting as ever.

It wasn't exactly dance music, but Gail didn't care. She clutched the photo to her chest and floated around the living room. At long last, Marissa's legs were pliant and supple and strong.

When the spirit is free, any body can dance.

"I'VE BEEN TRYING to call you for days. Your answering machine must be broken." At the far end of the line, Penny Skramstaad sounded exasperated.

"Sorry. I was away for a month working on a special project for Outrageous Press. I left the day after you called to tell me you were going to Plainfield to be with your dad when they put him in the hospital. I turned off my answering machine while I was gone. I didn't get back until yesterday afternoon. What's up?"

"My dad died week before last."

"Oh, Penny. I'm so sorry. How are you?"

"Numb, is probably the best word." Gail heard Penny suck in her breath. "And pissed."

"Why?"

"Because my brothers are such worthless jerks."

"Want to talk about it?"

"Not really. At least not long distance."

"Does that mean you're finally going to accept my invitation to come to Tennessee? It might do you good to get away."

"I'd love to take a break from this nuthouse, but I can't."

"Why not?"

"Because both of my brothers blew into town the day before the funeral, didn't help with one minute's worth of the planning for the service, and haven't helped me with anything since. The way things are going, it will take me two months to have Dad's house ready to list with the real estate agent."

"If your dad died ten days ago, what's left to take care of?"

"Oh, just eighty-six years' worth of junk my dad piled in every corner of his house."

"I thought you guys would have done a lot of that when you put him in the nursing home."

"I wanted to, but Dale and Wayne said it wouldn't be right. What if Dad got better and came back home?"

"From what you told me when you put him in the home — what was it? More than a year ago, wasn't it? — there was never a chance he'd recover."

"Right. I know now it was their way of putting it off until they could stick me with doing all of it."

"And now?"

"And now they're riding my ass to get dad's house cleaned out and put on the market so they can get their share of the inheritance."

"You're the executrix?"

"Yeah. At least my dad was smart enough not to trust either of his sons with anything requiring thought or action."

"Where are they living now?"

"Dale is in Indianapolis and Wayne lives in Milwaukee."

"Did they come home to help with your dad after his stroke?"

"You've got to be kidding."

"It seemed you were sure this was going to be the end of the line for your dad."

"Yes, the doctor was real clear right from the start. Wayne said there'd be no point in coming because Dad wouldn't know he was here."

"Do you think that's true?"

"You couldn't have a conversation with him, but I think he could tell when I held his hand and talked to him, even if he couldn't talk back."

"What about Dale?"

"Said he couldn't afford to be away from work."

"What does he do?"

"He sells patio furniture."

"Guess there must have been a hush-hush international wicker emergency. I'm sorry your brothers weren't more supportive, Penny, for your sake and your dad's."

"Thanks, but why should they change now? I didn't care so much for me, although heaven knows I could use some help around here. I hated it for Dad, though."

"I always liked your dad. He never made me feel like I was some kind of freak."

"What do you mean?"

"Most of the other dads in Plainfield seemed to sense I wasn't like all the other girls. They knew I wasn't going to marry a nice hometown boy and raise kids. And they made it clear I didn't belong. Maybe they worried I'd lure their daughters into my debaucheries. Your dad didn't seem to care. He treated me like a regular kid."

"I don't think my dad knew there was such a thing as a lesbian. You're probably giving him credit for kindness when ignorance is more likely the explanation."

"Doesn't matter why he was nice to me. He was. And I'll always remember him for that."

"How about putting your remembering to good use?"

"Doing what?"

"I'm on the verge of slitting my wrists. I've been working at cleaning this house out for more than a week, and I've barely made a dent."

"I could send you money for a blow torch."

"Believe me, I've already considered it." Penny paused and Gail waited.

"Come up to Minnesota and help me, Gail. Maybe it's because I've been staying in this house for weeks on end, or because I've been breathing the Plainfield air, or maybe it's nothing more than a strange version of grief, but if I'm in Plainfield, you should be in Plainfield, too. Every time I drive by the monument to the city's founding fathers in the park across from the high school, I remember the time you and I dressed the statues in bras and hung purses off their arms. Or how about that night we went out to the lake where all the popular couples went to neck and got your dad's car stuck in the sand? C'mon back and help me relive our misspent youth."

"Gee, I don't know."

"I can send you money for the plane ticket."

"It's not that. What about my job? And my cats?"

"I hadn't thought about the fact you have a life."

Gail could picture the crestfallen look on Penny's face. The effect it had on her was no different from when they walked the hallways of Plainfield High almost forty years earlier.

"Give me a couple of hours to see what I can work out, okay? I'll call you later."

"Let me give you the number here at Dad's house."

"No need. I called there so many times it's forever etched in my mental phone book."

Gail hung up the receiver and looked around the main room of the cabin as though she were seeing it for the first time. The month in Atlanta with Connie Martin had somehow warped her perception of home. What else could make her feel so alienated in her woodland retreat? She saw Marissa's funeral pamphlet still lying on the sofa where she had dropped it the previous evening.

Come to think of it, Plainfield, Minnesota, in the early fall seemed like a perfect idea.

"HOW WAS THE trip?"

"Next time I say I'm going to drive non-stop from southeastern Tennessee to north central Minnesota with two neurotic cats in the cab of my pick-up truck, please feel free to have me institutionalized." Gail flopped into an overstuffed chair in Penny Skramstaad's childhood home. "The louder I played the radio to try and drown them out, the louder the cats yowled. Now I know what the Muzak system in the elevators in hell will play."

"How long did it take you to get here?"

"In people time, about twenty-six hours, but this trip really should be measured in dog years, which would make it a little over a week." Gail rolled her head on the rounded back of the chair. "I know I need to go out to the truck and bring them in here, but I wanted at least five minutes of peace and quiet."

"Do you think they'll get along with my dogs?"

"Who knows? I don't think they've ever seen one. The way I feel about them right now, I might gladly offer them up as a canine appetizer. Where are your dogs?"

"Out back. You know, it seems really strange to see Cookie and Rounder running around in my old backyard. I keep thinking I'm going to see Scruffy or Buzzie or Knickers instead of these guys."

"I bet. Kind of a time-space warp or something, huh?"

"Yeah. And how the hell did I get so old? If I'm on Vasa Avenue in Plainfield, Minnesota, I shouldn't be more than eighteen."

"Now that all four of our parents are dead, I guess we must be the old farts we used to make so much fun of when we lived here." Gail's voice dropped a notch. "I really am sorry about your dad, Penny."

"It will sound heartless, but for the most part, I'm glad it's over. He hasn't had much of a life these past few years."

Gail heaved a sigh and rose from the chair. "If I sit any longer, I'll fall sound asleep, so I'd better unload the truck. Where do you want me to put the cats?"

"If it's okay with you, I'm going to have you stay in Mom and Dad's bedroom. Will the cats be all right in there?"

"Sure. We'll keep the door to the room closed. I'll set up their litter box in a corner, and we'll be fine."

"Remember, my parents added a bathroom off the back when Dale was in high school. You could put the box in there."

"Okay. That'll be great."

Gail brought her road-weary cats into their new temporary quarters. Penny helped with suitcases and paraphernalia for the cats, and then excused herself to finish fixing dinner. Gail opened the carriers and sweet talked Cubbie and Annette into venturing out. First, it was a month in the Magnolia Suites with Connie Martin, and then it was only one night back in their familiar cabin in Sweetwater before they were crammed in their crates for another interminable ride. They had had, Gail feared, more than enough time to plot their revenge.

She splashed some water on her face, then went to the kitchen to join Penny.

"I can't believe you went to the trouble to cook something."

"I'm badly out of practice. We'll probably end up at the emergency room having our stomachs pumped later," Penny said. "It's a chicken and vegetable dish I'll serve over basmati rice. I've got a green salad and some fresh bread to have with it." She picked up a cruet from the counter top. "This is oil and red wine vinegar with some herbs. If you'd prefer some other kind of dressing, check the shelf on the refrigerator door."

"The oil and vinegar will be fine. Can I help with something?"

"No, I've got it under control. The salad is in the fridge ready to go. The chicken will be done in a little while, and the rice will sit here and simmer. I'll pop the bread in the oven now so it can heat through while the chicken finishes, and that will about take care of it."

Penny rinsed her hands in the sink and wiped them on a towel draped over the handle of the oven door. "Do you want some wine or a beer maybe?"

"Some wine would be nice."

Penny opened a bottle of white wine and poured them each a glass.

"To old friends," she toasted as she handed Gail her glass.

"I'll drink to that."

"Let's go sit in the living room until dinner is ready." Penny led the way from the kitchen to the big room occupying the front half of the house. "I really appreciate your coming all the way up here to help with this." Penny sat next to Gail on the sofa. "I hope you didn't have too much trouble getting things arranged so you could be away."

"I needed a change." Gail laughed cynically. "That sounds kind of strange since I was just down in Atlanta for a month."

"What was that about anyway?"

"My managing editor had me working on a special project with one of Outrageous Press's most popular authors."

"Sounds exciting. Tell me about it."

"Some other time, maybe. It's too complicated to go into tonight."

They sat in silence sipping their wine.

"I almost hate to bring it up, but what's happening with Marissa? I've been so caught up in my own dramas with Dad, I've forgotten to ask."

Gail tilted her head back and stared at the ceiling.

"No change, huh?"

"Big change. Worst possible change. She died."

"Oh, Gail. You should have called me." Penny laid her hand gently on Gail's forearm.

"Why? No one called me. Marissa's sister sent me the folder the funeral home printed. She'd been dead for weeks before I knew she was gone."

"That must have been hard on you."

"Not really. Because of how her parents cut me off, it was almost as if she died two years ago." Gail gulped the last of her wine. "I know it sounds stupid, but I always held on to this crazy notion she'd get better, and one day, she'd show up at our cabin in Sweetwater."

"When did she die?" Penny's voice broke as she asked.

"July thirtieth."

"While you were in Atlanta?"

"Right, but it wouldn't have mattered if I'd been on Mars. As far as the Adlers were concerned, I didn't merit a footnote in their daughter's life."

"They knew about — about the two of you?"

"About our being lovers, you mean? Sure. Marissa had told her parents she was a lesbian long before she and I got together. They simply closed their eyes tight and wished it away." Gail paused. "And I guess they succeeded. In their perception, the fourteen years she and I shared never happened."

"That sucks."

"No shit."

They heard the oven timer sound.

Penny stood and offered her hand to Gail.

"Come on. After what the two of us have been through, we could use more wine."

Gail grasped Penny's hand. Wine wasn't what she wanted or needed, but it would have to suffice.

"THANKS FOR DINNER. It was great. I had forgotten how nice it is to sit with someone who's known you forever — but still likes you anyway — and talk. I'd better go to the bedroom and check on the cats. They're not used to being cooped up for so long."

"I need to bring the dogs in. I'll put them in the basement for the night. That way, you can let the cats come out here with us for a while."

They set off to deal with respective pets and met back in the living room a few minutes later. Cubbie and Annette gingerly inspected every piece of furniture and, with their mouths hanging open, sniffed the bottoms of Penny's shoes.

"Eau de canine," Gail said as she gestured to Penny's feet.

"And probably rabbit poop and squirrel dookey and bird manure, too."

"An olfactory smorgasbord."

"Apparently."

"Much as I'd love to sit here and talk the night away, Penny, I'd better hit the sack. How about you?"

"One of the old movie channels is showing one of my favorites tonight. I think I'll sit up and watch at least a little of it."

"What's on?"

"'Urban Cowboy.'"

"You're a John Travolta fan?"

"It's not so much the movie as the sound track. I've always loved a bunch of the songs."

"I'm not sure I could name a song from the movie if you paid me to."

"I bet you'll remember them once the movie starts." Penny pulled her feet under her as she wedged herself into the corner of the sofa.

"What the heck. If I fall asleep, I hope my snoring doesn't drown out the music." Gail kicked her shoes off as she rearranged herself on the other end of the sofa. The two cats scrambled for prime lap space.

Conversation stopped while they watched the opening scenes. Soon they were lost in the story line. Mid-way through the movie, Penny glanced over at Gail. Gail did her best to hide her brimming eyes.

"I didn't think you'd let a schmaltzy movie get to you," Penny said.

"It's not the movie. It's the song."

"Could I Have this Dance?"

"Uh huh. Marissa and I used to dream about a medical breakthrough that would give back the use of her legs. We always said this would be one of the songs we'd play the first time we could hold each other and dance."

"If I had known, I'd never have suggested we watch this movie."

"No, it's okay. We knew it was nothing more than a crazy dream and that she'd always have to use her leg braces. Funny, though. We got so good at picturing it in our minds that, sometimes when we'd play the songs we'd picked for our dance card, I could almost see her in my arms, light and responsive."

"You loved her a lot, didn't you?"

"Yeah, I did."

"Was there ever anyone else? Anyone before Marissa?"

Gail caught the look on Penny's face. She felt her pulse leap into overdrive. She leaned forward, tilted her head, and dropped a kiss—so gentle it was almost imperceptible—on Penny's lips.

In a flash, Gail came to her senses. She was on her feet, out of the living room, and down the hall with the cats close on her heels. She slipped into the bedroom and closed the door behind her. Gail slid silently down the back of the door and gathered the cats to her. "No fool like an old fool, huh guys?" The tears that had started on the sofa fell in full force in the darkened room.

BACK IN THE living room, Penny sat slack-jawed and pensive. It had all happened so quickly she wasn't sure anything *had* happened. The last few strains of the movie's love theme came from the television. Anne Murray asked again if she could have this dance.

"HAVE YOU EVER known me to be attracted to women?" Penny's voice sounded as though it were coming from another planet instead of from a few feet across the room.

Gail nearly dropped the painted figurine she was wrapping to put in the box of things to be donated to the church for their next rummage sale. She didn't dare look at Penny. It had been two days since she had planted the ill-advised kiss on Penny's lips. Since then, they had kept busy sorting, packing, tossing—often in different rooms—for hours on end. When neither of them had mentioned the kiss in forty-eight hours, Gail hoped it had been relegated to the category of over and forgotten.

"So have you?" Penny stopped piling towels and sheets into the box at her feet and took a step toward Gail.

"Have I what?"

"Have you ever known me to be attracted to women? Tell me the truth."

Gail felt her mouth go dry as adrenalin poured into her bloodstream. If there was one thing fifty-plus years of living had taught her it was when someone insisted you tell them the truth, the last thing they wanted to hear was anything approaching unvarnished reality.

She catapulted through a hasty mental recap of her forty years of friendship with Penny. In their first year of high school, there was Karen, the doctor's wife Penny did babysitting for. She had talked about that woman as though she were Aphrodite incarnate. Then there was the requisite crush on the gym teacher, Miss Conway, in their junior year. Of course, Penny would deny any such attraction, but Gail knew better. (She'd had a crush on Miss Conway, too.) Gail couldn't forget Penny's senior year puppy love fascination over the cheerleader, Kim, who didn't know Penny drew breath. How many times had Gail and Penny—at Penny's suggestion—driven to the practice field to watch Kim and the rest of the squad jump and shimmy and exhort the Plainfield Panthers to "Go! Fight! Win!"? For her part, Gail had feigned nonchalance as she and Penny slouched on the chain link fence eyeing the popular girls honing their skills in pompom shaking, pyramid building, and foot stomping. Every time they went, Penny dreamed up new ways to try to catch Kim's attention. Penny had pocketed one of Kim's maroon and gold pompoms she'd accidentally left behind one afternoon as the squad left practice to head for Shaggy's Malt Shop. Penny sealed the pompom in a zip-top bag and held on to it for who knew how long—a cherished collector's item.

In later years, it was the woman who managed the hotel where Penny worked for a while who was the sure bet topic of conversation every time Gail and Penny spoke. Then it was a divorced neighbor lady who brought Penny baked goods and helped her in her flower garden. Last year, it was a female customer who kept coming into the financial planners' office where Penny worked. Gail was sure she could add more women to the list if she thought about it. As best Gail could tell, Penny had *always* been attracted to women, but she had never admitted it to anyone—especially not to herself.

"If that were the case, how would you explain Richie and Larry and Russell?" Gail put the figurine in the box and sat on the edge of the nearest chair.

"See? That's what I mean." Gail saw the look of relief on Penny's face. "If I liked women, how could I have slept with those guys?" She sat down in the adjacent chair and avoided making eye contact with Gail.

Gail chose not to remind Penny of the fact Richie was one of her brother's best friends, and that he had done the deed with any and every girl in the high school who would lift her skirt for him. Larry was a married man with whom Penny had carried on for five years or more—a non-issue in Gail's estimation because he had told Penny right from the start there was no way he was leaving his wife and getting stuck with alimony and child support. As for Russell, twenty-five years ago, Penny and Linda Hughes, another of their Plainfield High classmates, had dated the same man for months on end. In the end, he married Linda, and Penny was her maid of honor. Penny claimed she still carried a torch for him, but if she did, the flame didn't throw much light.

Gail would wager there had been other heterosexual liaisons in Penny's past, which Penny had opted not to tell her about, but odds were in favor of them all being flashes in the pan. Penny beamed out an unmistakable signal that said, "Just browsing in the penis section. I don't plan to sign a long-term contract."

"But still…"

Gail took a deep breath and willed herself to speak. "What's on your mind?"

"Well, there's this woman at work."

Gail felt the medicine ball slam into her stomach. "Oh? What about her?" She knew she didn't sound as nonchalant as she wanted to.

"Her name is Andrea. Andrea Martinson. She was the queen bee in our office in Santa Fe, but she transferred up to the Minneapolis office about eight months ago."

"What's her story?"

"She's been with Worldwide Financial for years and years. She started there right out of college. She's got a couple of grown kids—boys, if I remember right—and a husband who, a few months back, took early retirement from his job with one of the big feed and seed companies."

"So, a happily married woman?"

"Oh, yeah. She talks about good old Bob all the time."

"But?"

"You'll think I'm being foolish."

"Try me." Gail willed her voice to sound light and inviting.

"You'll tell me I'm being dumb."

"As I said, try me."

"Turns out we live on the same transit line. We almost always catch the same bus into downtown every morning. She saves me a seat, and we talk the whole way to the office. She bakes muffins and brings two in, so we can each have one when we take our coffee breaks. She knows way more about how our office runs and what recommendations to make to clients, but she's constantly bringing files to me and asking for my opinion."

"And these things are making you question your sexual orientation? It doesn't sound like enough evidence for you to start shopping at Dykes-R-Us."

"It's more than that."

"Such as?"

"For one thing, when we sit together on the bus, she always presses her leg up against mine."

"What else?"

"When she comes to my desk to ask me questions, she leans down real close so our heads are almost touching. Or she'll put her hand on my arm or on my shoulder when she's talking to me."

"And what do you do when she does these things."

Penny's laugh reminded Gail of a grade-school girl who'd been caught under the bleachers sneaking a peak at a little boy's wee-wee. "I slide over farther to my side of the bus seat or push my chair away from the desk and act as if I need something from the file cabinet."

"I see. Giving her every indication the attraction is mutual."

"C'mon, Gail. She's a married woman."

"So? You've never heard of anyone figuring out they made a mistake and changing their mind?"

"But I'm not gay!"

Only for lack of action, not for lack of desire. "Yes, but Andrea might be."

"As I said, she's a married woman."

"Who could very well have slept with three, seventeen, or a hundred and nine other women since the day she stood at the altar with — what did you say his name was? Bob? Anyway, maybe it's a case of he's none the wiser, and she's able to keep her sanity because of it."

"Do you think?"

"How should I know? Up until two minutes ago, I didn't know Andrea Martinson existed. You're the one who seems to be seeing something in her tea leaves."

"But you're gay, Gail."

"And that somehow grants me the clairvoyant ability to detect other lesbians, sight unseen, based on a cursory description from a woman who has suddenly found the cotton crotch in her nylon bikini briefs inexplicably moist?"

"When you put it that way…"

"What way would you rather I put it?"

"Damned if I know."

"You wouldn't have brought it up if you didn't think I could help you."

"Isn't there some kind of guide book or user's manual?"

"You bet. I'll run right downtown and buy you a copy of *Ten Sure-Fire Ways to Determine if a Woman You Think is Straight is Really Trying to get in Your Pantyhose*. It was on the best seller list for almost a year."

"Very funny, Ms. Larsen."

"Actually, there are a couple of books you might want to take a look at. If I had known you wanted them, I would have brought them along. One of them is called *And Then I Met this Woman*. It's a collection of stories, each one a true life tale of someone who discovered she had been drinking from the wrong fountain. Another one that might help you think this through is a book of poetry by Rita Mae Brown — *Songs to a Handsome Woman*."

"You can bet old man Lundquist won't have them on the shelves of the only bookstore in Plainfield, Minnesota."

"I'm sure you're right, but the library has public use computers. I bet we can order them on-line and have them here in a day or two."

"Oh, I don't know."

"Don't worry. They won't label the package 'lewd lesbian literature.' The mailman will never know what's inside."

"You think I'm off my rocker, don't you?"

"Not at all. I'd say you're dealing with some tough issues."

"So you think I'm gay?"

"Doesn't matter what I think. Your vote is the only one that counts."

Penny stood and wandered aimlessly around the room. Gail hated witnessing Penny's embarrassment.

"Let's order the books," Gail offered. "When they come, turn a few pages and see if you see yourself in the stories or the poems. If it creeps you out, you can probably give yourself a pass on joining the Better Late than Never Lesbian Society."

"I READ THE book of poems and part of the other book last night." Gail and Penny were sitting in the breakfast nook at the back of the house on Vasa Avenue. Cubbie and Annette had long since made peace with Penny's dogs, Cookie and Rounder. All four animals were sprawled in sunny patches on the linoleum floor.

The on-line discount bookseller had rushed Gail's recommended volumes to them in Plainfield. In the intervening days since their conversation about Andrea Martinson, Gail had studiously avoided bringing up the topic and had, instead, intensified her efforts to get the house ready for sale.

"Good. Your second grade teacher would be proud. What did you think?"

"It's confusing."

"Confusing how?"

"Like I'm watching a disaster in slow motion."

"Meaning?"

"I don't want to keep looking at it, but I can't seem to help myself."

"So you don't feel the need to march out of this house and go in search of a man who could help you put the world back on its axis?"

"No. But while I was reading, I did catch myself wondering what Andrea might be doing."

"Did you call her and ask her?"

"No! What if her husband answered the phone?"

"Gee, I don't know. How about ask to talk to Andrea?"

"I'd probably have passed out."

Gail launched into her rendition of an old Supremes song about getting bitten by a love bug.

"Oh, stop. What did Diana Ross ever do to you?"

"All I'm saying is you seem to know where you need to go, but you want someone else to tell you to get on the train."

"Do you really think so?"

"I'm no expert, but if reading love poems written by one woman to another woman makes you—a woman, or at least so you claim—ponder and pine over yet another woman who takes every opportunity to be in physical contact with you, then yes, I'd have to say there's at least a glimmer of possibility there."

"So what should I do?"

"Go to the depot and buy your ticket to Andreaville."

"What if she laughs at me or tells me to go to hell?"

"Wouldn't that be better than spending night after night pitching and tossing in your lonely bed, telling yourself you're not imagining how it would feel to have her lying next to you?"

"But we work together."

"So?"

"What if she tells everybody in our office I'm some despicable pervert?"

"My crystal ball isn't back from the repair shop, Penny. I can't predict what's going to happen. I'll tell you this, though. If you make an overture and she rejects it outright, I'm guessing she'd be too embarrassed to say anything to anyone. I mean, after all, you could point out she's the one who's been initiating all the touchy-feely stuff, and you were taking your cue from her. If, on the other hand, she rips your clothes off and asks what took you so long to make your move, I can't picture her hanging posters in the office proclaiming you rode her like a pinto pony and yelled 'Bingo' at a particular moment of ecstasy."

"You make it sound so inconsequential—nothing but an everyday occurrence."

"Quite the contrary, m'dear. Falling in love is monumental—and an occurrence you really shouldn't thumb your nose at."

"So now you're accusing me of being in love."

"It's not an accusation in the least. It's a fond wish for a lifelong friend."

"Why does life have to be so hard?"

"Sometimes it's only as hard as we make it."

"I really wish Andrea would give me some sort of sign."

"Do you remember the old joke I always used to tell about the guy who was trapped in the flood?"

"Not really."

"Then humor me while I refresh your memory." Gail cleared her throat for dramatic effect. "The flood waters are rising and this guy — let's call him Fred — is standing on the front porch of his house. A neighbor comes by in a four-wheel drive jeep and tells Fred to get in. 'No, no, my help is in the lord and he'll save me,' Fred says. Soon, the flood gets worse yet, and Fred has to go to the second floor of his house to keep from getting swept away. Two firemen come by in a rowboat and tell him to get in. 'No, no. I believe in the power of the lord, and I know he'll save me.' Sure enough, the flood swells even higher, and Fred has to scramble up to the roof of his house. A helicopter flies over, and a man inside shouts at him with a megaphone to grab the rope ladder they're dangling down to him. Once again, Fred waves them off shouting, 'No, I've always believed in the strength of the lord, and I've prayed for him to save me.' An hour later, the flood crests higher than Fred's house, and he washes away and drowns. Next thing he knows, he's in heaven standing face to face with the lord, and he's in absolute disbelief the lord has let him die.

'How could you let this happen?' Fred demands. 'I believed in you all my life, including in a time of dire peril. I put all my trust in you, but still, you let the flood take me away and kill me. Why didn't you help me?'

'Now, Fred' said the lord, 'I sent you a jeep and a rowboat and a helicopter. What else were you expecting me to do?'"

Penny chuckled as Gail finished the story. Gail held Penny's gaze with her eyes.

"Andrea has sent you a fleet of jeeps, an armada of rowboats, and at least a couple of helicopters, Penny."

"I guess."

"I might remind you of one other thing, too."

"What's that?"

"You never did learn how to swim."

Chapter
Four

"IT WAS REALLY nice of you to stay here in Plainfield with the dogs while I went back to my house in Minneapolis."

"Not a problem. Rounder and Cookie and I got along fine for the day and a half you were gone." Gail bent down and scratched Cookie's underbelly. "Didn't we, cupcake?" Gail stood and arched her back. "It got a little crowded on the bed last night with four animals jockeying for space, but we worked it out. Besides, your being away gave me a chance to get your dad's clothes out of here. I know you'd have had a hard time sorting through his personal belongings."

"You're right. I would have. Thanks for taking care of it." Penny eased onto the sofa. "I can't believe how many pieces of paper it takes to put one stinking house on the market." She began pulling sheaves of paper from her shoulder bag. "Dad's power-of-attorney. Deed and title for the house. Mom's death certificate. Sheesh. She's been dead for fifteen years. Did they think she'd come back from the grave and file a complaint? I still need to get a notarized copy of Dad's death certificate, and the real estate agent said she wants notarized statements from my brothers saying they aren't contesting the sale of the house or the terms of Dad's will."

"It's a complex world."

"No joke. I should have thought to bring all my file folders for Dad's affairs with me when I came up last month, but I was in such a rush to get up here, it completely slipped my mind."

"As I said, I was glad to do it. At least you didn't have to haul the dogs with you up and down I-94." Gail opened her arms expansively and gestured around the living room. "I hope one more day will be enough to get everything left boxed up and out of here. You should be able to list the house by Monday, at the latest."

"It will be so strange never to set foot in this house again." Penny's lower lip trembled.

"I know." Gail dropped down next to Penny and looped an arm around her shoulder. "During our high school days, I spent almost as much time in this house as I did in my own. Good thing we'll always have our memories."

"I could use a drink. How about you?"

"Sure. What do you want? I'll get it."

"Is there still some beer in the fridge?"

"I picked up another six-pack last night. I'll be right back."

Gail went to the kitchen and pulled two long-necks from the refrigerator.

"Everything okay at your house down in the Cities?" Gail sat down cross-legged on the floor and faced the sofa.

Penny took a long swig from her beer. "Yeah, the house was fine. Too bad I don't have the brains God gave a turnip, though."

"Why do you say that?"

"I saw Andrea last night."

Gail studied the label on her beer bottle. "How'd it go?"

"Not at all like I hoped it might."

"Tell me about it."

"I guess I was thinking about her on the drive down. You know, I've been away from work for almost a month now, so it's been that long since I've seen her. I've talked to the office manager a couple of times to keep him up to date on what's going on. He's been good about letting me use my sick days and vacation time, and I know he's told everybody in the office about Dad dying and all. Andrea sent a nice sympathy note to me here at Dad's house."

"You had her on your mind as you cruised down the interstate, and your little heart was going pitty-pat, and other anatomical parts were doing other things you found hard to ignore."

"Something like that."

"So you called her."

"So I called her. After I'd found all the papers I needed to get this house deal moving, I sucked up my courage and called her. And right off the bat, she invites me to meet her for dinner."

"Which you accepted."

"Of course." Penny snorted out a half laugh. "If I had only known."

"Known what?"

"She meant dinner with them, not her."

"Bob, the wonder husband?"

"One and the same."

"What did you think of him?"

"South end of a north-bound horse."

"You base your assessment on what?"

"He was rude, he was crude, he was a conversation hog."

"Oh, you mean he was a man?"

"Yeah. And what really honked me off was how he kept doing really mean things to Andrea."

"Such as?"

"The whole time we were at the restaurant, when he was talking to her, he'd pinch the backside of her upper arm where the skin is real thin and bruises so easily. Or he'd insult her by making fun of her weight and belittling her family members. Little barbs like that."

"And she sat there and took it?"

"Sort of, but I got the feeling she was really mortified by how he was acting."

"Can you blame her?"

"No, but I felt something else was going on, too."

"What do you mean?"

"I got the feeling she was used to him being an ass in public, but not to the degree he was last night."

"Maybe he was staking his claim and issuing a warning to anyone who might have designs on his little woman."

"Oh, shit."

"I know you and I have differing views on how big a role intuition plays in human behavior, but it sure sounds as if old Bob—although he's a member of the gender not renowned for paying much attention to gut feelings—picked up on vibrations in the air and felt compelled to pee on his property so there'd be no mistaking who owned it."

"C'mon, Gail. Why would he get all defensive about me?"

"From what I understand, that's the worst possible situation. It would be one thing to lose his wife to another man, but losing her to a woman—I mean, really, what would that say about his machismo?"

"Huh. I never thought about that."

"It's only a hunch. I wasn't there, but what you described seems to be jealous, over-protective posturing."

"Which probably about finishes my chances with Andrea."

"Why?"

"If she'd bring her husband along on our first date..."

"First of all, maybe Andrea didn't know it was supposed to be a date, and secondly, for all you know, Bob pitched a holy fit and demanded to be included. She might have wanted to come alone."

"Who knows? I don't think I'm cut out for this woman-to-woman scene anyway. Driving from my house to the restaurant to meet her—at least I thought it would be just her—I was almost sick to my stomach."

"If you thought all you were doing was meeting a friend from work, do you think you'd have had a similar reaction?"

"No, that's my point."

"And that's *my* point, Penny. Your guts—quite literally, I might add—are telling you to go for this because it's your big chance, and you're still fighting it every inch of the way."

"Easy for you to say. You know what you're doing. You've always been gay. It's no big deal for you."

"Sorry, but you're wrong. Not about the being gay part. I've known that since I was five years old, but laying your heart out there for someone else to accept or to stomp on is a major leap of faith. Rejection hurts whether you're gay or straight. Probably the only thing worse than having someone turn you down is never knowing for sure if she might have said yes if you'd only had the courage to ask."

"You don't strike me as the kind of person who ever walked away without knowing, Gail."

"Wrong again."

"Hard to believe."

"Maybe so, but nonetheless true."

Penny drained her beer bottle. "Anyone I know?"

Gail had known Penny long enough to recognize every nuance in her voice. Her attempt at detachment failed.

Gail rose from the floor and picked up the book of Rita Mae's poems from the end table by the sofa. She handed the book to Penny. "Change the cover so it says 'Songs to Penny,' and you can probably figure out what name to substitute where it says Rita Mae Brown."

As she had done on her first night there following the much-regretted-but-never-again-spoken-of kiss she'd given Penny, Gail walked down the hallway to the back of the house and closed the bedroom door behind her.

GAIL LAY ON the bed and strained her ears, waiting for Penny's knock at the bedroom door. She knew exactly how Penny must have felt when she was driving to meet Andrea at the restaurant down in Minneapolis. She wished she hadn't had that bottle of beer. It was turning to acid in her stomach. To distract herself, she rehearsed dozens of opening lines. Whatever she said to Penny, it would have to be memorable. She didn't want to blow a dream four decades in the making.

The distraction wasn't working. The minutes dragged by. An hour. Then another. Gail had to admit to herself Penny wouldn't be coming to her door that night. Gail struggled against the tears burning the backs of her eyelids.

"Idiot. Couldn't leave well enough alone, could you?"

She wished for sleep but was too agitated for that comfort. Her mind reeled back to a distant memory. It was another time when sleep had eluded her. And every detail came back to her as though it had happened only a day before.

HER SKIN WAS on red alert feeling the warmth of the sleeping body next to her. She heard the rise and fall of the measured breaths of her companion, lost in well-earned slumber. Her lips tasted of the residue from unfamiliar but endlessly inviting places. The fragrance from those newly-explored openings lingered on her fingers. As she propped herself up on her elbow, her eyes were filled with the vision of Jill Woodhouse — the woman, the child, the wonder — entwined around her torso.

Gail slid out from under the covers of the bed in Jill's thirteenth floor dorm room. The mattress on the webbed spring frame was meant for only one person, but she and Jill hadn't taken up more than a single body's worth of space. The thinnest slice of gray-green morning light was coming through the window. November mornings in Colorado weren't known for their brilliance. She stared attentively at Jill as though it were the only way she could convince herself the night was real, not another fruitless fantasy. Silently, Gail began slipping into her clothes, which were lying in a jumble on the floor beside Jill's bed.

As she dressed, she gazed at Jill, and all of the emotions of the night resurfaced and fought for attention. Her pulse thudded in her ear as she remembered the evocative power of their tender, tentative touches. Then she recalled the fear that any second they might be caught or that one of them would flee. She relived how, only hours earlier, she and Jill had both ached for more — for consummation — and she felt again the frustration of not knowing how to accomplish it. She found herself awash in the tangle of feelings she had experienced all through that mystical, surreal night. It was awkward and abortive and unsettling. It was thrilling and consuming and exhilarating.

Gail found a pen and a piece of paper. "November 4, 1974, seven-forty A.M.," she began. She lifted her eyes from the notepad to glance over at Jill one more time. "I don't know what to say except thank you and good-bye. It was so beautiful. So are you. I hope you don't hate me for what we've done." She propped the note against a stack of books atop the desk, picked up her shoes, and crept to the door. She allowed herself one last look at the virgin angel — her first lover — dreaming peacefully, her long sandy blonde hair scattered across the pillow.

There was no instruction manual for what to do after spending her first night in the throes of physical passion. Routine was her safest bet. She went to her "Writers of the Transcendental Age" class and feigned appreciation for Thoreau and Emerson.

Jill was waiting for Gail when she got out of class.

"Gail, I need to talk to you."

"There's nothing you can say to me I haven't already said to myself." Gail started to walk away, but Jill caught her by the arm.

"Why are you doing this?"

"Don't you know what we've done? Don't you know what people will say about us?"

"What about what I'd say about us? Don't I have a right to some feelings, too? Let's go back to my room. We can talk there. My roommate won't be back 'til tomorrow."

They walked across campus without speaking. The set designer had done an outstanding job. The November sky was slate-gray, and the cold wind blew the brittle leaves around their feet. If only they could have walked into a rustic cabin with a blazing fireplace.

Jill's room was on the top floor of the dormitory. They continued in silence as they rode up on the elevator. Once inside the room, Jill flung her arms around Gail and kissed her fervently. She led Gail to her bed and they sat down on the edge.

"I don't know if what we did is wrong or right," Jill said. "I don't care if what we did is wrong or right. All I know is last night was the best thing that's ever happened to me. I always wondered why I felt so cold when my dates kissed me. It's because they were guys. With you, everything is so warm and so real. It's exciting, and it makes me feel alive. I don't care what people will say about us. I just want to be with you."

Gail's heart raced. She had known since she was a child she was gay, but she doubted she would ever find anyone who would let her act on that feeling. Now, there was this live, adorable young woman almost pleading with her to be what she had always wanted to be. A tiny voice urged her to be cautious, but the years of pent-up longing were too great. The truth will out.

"You're sure, Jill?"

"Yes," she said simply.

They fell together on the bed and began the age-old ever-new exploration of young lovers. Wasn't it Goethe who said the true measure of love is the belief we alone can love and that no one has ever loved this way before?

Gail and Jill didn't need a cabin with a fireplace. They made their own pure, intense, warming blaze again and again.

TOO BAD ALL her memories of Jill couldn't be as happy as those of their first night. It was less than a year later her bliss with Jill turned to dust. They were sitting in the tiny off-campus apartment they had rented together for the summer.

"I'M TIRED OF feeling like less than a whole, real person, Gail."

"What's that supposed to mean?"

"I hate lying to my family and everyone here at school."

"So tell them the truth."

"I don't think you know what the truth is."

"I know you and I lie naked in our bed most nights, and I know you enjoy what we do there."

"But it's not something I'd have ever done if you hadn't come into my life."

"So now it's my fault you're a lesbian?"

"You're wrong on both counts."

"Both counts?"

"It's not your fault." Jill cleared her throat and struggled to finish her statement. "And I'm not a lesbian."

"What do you call making love with me?"

"Starting right now, it's something I used to do."

"What are you saying?"

"I'm sorry, but I can't do this anymore."

"You've found somebody else—is that it?"

"Not somebody else— not really a somebody—something bigger and better."

"Oh, come on. I'm the one you've been opening your legs for since last November. You've told me a hundred times nothing could be better than what we do to each other."

"I was okay with all that for a while, but I know now it's not who I really am."

"And who do you think you really are?"

"I'm someone who has been accepted as a novitiate at St. Margaret's convent."

"The hell you say."

"No, I'd say the road to heaven."

"Bullshit."

"It happened three weeks ago, but I couldn't find the right time to tell you."

"And you've been upside down on me making me come at least twice a week for those three weeks."

"I kept hoping I could feel close enough to you to tell you without hurting you."

"And you've decided this is the perfect moment?"

"There won't ever be a perfect moment. I report to the convent on the first of the month. I needed to let you know so you can find another roommate if you want to keep this place."

Gail leaped out her chair. "A roommate? For chrissakes, Jill, you and I aren't roommates. Maybe I should call the Mother Superior and tell her the church is planning to marry a lesbian. That should go over real well."

"Stop it, Gail. I'm not a lesbian. I'm one of God's chosen women."

Gail wasn't sure which hurt more—Jill's tone of voice when she said "lesbian" (akin to leper, pervert, damned, unclean) or the knowledge she was losing Jill—losing her to a force she could never hope to compete with.

"How could you, Jill? You're supposed to be my lover."

"You'll always be my only physical lover, Gail. I'll never forget you, but I've got to follow my calling and fulfill my life. And you should do the same."

WITH WHAT WAS left of her heart, Gail Larsen had tried to do as Jill suggested. She wandered the country for several years looking for a way to anchor her life, but until she met Marissa Adler, everything was worthless. Now Marissa was dead.

And almost worse than that, Gail was sure she had ruined her chances with Penny Skramstaad.

"GAIL, ARE YOU awake?"

Penny's voice startled her. She had fallen asleep while reliving her time with Jill. The crick in her neck made it hard for her to lift her head. She heard Penny take a couple of steps farther into the bedroom.

"Yeah, I'm awake." Gail sat on the edge of the bed and rolled her head from side to side, trying to ease the cramp running from her shoulder to her ear. Penny was silhouetted in the light falling through the open doorway to the hall.

"There's a phone call for you."

"What time is it?"

"Almost midnight."

"Who the devil is calling me here in the middle of the night?"

"She didn't tell me her name. I figured if anyone knew to look for you here, it must be important."

"I'm not sure anyone knows I'm here."

"When she asked to talk to you, she used your full name and said 'the one from Sweetwater, Tennessee.' I guess there must be other Gail Larsens in her life, and she wanted to be sure she had the right one."

"I can't imagine." Gail stood up and started for the door. "I'm sorry whoever it is woke you up."

"I hadn't gone to bed, so the call couldn't wake me up."

Penny stepped aside, letting Gail pass through the doorway.

"There's still only the one phone—out in the kitchen by the fridge."

"Right. I remember."

Gail picked up her pace through the living room to the kitchen.

"Hello?"

"Oh, good. Lydia had the right number for you."

"Pardon?"

"Lydia LaGrange. I got this number from her."

"Who is this?"

"I refuse to believe you've forgotten me already."

"Believe it."

"Gail, it's me—Connie. Connie Martin."

"Holy cannoli."

"I usually only go by that name on Sundays when I'm in Italian neighborhoods."

Gail pulled the phone away from her ear and stared at the receiver.

"Are you still there? Gail? Hello?"

"Yes, I'm here."

"I bet you're surprised to hear from me."

"There's an understatement."

"I wanted to call to say you were right."

"Pardon?"

"The scene in my new book where the protagonist confronts her boss about denying her request for time off to take care of her partner after she has surgery."

"Oh."

"Don't you remember the fight we had about that the last night we were at the Magnolia Suites?"

"Uh huh. I thought you should have her tell him the truth."

"I took your advice and talked to Lydia. She agreed with you completely."

"Okay." Gail contorted her face in confusion. "Uh, thanks for letting me know."

"I'm sorry I was so bull-headed about it."

"Don't mention it, Connie. We were both so worn out by then it's a miracle we didn't kill each other."

Connie laughed nervously. "You're right. It got rather intense at times, didn't it?"

"That's for sure," Gail replied.

"You really did a great job editing the book. I don't think I ever thanked you for all your help."

"It's what Lydia pays me to do. I'm glad you're happy with how it turned out."

"I am, but..."

Gail waited for Connie to finish the thought. After a long pause, she prompted her, "But what?"

"But I had another reason for wanting to call you."

"Oh?"

"After I've finished writing a book I go into hibernation for a while. I think I told you that while we were working together."

"Uh huh. You did."

"This time was different though."

"How so?"

"I really couldn't come down from the high."

"I see."

"I kept thinking it was because I knew this book was going to be rushed to print to coincide with the writer's award I'm getting next month, but I eventually figured out that wasn't it."

"No?"

"No."

Again, Gail waited to see if Connie would offer anything further.

"Something happened while we were at the Magnolia Suites." Gail remembered all too painfully what had happened at the Magnolia Suites and wasn't eager to have it in the forefront of her mind.

"I met this woman..."

"You mean someone besides me?"

"You know better than that, Gail. We were together every minute."

"So it seemed."

"I can't get you out of my head. I see your face when I wake up in the morning. I can hear your voice when I turn the pages in my manuscript and remember what you told me to change. If I go to the restaurants where we ate, I keep thinking you should be sitting across the table from me."

"As you just noted, our time together had a number of intense interactions."

"No, Gail, it's more than that. More than our working on the book together." Connie seemed to struggle to find the words she wanted. "I'm not very good at this sort of thing. What I want to say is...I miss you. I'd love to see you again."

For the second time in the conversation, Gail held the receiver in front of her face and stared at it in disbelief. She could still hear Connie's voice.

"I sent you a hundred e-mails, but you never answered them. I drove up to Sweetwater to find you, but your house was all closed up. I was afraid you'd moved away — left Outrageous Press. I worried I'd never know what happened to you. I managed to convince Lydia to tell me where you were."

The lull in the conversation was excruciating.

"Did you hear what I said, Gail?"

"I heard you."

"And?"

"And...I don't know."

"Please tell me that you've been thinking about me, too."

"I don't think I can."

"Why not?"

"Because I don't think I have."

"But we were so good together when you were here in Atlanta."

"It was all like a dream, Connie."

"That's what I mean. It was so wonderful. We seemed to fit together so perfectly. I'd never felt what I felt with you."

"No, what I meant is it was all just illusion — we were caught in the heat of the moment. It was a 'Twilight Zone' rerun, not the final scene of a new movie where we hold hands and walk into the sunset."

"I'm sorry to hear you say that. I thought there might be a chance for something more between us." Gail heard Connie suck in a deep breath. "I should have known someone as good looking as you couldn't be interested in dumpy me."

"That's not it at all, Connie. Listen, I was in over my head. I had been yanked out of the woods and plopped into the big city, where I was working with the hottest author in lesbian romances. I kept thinking any minute I'd look up and see the crew from Candid Camera laughing their asses off at what a fool you'd made of me."

"You couldn't have been any more surprised than I was. I write about that sort of thing. I don't live it. That's why it's freaking me out so much."

"I suppose we ought to talk about this some more some time, but this isn't the right time for me. I'll probably be heading back to Sweetwater in a few days. How about if I call you when I get back home and have some time to get settled?"

"Promise? Please don't hang up and walk away from this."

"Yes, I promise."

"When can I hope to hear from you?"

"A week. Maybe ten days. But I've told you I'll call, and I will."

"All right. I'll be waiting for your call. Thanks for talking with me tonight. I'll look forward to hearing from you soon."

"Good night, Connie."

Gail put the receiver on the hook and leaned her head against the back of her hand still cupped around the handset.

"Bad news?" Penny eased into the dimly lit kitchen.

"All a matter of perspective." Gail dropped her hand from the phone.

"How's that?"

"You don't really want to hear about it. At least not at one o'clock in the morning."

"What the heck? We can make believe we're teenagers again. Want some coffee?"

Gail rubbed the back of her stiff neck. "Why not? I'm already too buzzed to sleep."

"SO DO YOU have feelings for Connie?" Penny asked as she poured the last of the second pot of coffee into their mugs. The first weak rays of the mid-September sun were beginning to show themselves through the east window. She put the carafe in the sink and reclaimed her chair in the breakfast nook.

"Sure, but I don't think they're the feelings you're talking about."

"Would you say you love her?'

"No, I wouldn't say that."

"What then?"

"My first impression of her was she's a total maniac, completely self-centered and on an ego trip that lasts all day, every day."

"And your last impression?"

"She certainly is driven. When she has a deadline, God love you if you want to draw breath for anything other than making sure she meets it."

"Lots of people are really engrossed in their work. And if she's an artist — a writer — that's not really a surprise, is it?"

"No I suppose not."

"That still doesn't tell me what you feel for her, Gail."

"I feel sorry for her."

"Sorry for her? Why?"

"She puts on this big show about being so totally in control, but I got the feeling that's all it was—a show."

"Wouldn't that make her about like the rest of us? Do you feel you've got this big game of life figured out?"

"Not by a damn sight, but I hope I don't go marching through other people's lives as though I'm special and they're chopped liver."

"You don't, but what I meant was don't you think we all bluff our way through situations every day? Look at me. I've spent however long acting as if I knew how to deal with my dad's illness and death, and now I'm stumbling along, tying up the last loose ends of his life. I don't know any more about being an executrix than I know about splitting the atom. But every day, I talk to the bank or the insurance company or the people down at the courthouse as if I know my ass from my elbow. Funny thing is, half the time, I don't think they're any smarter about these things than I am."

"Oh, sure, we all use words we don't quite know the meaning of and fudge our way through unfamiliar circumstances, but with Connie it was as though she knew some giant secret of life and everyone else was put on the planet to serve her while she revels in her glory."

"But a minute ago, you said you thought she was faking."

"Not faking so much as pretending."

"What's the difference between faking and pretending?"

"To me, faking suggests an ulterior—probably sinister—motive. Pretending is more hiding out from what she knows is real. I got the sense she felt if she kept barking out orders and holding on to the illusion of making progress, she could pretend it wasn't all about to spin out of control and leave her in the dust."

"Maybe it's a classic inferiority complex."

"Maybe. All I know is I kept getting the feeling what I saw wasn't really the whole picture."

"How did she handle it when you told her about Marissa?"

"You'll love this wrinkle. I didn't tell her."

"But Marissa wasn't—I mean she hadn't—she was still..."

"Come right out and say it, Penny. Marissa wasn't dead, and I was carrying on with Connie Martin while Marissa was in a coma in Pennsylvania. Not exactly the kind of thing I'm likely to get any medals for."

"Still, Marissa never knew."

"That doesn't get me off the hook, and you know it. The worst part is I wasn't attracted to Connie in the least. All of a sudden, there we were naked. Naked and doing things I hadn't done in more than two years. I hated myself every time I so much as kissed her, but before I could build up a good case of guilt, I'd be back in her arms, on the verge of doing it all over again."

"So how did you and Connie leave things?"

"We were both so sleep-deprived by the time I left Atlanta I barely remember the drive back to Sweetwater. I do remember loading all my crap into my truck at the hotel and her leaning through the window to kiss me good-bye, but everything else is a blur. And don't forget, it was that night when I got back to the cabin I got the note from Marissa's sister telling me Marissa had died. I swear I haven't given Connie a moment's thought since."

"But from what you told me about the call you got from her," Penny looked at the clock on the wall above the stove, "four hours ago, she's been thinking about you."

"So it seems."

"What are you going to do?"

"I told her I'd call her, and I will."

"Yeah, but what are you going to tell her?"

"I'm a cheat and a whore and a sorry excuse for a human being."

"Planning to paint yourself in your very best light, I see."

"What choice do I have? At least it would be the truth."

"Okay, I'll grant you did cheat on Marissa, technically, but I'll bet you anything you want to wager, if we asked her, Marissa would tell you she doesn't hold it against you."

"She can't hold anything against anyone anymore."

"No, I mean even then, while she was still legally alive and on the respirator and all, she wouldn't have been angry with you. She would have wanted you to have a life, have a lover, have something better than just a memory of what used to be."

"Maybe. But a decent person would have waited until she died to start doing anything about it."

"You told me when you found out she was dead, you already felt as though she'd been gone for two years."

"It was because her parents wouldn't let me be part of her life anymore."

"Can you honestly call what she's had since that day on the lake 'life'?"

"She might have come out of the coma."

"And been a shell or a shadow of the woman you knew. She was brain dead from the day of the accident, Gail. What would it have gained you to wait for another hundred years? She couldn't ever come back to you."

Gail waited a long time before she spoke. "But I should have been able to help her."

"And I never should have let my dad eat the fatty part of his steaks and clog up his arteries. Things happen. We don't always like them, but once they're done, that's that."

"Maybe I couldn't help her that day on Tellico Lake, but I should have been sure we had our papers done so her parents couldn't have dragged her away."

"Different example, same deal. Could have, should have, would have, might have. But didn't."

Gail lifted her head to look at Penny. Penny's compassionate expression nudged at her heart.

Penny continued. "Let it go, kid. You loved her with all your heart for as long as you could. You're the only one who thinks you let her down. From what you've told me about her, she'd be the first one to kick you in the butt for all of the second guessing you're doing."

"You're probably right."

"So I'll ask you again, what are you going to tell Connie when you call her?"

"I'll tell her I'm flattered she's been thinking about me, but Atlanta was a passing schoolgirl fling."

"You're sure?"

"Compared to her, the Energizer bunny is an underachiever. I can't picture me ever being in a relationship with someone like her."

Penny drank the final swallow from her mug. She arched back and stretched in her chair. "Speaking of schoolgirl flings, I've got a proposal for you."

"What?"

"It's homecoming at Plainfield High tonight."

"Can't be. Homecoming was always the last week in September. Today is only the fourteenth."

"You're stuck in the old days. They do homecoming earlier than they used to. I saw it in yesterday's newspaper. We should go to the game and then hit the dance afterwards."

"You've got to be kidding. We never had dates for homecoming when we were in high school. Why the heck should we go now?"

"Precisely my point. This might very well be the last time either one of us is in town for homecoming. If we don't go tonight, we'll probably never have another chance."

"We won't know anybody there."

"Don't bet on it. The paper said Jessica Schoening is homecoming queen."

"So?"

"It also said she's the daughter of Kim Galloway Schoening, homecoming queen, class of 1970."

"Cheerleader Kim Galloway from our class?"

"It's got to be. Come on, Gail. Let's go tonight. It can be our reward for getting this house cleared out. It will be a gas. I can't wait to see what Kim looks like after all these years."

Gail couldn't help but wonder if Penny still had Kim's pompom in a box of memorabilia somewhere.

Chapter
Five

"THEY CALL THIS music?" Penny said. Gail and Penny were off to the farthest edge of the high school gymnasium, which had been transformed into a grand ballroom for the homecoming dance. Maroon and gold streamers hung from the overhead girders. Signs proclaiming the prowess of the Plainfield Panthers decorated the walls. A huge banner welcomed the visiting alumni.

"Apparently. Look at all the kids dancing." Gail said as she swept an open palm toward the mass of young humanity flailing about on the gym floor.

"I'm reminded of the sounds of someone being tortured in an abandoned mine shaft."

"Our parents said the same thing about the music we liked when we were in high school."

"At least you could understand the words."

"It wasn't lyric poetry."

"No, I guess not, but we might as well be listening to a foreign language for all I can make out from this racket."

They watched the dancers while the DJ found new ways to assault their ears.

"I haven't recognized one single thing he's played so far. Have you?" Penny asked.

"This one is Jessica Simpson, but I don't know the name of the song."

"Every week they put the top ten list in the entertainment section of the paper. I knew I was getting old the first time I didn't know which was the name of the artist and which was the name of the album."

"You *are* old, Penny. They haven't called them 'albums' in fifteen years." A new crowd of people entered the room. Gail pointed at one of the newcomers.

"I know it's not polite, but I can't help myself. Soo, piggy, piggy. Soo pig." Gail imitated her grandfather calling his hogs at slopping time. The music was so loud only Penny, who was standing right beside her, could hear the comment.

"No, it's not polite," Penny said. "So Kim has put on a few pounds. We're not the same slim beauties we were in high school, either. At least she's got a knock-out of a daughter to show for it."

"She's had plenty of time to lose what she put on when she was pregnant with Jessica. Face it, Skramstaad, you've still got the hots for her."

"I do not. And furthermore, I never did."

Gail was sure Penny was blushing, but the light in the gymnasium was so dim she couldn't prove it.

"You're right about her daughter, though. She's as striking as Kim was back in high school," Gail said.

"And a little while ago I heard somebody over by the punch bowl say she's got another daughter a year or two behind this one who's every bit as good looking. She'll probably have to build an extension on her mantelpiece to hold all the crowns and trophies."

"Did she marry someone from our class? We graduated with a Schoening, didn't we?" Gail asked.

"Uh huh, but I doubt Kim married Kathy Schoening—she's the Schoening who was in our class. Kim married Kathy's brother, Kenny. He was a couple years older than us."

"Kept up with all this, I see."

"Not really. After we graduated and I moved to Minneapolis, I came back to Plainfield a couple of times a year to see my parents. After mom died, I spent a lot more time up here with Dad. You can't help but run into people at the grocery store or whatever. You know what a bunch of blabbermouths live in this town. Everybody knows everybody else's business and is perfectly happy to tell it to anyone who'll listen."

"So what you said at the house this morning about wondering what Kim looked like after all these years was blowing smoke. You've probably seen her at least three times a year since graduation."

"I've seen her around town a few times, but I haven't talked to her. We didn't run in the same circles or anything."

"I'd say that's about to change." Gail gestured to a woman approaching them.

"It really is you two. I thought I saw you at the game earlier, but I figured my eyes must be playing tricks on me." Kim Galloway Schoening was grinning like the homecoming queen she used to be. "Just like the old days. You never saw Penny Skramstaad but what you saw Gail Larsen." The three women exchanged hellos. "I saw your dad's obituary in the paper, Penny. I'm so sorry. How are you holding up?"

"I'm fine, thanks. He had been in a nursing home for more than a year, so it wasn't a surprise. Since he died, I've been getting his house cleaned out to put on the market. I don't know that I'd ever have gotten it done if Gail hadn't come to help me."

"So, do you live right in Minneapolis, or are you out in one of the suburbs?"

"Oh, no. I live down in Tennessee—between Knoxville and Chattanooga. I don't think I could survive a Minnesota winter any more." Gail gave a shiver to emphasize her point.

"That must make it hard for you." Kim looked at Gail, then back at Penny. "How often do you get to see each other?"

"It's been more than a dozen years since Gail and I were in the same room. As best I remember, the last time we saw each other was the spring when Gail's mom died — ninety-four, wasn't it Gail?"

"Ninety-three, actually. She died about four years after your mom did."

"Oh, dear, my mistake. I thought — you know — what with the two of you being — well, I mean..." Kim's obvious discomfort made all of them uncomfortable.

"Congratulations to you on your daughter being named homecoming queen." Gail tried to salvage the moment.

"Oh, why, thank you, Gail. There were so many other girls who were equally as deserving as she was. I am proud of her, of course." The way Kim smiled made Gail wonder if Kim hoped the Plainfield *Gazette*'s news reporter was lurking nearby for a candid shot.

"Yeah, she's a very attractive girl, Kim," Penny added.

"You two would certainly know." Gail thought Kim's smile looked forced and fake. "Oh, look! There's Valerie Murdock. She was one of my attendants at our class's homecoming. Excuse me, won't you? I need to go say hello." Kim hastened off to hug the woman who had been part of the royal court when she was queen.

"What the hell was that all about?" Penny motioned toward Kim and Valerie.

"The queen and her princess."

"No, I mean Kim's remark about it being hard for us not to see each other."

"You're pulling my leg, right?"

Penny shook her head. "She made it sound like she thinks we're living together or something."

"I'm sure that's exactly what she thinks."

"Why in the world would she think that?"

"Because for the entire time you and I walked the hallowed halls of this educational institution, everyone assumed we were lovers."

"Get out of Dodge!" Penny reeled backwards and stuck her hand out against the wall to catch herself.

"You can't honestly tell me you didn't hear the snickers and whispers."

"I am telling you precisely that."

"Maybe our worthy classmates didn't despise you quite as much as they did me. I heard enough for the both of us."

"Why didn't you ever say anything to me?"

"Penny, you were practically my only friend in high school. I knew we weren't doing the nudie rumba, and I also knew the more I tried to convince people we weren't, the more likely they'd presume we were. If

I had told you about the rumors, you would have vanished, just like everyone else."

"Turds."

"We've known for a long time this part of Minnesota isn't renowned for embracing liberal leanings, m'dear."

"Still, why would anyone give a holy fig?"

"Do you remember *anything* about high school, Penny? The kids cared about everything from what color benchwarmer you wore to the football games to how many times you chewed each forkful of ptomaine potatoes in the cafeteria. It was conform or be exiled."

"I never felt that way."

"You had friends you'd gone to grade school with, been at junior high with, grown up with from the time you could talk. I came in after eight years in the rural school system. You were in band and chorus and pep club and all the extra curricular activities. I was an alien from day one and never found a place where I belonged. And of course, the minute my — shall we say *glaring abnormality* — was suspected, I might as well have had contagious pellagra."

"That truly stinks."

"Sorry to ruin your idyllic memories, but it's probably better to get some of this out in the open."

"You mean the entire class thought I was a lesbian?"

"You give them too much credit. At least half of them never gave you any thought at all."

"You really should have told me."

"I just did."

"You know I meant you should have told me when we were in school."

"What good would it have done? I was miserable enough for both of us. You had a great time in high school, and up until this very minute, believed there wasn't a single thing not to adore about our beloved classmates."

"Perfect, snotty Kim Galloway still thinks we're lovers." Gail wasn't sure if Penny was posing a question or making a statement, so she waited.

"To hell with her. To hell with all of them." Penny grabbed Gail's hand. "Come on." She half-dragged, half-led Gail onto the dance floor. As they were about to try to fling their bodies around in a way approximating the younger dancers already there, the DJ finished his crescendo medley of hits. He turned up the microphone. "Okay, ladies and gentlemen, let's change the tempo a little. I've been told the mother of tonight's homecoming queen was homecoming queen herself right here in this very auditorium a few years back. Let's go back in time and reminisce with that queen — Kim Galloway Schoening — with some of the songs that made her night so special."

The box-step ballads of Neil Diamond echoed off the walls. Penny pulled Gail into a snug embrace. "This should give the town a little something to talk about," she said as they began to sway to the beat. "Oh, by the way, can I have this dance?"

"You're not used to leading, are you?' Gail did her best not to giggle as she tripped over Penny's feet for the tenth time in as many seconds.

"Leading? Criminee, I'm not even used to dancing."

"Here, let me give it a try before one of us ends up in traction." Gail swapped arm positions with Penny and found a more comfortable cadence to fall into step with. Soon they were gliding smoothly among the other couples — any number of whom stopped dead in their tracks to see two women old enough to be their mothers — mothers? make that *grandmothers* — floating on air as the DJ segued from Neil Diamond to songs from the Carpenters.

"You're so light on my feet," Gail said with a laugh.

"Now that all I have to do is slide along wherever you steer me, I have a whole new appreciation for the concept of dancing all night."

"You're making quite an impression on the locals."

"You mean the slack-jawed stares?"

"Don't overlook the pointing and whispering."

"Good thing my only remaining piece of business here is to get Dad's house sold. I don't think I'd be welcome at the ladies' sewing circle or Chamber of Commerce picnic."

"They'd learn to cope."

"Don't bet on it."

They danced in silence for a few minutes. The Carpenters gave way to the Fifth Dimension.

"Can I ask you something, Gail?" Penny's lips were tight against the side of Gail's head. She quivered from the sensation of Penny's breath on her skin.

"Blow in my ear that way again, and I'll sign over my bank account to you. Ask away."

"Is this some weird time-travel, out-of-body flashback, or do you smell exactly how I remember you smelling when we were in high school?"

"I can't believe you'd remember that."

"Believe it or not, I do. You always wore a certain perfume. I don't think I ever smelled it on anybody else. And now, tonight, out here on this dance floor with what I'd swear to be at least a thousand pairs of eyes boring holes in us, it hit me. You smell exactly the way you did the last time I was in this building with you."

Gail pulled free from Penny's embrace sufficiently to catch a glimpse of Penny's face. She snuggled back, and they kept dancing. "It's called Golden Autumn. It was a fragrance by Prince Matchabelli. It came out about the same time as Wind Song and Beloved and Woodhue. In typical fashion, I was drawn to the one no one else seemed to care for."

"Now that you say them, I remember those names, but I haven't seen any of those on the shelves in ages."

"No, they quit making them years ago. Or at least stopped calling them by those names. I was looking at a mail-order catalog of oddball products one day a couple of months back, and there it was, good old Golden Autumn. The write-up in the catalog said customers kept asking for it, so they'd scoured the planet until they found it. The ad went on and on about how the perfume has smooth top notes of lavender, underscored with patchouli and accented with musk. You know how ridiculous they can get with their descriptions. I ordered a bottle, for old times' sake. I don't think it's exactly the same as what I got at the drug store here in Plainfield, but it comes darn close."

"My sense of smell seems to affect me the most. I still remember the perfume the lady funeral director was wearing the night my dad and brothers and I went to view my mom's body the night before her funeral."

"I remember, Penny. I was there with you."

"I know."

They let the ghosts and the memories and the scents roll in their minds as the music took them back to another time.

"Let's make this a real homecoming, Gail."

"What do you mean?"

"You'll see."

Penny slipped free of Gail's arms, took her hand, and led her out of the auditorium. They walked the long hallway to the double doors that opened to the walkway to the parking area. The cool (almost frosty in Gail's estimation) September air jolted them as they exited the building. The gravel crunched underfoot on their way to Penny's car in the lot.

"Do you remember the way to Anderson Lake?" Penny asked as she put the key in the ignition.

"Sure."

"Good. There should be quite a crowd there tonight."

"THIS IS THE right place, isn't it?"

"If you mean the place where the in crowd used to go to neck, yes, this is the correct geographic location. If you mean is it where kids go today to do that sort of thing, then, no, I'd have to say it's not."

With some prompting from Gail for which turns to make, Penny had driven them four or five miles out of Plainfield to the public access road to Anderson Lake. When they were in high school, it had been a deserted stretch of unpaved road with lots of wide pull-offs and half a dozen dead-end feeder roads. On any Friday or Saturday night, they could count on finding at least ten couples in parked cars with steamed windows. What they found this time was quite different.

"A freakin' miniature golf course." Penny stared at the amusement park from their vantage point in the partially-lit parking lot. "And it's still open."

"Probably hoping to get a little late night traffic from the losers who didn't have dates for the homecoming dance. It can't be more than forty degrees out there. How do they keep their hands warm enough to hold on to the putters?" Gail asked.

"You've been away too long. Forty degrees is almost summer up here. I bet this place doesn't close for the season until there's too much snow to see the fake grass on the fairways. Do you remember there being all those houses along the road on the way out here?"

"The last time we were here, there weren't any houses at all. Obviously, the old lover's lane has fallen prey to the capitalists' mantra: god the father, god the son, and god the almighty dollar."

"I wouldn't have dreamed it could change so much."

"Everybody thinks their hometown will escape the march of time, hang forever in suspended animation, and stay the same as when they lived there. You've at least been back here to see your dad all along, so you've had a chance to see the changes a little at a time. When I rolled into town two-and-a-half weeks ago for the first time since your mom's funeral, I thought I had taken a wrong turn at Iowa and wound up in purgatory. Downtown is nothing but empty storefronts. The highway between the interstate exit and the edge of town is an endless string of fast-food chains. There's a mall out west of town with a sixteen-screen theater. When we lived here, the same out-of-date movie played on the postage stamp screen at the Bijoux for two weeks at a pop."

"You're right. I remember the first time I came to town and saw that Shaggy's Malt Shop had been turned into a fabric store. I think I actually cried."

"Think what it did to old man Shagovin."

"He was older than dirt when we used to hang out there. He's got to be dead by now, don't you think?"

"Oh, I'm sure he is, Penny. The grease from his burgers and fries has to have long since taken its toll."

"No more Shaggy's. No more passion pit at Anderson Lake. I wonder where the kids go to make out now?"

"Probably their bedrooms at their parents' houses."

"I doubt it. Not here in a town where you have to turn out the lights in your living room and draw the shades if you want to have a beer on a weeknight."

"I suspect the town's rather conservative approach to alcohol has changed, too, my friend. There's not much about Plainfield, Minnesota, that's quite what it used to be."

"Unless you count you and me together on a Friday night driving around looking for the cool kids cramming their tongues down one another's throats."

"Thank goodness for at least one enduring tradition."

The banks of floodlights illuminating the clown's mouth, windmill, loop-de-loop, and other features of the golf course flashed on and off twice. A voice boomed over the loudspeaker. "Ladies and gents of all ages, take your last strokes and head for the clubhouse. The course will be closing in ten minutes. Anyone with five or more holes remaining on your scorecard, please see the cashier for a refund or a voucher for a free game. Thanks for your business, and have a safe drive home."

"I guess we should go." Penny leaned forward and reached for the key in the ignition.

"No, let's wait a minute."

With a shrug, Penny obliged.

The few golfers straggled out, climbed in their cars, and pulled out of the lot. A few minutes later, the floodlights went dark and the park's two employees came out of the office, locked up, and drove away.

"Look." Gail pointed across the golf course. "You can see the lake from here."

Penny shifted to get a better view. "Oh, I get it. This is the hill right above the shore. We used to sit here and look at the lake for hours. What a shame to ruin the view with a tacky golf course."

"You can't make money off a breathtaking view, Skramstaad. Think how much better this little diversion is for the tax coffers of the city fathers."

"And after all, isn't that what it's all about? So, do you want to see if we can find the new place where lovers go to give each other hickies?" Penny asked.

"Not really. I don't think shining flashlights through car windows and scaring the starch out of young men's pointers would have the same laugh quotient for us as it did in the old days. Besides, look at us. Someone would probably use their cell phone to call the police and report two escapees from the old folks' home. We got away with it when we were teenagers, but I don't think we can pull it off any more."

"Poor choice of words, I'd say."

"You at least did yank a few in your time," Gail replied.

"Yeah, a few, I guess." Penny flipped the key and buzzed her window down a little. "You know what the best part about hunting down the lovebirds out here was?"

"What?"

"After we'd laughed ourselves sick over peeking in a car window and seeing one of the jocks with his face buried in a cheerleader's breasts, we'd find an empty cul-de-sac out here and park the car. Then we'd listen to the radio and talk."

"Cheaper than a shrink and probably lots more beneficial."

Penny punched the control for the CD player in the dash. Dionne Warwick's voice filled the compartment.

"Any chance Doctor Larsen would consent to seeing a client tonight?"

"WHEN DID YOU figure out about being gay, Gail?" A long interval had passed since Penny posed her question about "Doctor Larsen." Gail knew time was her only ally if Penny were ever to reveal what was plaguing her.

"I don't think I ever figured it out. It's just how I always was."

"You don't think there was some big life event that made you turn out to be a lesbian?"

"Not that I remember."

"What do you remember from when you were little?"

"For one thing, I remember asking for both a truck and a doll every Christmas."

"You played with dolls?"

"Sure, but when I played with them, they were kids who had somehow managed to survive when the Indians raided their village, and I had to look out for them 'til I could get them to a town where some nice lady would offer to take them in. Of course, the nice lady always wanted me to stay, too, and I'd tend her farm or brand her cattle or patch her roof."

"Not exactly a dainty little homemaker in your fantasies, were you?"

"Seemed to make perfect sense to me. The nice lady was already cooking meals and keeping house. She didn't need a maid; she needed someone handy in the great outdoors."

"What else do you remember?"

"I hit a lot of game-winning homeruns."

"For real?"

"At country school, we played softball in the spring and fall. There were never enough kids to have two real teams, so the teacher made the best hitter and the best fielder in the school play on both teams to try to keep things a little more even. From about fourth grade on, I swung the bat as well as anyone in school, so I batted at least twice every inning, once on each team. When I'd practice at home by myself, I'd dream up this scene where I was a kid picked at random from the stands at one of the Twins' baseball games, and I'd amaze the crowd by hitting a home run at Metropolitan Stadium down in the Cities. It wouldn't have nearly the panache at the Hubert Humphrey homer dome today."

"No, probably not. What do you mean when you'd practice by yourself?"

"I'd take my bat and ball and go out to one of the pastures. I'd hold the bat on my right shoulder, toss the ball straight up into the air with my left hand, grip the handle, then smash the ball when it got to eye level. It did wonders for my eye-hand coordination—not that I ever put it to good use."

Penny looked out the side window briefly. "Girls weren't allowed to play baseball at Lincoln Elementary. Only the boys."

"Yet another reason why I'm glad I went to school in the country.

You had to wear dresses to school, too, didn't you?"

"Even in the winter. And then remember, our mothers made us wear snowpants under our skirts so our legs didn't freeze and fall off."

"It would have made a lot more sense to wear nice warm corduroys."

"Yes, but in those days, only tomboys wore pants."

"I rest my case, Penny." They listened to Dionne croon for a moment. "So what do you remember about being a kid in Plainfield, Minnesota?"

Out of the corner of her eye, Gail saw Penny tense up. She hummed along with the CD and waited.

"If I said 'Roland Dekeman,' you'd say?"

"I'd say the guy we used to joke about being your mom's boyfriend. He lived with his old maid sister. What was her name?"

"Minerva," Penny supplied.

"Right. Minerva. Roland and Minerva Dekeman. They were at your parents' house six days a week, or so it seemed. She was so quiet and mousy, and he was such a blowhard. Gawd, I used to hate it when I'd get trapped listening to one of his endless stories about how he single-handedly saved the entire nation from the Germans when he was in the war. Neither one of them ever got married, did they?"

"Nope. They lived in the same house they'd grown up in and then inherited when their parents died."

"I don't think I ever knew how it was they got to be such good friends with your parents."

"Funny thing is I don't know, either. As best I can recall, they were fixtures in my parents' living room from the time I was old enough to walk. Minerva sat in the corner drinking cup after cup of strong, black coffee, and Roland stomped around the house retelling the same stories day after day, week after week, year after year."

"What ever happened to them?"

"Minerva died right around the same time my mom did — a couple months later, I think."

"And dear old Roland?"

"If there is a fair god, he continues to burn slowly and painfully in a very hot corner of hell." The edge of rancor in Penny's voice took Gail by surprise.

"Not one of your favorite people, I take it?"

"Sorry bastard."

"Care to elaborate?"

Gail knew Penny was sifting words carefully in her mind. Trying to rush her would only make her more reluctant to speak. She let Dionne's melodies caress her ears.

"As you said, they were always at our house."

"Uh huh."

"You know no one ever locked their houses back then unless they were going to be gone for a week or more. Roland and Minerva, alone or together, would show up at the house and let themselves in. I'm sure neither of them ever knocked. They walked in and made themselves at home."

"Annoying, I'm sure, but hardly cause to wish eternal damnation on them."

"Minerva wasn't so bad. For the most part, she was like an extra piece of furniture—silent, useless, and dust-encrusted."

"But Roland?"

"I haven't talked about this in a long time, Gail."

"It's okay. Tell me what you want to when you want to."

"You probably already know."

"I've got a feeling, but I'd rather not say anything, in case I've got it all wrong."

"I'd rather you say it than me."

"Roland tried some funny uncle stuff with you."

"Tried and succeeded."

"How bad was it?"

"About as bad as you can imagine." Penny's voice was a hoarse whisper.

"Want to tell me about it?"

"Yes and no."

Gail spoke levelly, reassuringly. "And as I said, you can tell me whatever you want to whenever you're ready to."

Penny dropped her head back on the headrest and contorted her face.

"At first, it didn't matter to me. I'd come home from school, and he'd be there. He'd tell me Mom was at her ladies meeting at church or she'd gone to the store and he would stay with me 'til she got home. He'd make me sit on his lap and tell him what we'd done in school."

"How old were you?"

"I don't know. Second grade, maybe."

"But it didn't stop with sitting on his lap?"

"No. If it hadn't been for those damn snow pants we had to wear under our dresses—" Penny's voice caught in her throat. "It was one day in the winter. I needed to go to the bathroom right when school got out, but I didn't want to miss out on walking home with the other kids, so I pulled my long pants on and hurried along with Darcy and Judy and Andy. When I got to my house, my mom was gone, but Roland was there. I needed to pee so bad my teeth hurt, and of course, I couldn't get out of my pants. They got all balled up around my ankles, and the harder I tried to get them off, the more tangled they got. The next thing I knew, I had wet myself, barely inside kitchen door."

"What happened?"

"At first, I thought it was going to be all right. Roland started saying things like, 'don't worry, we don't have to tell your mommy

about this,' and 'we'll get you a dry pair of panties, and I'll take these
wet ones home with me so no one will ever know.' He was patting me
on the head and on my back and telling me he'd take care of
everything."

"But?"

"But then he told me he'd have to wash my bottom so my mom
wouldn't smell the pee."

"What did he do?"

"He picked me up and carried me upstairs to the bathroom. He
undressed me and put me in the tub and used a washcloth draped over
the faucet to wash me between my legs." Penny trembled as she spoke.
"Remember, that was before my dad remodeled the house and added
the bath on the main floor, so there was only the one bathroom,
upstairs."

"Did he molest you that day, Penny?"

"I'm not sure. I was so embarrassed by what had happened. I felt I
was watching myself in a movie. I was there, but I wasn't there. I know
he spent a long time drying me off with a big blue towel, and I'm almost
sure he touched me. You know, *touched* me."

Gail feared Penny might throw up. "Open the windows and let
some air in, okay?" Gail suggested. The cold gust refreshed them both.

Penny swallowed hard and turned to look at Gail. "Do you hate me,
Gail?"

Gail slid across the seat and put her arm around Penny's shoulder.
"Oh, Penny. It wasn't your fault. And anyway, why would I hate you?
Hate him for being a filthy pervert, yes, but hate you? No, and neither
would anyone else."

"Says you."

"What?"

"I'm getting ahead of myself. Hold that thought."

"Okay, so what else happened that day?" Gail moved back to the
passenger side of the car.

"He took me to my room and helped me put on my play clothes. He
kept saying, 'Remember, we're not going to tell anybody anything
about this. This is our little secret.' Of course, I didn't want my mother
and dad and brothers to know I'd wet my pants, so it seemed the perfect
solution. I mean, so what if he had seen me naked and had put his
hands on my body, he was going to keep me from getting in trouble
with my family, so he must be my new best friend, right? We went back
downstairs, and he took my wet panties out to his car. Then he came
back inside and we sat down in the living room, and he read me some
storybooks. A little while later, Mom was home, and I figured I'd never
have to deal with it again."

"But obviously, you did."

"I can't stand to tell you every detail."

"I don't blame you. Have you ever told anyone every detail?"

"I tried."

"Who'd you tell?"

"I wanted to tell my mom."

"Right away?"

"No, I was hoping the wet pants thing would be the end of it."

"Go on."

"Not more than a week or two later, at least the way I remember it, Roland was always the only one at my house when I got home from school. I started staying at Darcy's house instead of going home, but my mom thought I was making a pest of myself over there, and she told me I had to come right home every day."

"Is that when you told her about what Roland was doing?"

"She wouldn't listen to me. She thought I was making it all up so I could go to Darcy's house instead of coming home."

"So things kept getting worse with Roland."

"Right. I mean my mother had practically given him license to do whatever he wanted. I never heard her say anything to him about it, but not long after I tried talking to her, he started threatening me. He'd say, 'Don't think you can go to Darcy's house instead of coming here to be with me.' I knew he knew I'd tried to tell. And I knew it made him mad."

"Did you tell your dad?"

"Picture our relationships with our dads, Gail. What I remember about my dad was him reading the paper at breakfast and then vanishing all day to go to work. He'd come home and sit in front of the TV until Mom put the meal on the table, and then he'd tinker in the garage or the basement after supper 'til he went to bed. Almost every weekend, he'd go hunting or fishing. It would take me a week to work up enough courage to tell him about breaking the strap on my shoes and needing a new pair. How would I tell him one of his best buddies was raping me in our own house a couple of times a week?"

"Was it really that often?"

"Who knows? While it was going on, it felt like it was happening twice a day. I've spent most of my life trying to wipe every memory of it from my mind. I'm not sure I could begin to reconstruct what was real and what my imagination made up."

"You said it started when you were in second grade. How long did it go on?"

"All through junior high and maybe the first year of high school."

"What made him stop?"

Penny laughed contemptuously. "His pecker betrayed him."

"Impotence?"

"If it had been twenty-five years later, he could have been the poster child for the 'before' picture in the Viagra ads."

"At least you were finally free of him."

"Not completely."

"What do you mean?"

"Every chance he got, he'd expose himself to me and try to make me touch him"

"Why didn't you report him to the police?"

"If my own mother wouldn't believe me, why would I fare any better with the Plainfield Police Department? He was still one of my parents' favorite people."

"Which was right about the time you and I started hanging out together. Back at the start of this conversation, I mentioned how you and your dad and I always called him your mother's boyfriend."

"Probably some wishful displacement activity on my part. If he had been dipping my mom, maybe he wouldn't have been raping me."

"Oh, my god, Penny. Do you think he was pulling the same stunts with your mom?"

"I've wondered about that for years. She was always so quick to defend him. And she was such a typical housewife. I don't think she ever had an original thought in her life. If she made chicken for dinner and dad came home and said he wanted pork chops, she put the chicken in the 'fridge and fixed pork chops. And of course, she was an absolute doormat for my brothers — waited on them hand and foot every day of her life. It would be easy to picture her not knowing how to tell Roland 'no' and mean it."

"But wouldn't your dad have found out?"

"How? Dad left for work about the same time we kids left for school. If Roland was at my house when I got home from school, who's to say he didn't get there twenty minutes after dad left the house every morning and then stay all day every day?"

"Okay, but wouldn't your mom maybe have told your dad and asked him to beat the daylights out of Roland?"

"Only if she wanted it to stop. Maybe this was one of those stupid jest-is-often-seed-to-truth deals. We probably started making jokes about Roland being Mom's boyfriend because that's how he treated her. Brought her presents, told her she looked nice, noticed if she did something different with her hair."

"If they were lovers, though, wouldn't your dad have been pissed off, big time?"

"You might think so, but as far as I could tell, Dad thought old Roland was about as big a hero as George Patton. I don't think I ever heard him say one ugly thing about him. Besides, you knew my dad. He was about as romantic as a stud horse. Chances are, he was perfectly happy to have Roland pay as much attention to my mom as he wanted to. It gave Dad more free time to go sit in his boat and fish for crappies in the summer or sit in his icehouse and spearfish for northerns in the winter."

"So, either Roland wasn't doing your mom, and he was this strange, attentive friend to her. Or he was doing her, and she didn't care. Or he was doing her, but your dad didn't care."

"Isn't that a lovely bunch of options? And now with all three of them dead, I'll never know for sure."

"Roland is dead, too?"

"Uh huh. About four years ago. Dad had already had a couple of strokes, so I had to come back to Plainfield and take him to the funeral. Damn near made me sick to hear everyone going on and on about what a wonderful man Roland was. Loyal friend, past president of the VFW, decorated war hero, steadfast member of the Lamb of God Lutheran Church. Took every bit of willpower I had not to stand up in the sanctuary and shout, 'And don't forget pervert, child molester, and all-around freak."

"Did you ever do any therapy to help you with what you went through?"

"I kept thinking I should, but I never could picture myself telling a total stranger about all this."

"Why, after all these years, did you decide to tell me?"

"I don't know. I suppose Dad's dying had a lot to do with it. Spending so much time in Mom and Dad's house didn't help, either. There've been times I swear I could almost smell Roland's stale, sour breath and hear the dragging sound his one foot made when he walked. He really was some kind of hero. He got shot in the hip pulling two other soldiers to safety over in Europe. They talked about it at his funeral."

"Some good even in the worst of us, I guess."

"Too bad the other guy wasn't a better shot, if you ask me."

"At the risk of stating the obvious, I guess this might explain why you haven't tied up with some nice man and done your version of happily ever after."

"Maybe. Who knows?"

Gail looked over at Penny. She looked much older than her fifty-five years. Her teeth started to chatter.

"Cold?"

"No." She paused. "Frazzled nerves."

"It can't have been easy for you to talk about this."

"No, but there's still one more skeleton to haul out of the closet."

"And that would be?"

Penny leaned forward quickly and started the engine. "You already know what, but no way in hell I'm talking about it here." She yanked the gearshift into reverse. "Let's go home."

Chapter
Six

PENNY MADE FOUR or five turns and got them back out to the main roadway.

"Hey, unless I'm totally turned around, shouldn't you have gone the other way to get back to your house?"

"It's homecoming, Gail. We really need to do something special to mark the occasion."

"If you think I'm climbing those stupid statues in the park across from the high school and hanging hula skirts and floral leis on the founding fathers, think again."

"No, I don't think either one of us has the muscle tone to make it up to the pedestals any more, let alone shinny up six feet of granite leg and boost ourselves up to their necks. I've got a much better idea."

"I know that tone, Lucy Ricardo."

Penny gave a devilish laugh. As had been true for all the many years she had known Penny, Gail was once again confronted with another instance where she wondered if Penny didn't suffer from something bordering on manic-depressive personality disorder. Not five minutes earlier, morose and heartbroken, Penny had laid bare her soul and told her deepest, darkest secrets. Now she was hell bent for leather to pull off some prank having about as much to do with what they had just spent two hours discussing as it did with the price of pork bellies on the Chicago Futures Exchange.

Penny wheeled into an all-night convenience store. "Need anything?" she asked as she flung the car door open.

"No, I don't think so."

"I'll be right back."

Five minutes later, Penny returned carrying three four-roll packages of toilet paper.

"Having some gastro-intestinal distress?"

"Nope. Hoping to cause a little." Penny tossed the packages into the back seat. She backed the car around and pulled out onto the main street through downtown Plainfield.

"Care to tell me where we're going at one-thirty in the morning?"

"A lovely little bungalow on Juniper Street."

"And it would be the home of?"

"Royalty."

"I'll bet it's not the get-away cottage of Charles, Prince of Wales and the lovely Camilla, Duchess of Cornwall."

"Right. This is local royalty."

Penny turned off her headlights and eased the car to a stop along the curb. "If we park here, it's only about three blocks. How's your pitching arm, Gail?"

"I haven't used it in years."

"Let's hope you haven't lost your touch."

Penny reached into the back seat and handed one of the four-roll packs to Gail. "You can get at least a couple of these inside your jacket. I'll cram as many as I can under my sweatshirt."

They got out of the car. A street lamp across the way cast a hazy pinkish light. "You look like the Michelin Man." Gail was trying not to laugh.

"You should talk. You look like the Pillsbury Dough Boy on anabolic steroids. Come on. We can cut through this yard and then hoof it down the alley between the next two streets. There shouldn't be any traffic out here this late."

Penny led the way. A few minutes later she pointed at a brick rambler with four or five big oaks and elms in the yard. "The palace of the reigning homecoming queen, Jessica Schoening and her equally regal mother, Kim-I'm-the-biggest-show-off-in-Plainfield Galloway," Penny whispered. "Load your cannons and prepare to fire." She extracted a roll of tissue from inside her sweatshirt and made sure the leading end was free. "Here's to you, Miss Homecoming 1970." She lobbed the roll toward the top of the nearest tree. It spun and whirled and tangled in the branches. She retrieved the roll from where it fell and tossed it again. "Come on, Gail. Get busy. This is our version of shock and awe."

Gail unzipped her jacket and grabbed a roll in each hand. She crept to the steps leading to the front door and began looping tissue back and forth from one side of the banister railing to the other. By the time she was done, it could have been a ribbon cutting site for a new Charmin factory. When she finished, she ran long streamers down the entire length of manicured hedges on either side of the front stoop.

Penny wasn't having much success in adorning the trees. Her first toss had been her best. Everything else was either missing the trees altogether or barely snagging the lowest limbs. Gail slunk over to where Penny was standing.

"Let me do the trees," Gail suggested. "You go wrap the cars. Remember to anchor one end around the outside mirror. Then it's easier to get the rest of it done."

Gail took her remaining ammunition and heaved the rolls high into the boughs. Meanwhile, Penny had both cars so covered over they looked like mummies with wheels. With the last two rolls, they collaborated on weaving the tissue into the curlicues of the wrought iron chairs sitting on a small flagstone pad under the largest of the oaks.

"I saw a light go on at the back of the house." Gail poked Penny in the ribs. "We need to get out of here."

They sprinted back to Penny's car, slapping at one another as they went and giggling as though it was junior year of high school again. Penny dropped the keys twice trying to get them in the ignition, which only made them laugh all the harder.

She pulled a U-turn in the middle of the street and drove without headlights for the first ten blocks. A light mist started to fall.

"Perfect. This rain will turn that toilet paper into gobs of glue. It will take them 'til Halloween to get it all cleaned up." Penny flipped on the headlights. "I always enjoy helping people remember the special days in their lives."

"The day Jessica Schoening was crowned homecoming queen at Plainfield High?"

"That too, I suppose, but I was thinking more along the lines of the day when Kim Galloway's assumption proved to be right."

"DO YOU WANT a beer? How about some wine?' Penny asked as she wandered around the living room, now devoid of everything except the sofa, one chair, and a couple of boxes of keepsakes she'd take back to Minneapolis with her. Her voice echoed off the bare walls.

"We sat up all night last night drinking coffee and talking about Connie Martin," Gail observed. "Are we going to have a repeat performance tonight, drinking something stronger and talking about something we should have talked about forty years ago?" She was on the sofa with Cubbie and Annette in her lap, Cookie beside her, and Rounder at her feet.

"I don't know if all the alcohol in the world would get me loose enough to be comfortable talking about this, Gail."

"At least sit down. All your pacing is making the animals dizzy."

Penny paused by the chair, but then edged over to the sofa and sat down. "Did you always think about me—uh—as a—you know—that way?"

Gail labored to find the right reply. "Please try to remember we met at a time in our lives when every hormone gland in our bodies was locked in the wide open position. For as long as I'd had conscious thought about anything having to do with love, or attraction, or sex, or any of those sorts of things, I knew I liked girls. Not once did I find myself dreaming about some cute boy or what a penis looked like. Of all the things that mystified me, probably the biggest puzzle was how girls could sit and sigh over movie stars or rock singers or basketball players or the new boy who moved into town."

"So you fantasized about girls?"

"As much as I let myself fantasize about anything, yes. It was real obvious my inclinations weren't going to be met with a round of applause or open arms. More than fantasizing, I sort of kept hoping one day I'd wake up with the feelings all the other teen-aged girls seemed to have, and then it wouldn't matter any more."

"But you've as much as told me you were attracted to me back in high school."

"It's ancient history, Penny." Gail stared intently into Penny's eyes.

"You were, though, weren't you?"

The look on Penny's face was more than she could bear, and she looked away. "I'm tempted to lie to you, but what would be the point?"

"Did you tell anybody?"

"Who would I tell? The Lesbians Anonymous group wasn't on the approved list of extracurricular clubs. The snide remarks and crude jokes encouraged me to keep it to myself."

"Then why did Kim Galloway know? And at the dance tonight, you said everyone assumed we were lovers."

Gail pursed her lips. "I overstated the situation. We were in the gymnasium where, on more than one occasion, our classmates had smarted off to me about how maybe I should be in the boys' gym class, or would I kindly stay out of the showers until everyone else was dressed. What I said to you was in reaction to flashing back on some rather painful memories."

"That doesn't explain why Kim thought we were living together. You said outright she had assumed we were involved in high school."

"Penny. Dear, thick-headed, still naïve Penny." Gail rubbed the top of Penny's head affectionately.

"What's that supposed to mean?

"Do you remember what else Kim said tonight?"

"She said she was sorry to hear my dad died."

"Yes, but she also said seeing us together tonight was exactly like it was in high school. If you saw one of us, you saw the other of us, too."

"So? You never saw Kim without Patty or Wendy."

"Not exactly. You mostly saw the popular girls in groups of at least three or four, or you saw them with their boyfriends. It was rare to see just the same two girls together at every ball game, in the cafeteria at lunch, cruising the drive-in burger joint Friday nights, or skating at the ice rink on Withrow Lake. The two of us were the equivalent of stink on pig poop." Gail held up her index and middle fingers so they touched and waved them side to side, like a dancing couple, in front of Penny's face.

"I can name at least a couple of other female twosomes who hung out a lot with each other."

"I know, but I also can promise you when the other kids overhead them talking, they were mooning over some dreamy guy or scheming how they could line up enough babysitting jobs to buy some special new outfit or a fabulous shade of lipstick."

Penny made an unhappy face. "What did we talk about?"

"Homework, books, movies, current events, what time I'd pick you up Friday night, if you wanted the sweater you'd left in my car the night before, would we eat at your house or go to Shaggy's, if we were going to ride the bus to the basketball tournament or if we'd take my car."

"What people who were dating might talk about."

"Uh huh. And my being unfailingly chivalrous didn't help, either."

Penny frowned. "I don't follow."

"I always held doors for you, usually bought both our tickets when we went to a game or a movie, took your books to your locker for you so you didn't have to climb clear up to the third floor, carried your lunch tray of dirty dishes to the conveyor belt, helped you get into your coat."

"But we didn't hold hands or do anything that would have made us seem to be anything more than just good friends."

"Which everyone construed as further proof we were buck naked and doing the wild thing when the lights were out."

"How come?"

"Oh, I guess it would be like the line from Hamlet: 'The lady doth protest too much, methinks.'"

"Translation for the less literary, please."

"People thought we were trying to cover up the real nature of our relationship by always being totally circumspect in public."

"Are you guessing at all this, or do you know it for a fact?"

"One of the girls I was in 4-H with talked to me about it once."

"Who?"

"Does it matter?"

"I guess not, but if there was only one..."

"There was more than one. She told me about some conversations she'd had. When I tried to convince her you and I really were nothing more than two people who spent a lot of time together — totally platonic in every regard — well, she's the one who told me the more I denied it, the more it appeared I was trying to hide something."

Penny leapt to her feet and glared at Gail. "How the hell could you *not* tell me about this, Gail?"

"Believe me, I wanted to, but I knew I couldn't."

"Why?"

She lifted her head to meet Penny's gaze. "Because you'd ask me if what I felt for you was more than friendship." Gail dropped her head and shook it morosely. "I could either lie to you and break my heart, or tell you the truth and risk breaking yours."

"What about tonight?"

"What about it?"

"What if I ask you if what you feel for me is more than friendship?"

"Is there a right answer?"

"The truth would be a good start."

Gail sucked in a breath, shut her eyes tightly for a moment, then spoke. "Penny Jean Skramstaad, you are my oldest friend. No, let me rephrase that. People our age need to be careful about calling each other 'old.' You are my friend of longest standing. I can't remember when you weren't a part of my life. I can't picture my life without you in it. We've had some long dry spells through the years where we didn't stay in touch much, but I always knew we'd find one another again."

"Doesn't really answer the question at hand, dear heart."

Gail delayed answering as long as she dared.

"All right, dammit. Yes, I used to hope one day it would dawn on you that I could be a whole lot more than the person you sat next to in Hannah Qualmberg's tenth grade English class. Yes, if you had ever given me so much as one tiny indication you'd let me hold your hand or take you in my arms or, God forbid, kiss you like I meant it, I would have. Hell, I'd have taken you to prom and homecoming and the winter snowball dance and any other stupid couples' thing in a fifty-mile radius. I'd have brought you corsages, sent you flowers, written you love sonnets, and carved our initials inside hearts on the trees at the park." Gail stopped to catch her breath. "And believe me, if I had known what that son-of-a-bitch Roland Dekeman was doing to you, I'd have tied a boulder around his neck and dumped him in the deepest lake in the county. And then I'd have done the prison time without a moment's regret, except for being separated from you."

"It's too late to save me from Roland." Penny moved so she was standing directly in front of Gail and squatted so she was at eye level with her. "But everything else is still a possibility." She stood and held her hands out for Gail to take. Gail pushed the cats aside and rose from the sofa.

"So kiss me already."

And she did.

GAIL AND Penny lay side by side on the queen-sized mattress in what once was Carl and Lillian Skramstaad's bedroom. Cubbie and Annette were at the foot of the bed. Rounder was on the floor next to Penny's side of the bed, snoring like a drunken sailor home on shore leave. Cookie was lying in the doorway, her head on her paws. She would occasionally lift her head and cock it to one side as if to say, "What the hell is this all about?"

It hadn't been more than four minutes since Penny had dug her fingernails into Gail's back as a four-decades-in-the-making orgasm had flashed around the room like a strobe light on a well-oiled swivel-topped barstool. "So this is how it's supposed to feel." Penny's words had pushed Gail over the top to a wonderfully sustained, toe-curling climax, but she hadn't dared speak for fear the words would wake her, and she'd find it was all only a dream.

Penny shifted slightly. "You were a big fan of the Mary Tyler Moore Show, weren't you?"

"Name the episode and I can probably do at least some of the dialogue. Kind of a strange topic to bring up now, isn't it, Penny?"

"Give me a sec to get my pulse back to a more normal pace. You'll know why I brought it up in a minute."

Gail waited. She knew that tone in Penny's voice. Maybe she should load up the cats and hit the road back to Sweetwater now. It would be daylight in another couple of hours anyway.

At last, Penny spoke. "Do you remember the running joke on Mary Tyler Moore?"

"They got a lot of mileage out of several of them. One of my favorites was how every party Mary gave was always a total disaster. Another one was Ted Baxter being so cheap he squeaked. He made Georgette wear a tuxedo at their wedding because he could get a discount on renting a second one when he got his."

"I remember that one. Georgette said they looked like the top of a gay couple's wedding cake."

"Right. Maybe the gag they milked the most, though, was how Mary never could seem to find a decent guy to date. They always were such disappointments."

"Then you'll remember the show where Mary has a date with Lou Grant."

"Of course. It was in the last season the show was on the air — 1977. Mary is complaining to Georgette how all the men in her life are such losers. Mary ticks off a list of characteristics she wants in a man, and Georgette points out there's someone already in Mary's life who meets all those criteria, namely Lou."

"So if you remember that much, I bet you remember how it ends."

Gail laced her fingers together and cradled the back of her head in her hands. "Mary and Lou have limped through an awkward evening and are back at Mary's apartment for a nightcap. They're sitting side by side on the couch, and it's time for the all-important lip-to-lip scene. They lean in toward each other and right before their lips touch, they both burst out laughing." Gail pulled her hands back down by her sides.

Penny reached out and groped for Gail's hand under the covers. "I hope you're not going to make me spell everything out."

"No, I think I understand. At least we made it beyond the kiss."

"Way beyond the kiss, it seems to me."

"But you hated it. Hate me."

"No, Gail. I didn't hate it, and I for sure don't hate you. It's just that..."

"Just that it's about the same as Mary Richards kissing Lou Grant."

"Back in the living room a while ago, you said you couldn't picture your life without me in it. The same is true for me. Like Mary and Lou, we've got too good a friendship to go messing it up with romance. I've loved you forever, and I'm going to go on loving you for as long as I draw breath, but I'm real sure we aren't meant to be lovers."

Gail tried to reply, but she couldn't push the words past the knot in her throat.

Penny squeezed Gail's hand. "It's probably a really good thing we didn't do this back in high school. I was already so torn apart by what Roland had done to me, this would have been more than I could handle."

"What about Richie?" Gail's voice was little more than a whisper.

"Wayne's friend? Different chapter in the same book. My brother hung out with some real low-lifes. After what Roland had done to me, it wasn't like I could save myself for my husband. At least Richie was from the right generation."

"And you and me?"

"If I had had a normal childhood — one free of what Roland did to me, I mean — you and I might have had an experiment or two with sex and might have gone so far as to set up housekeeping for a while. Who can say?"

"A little while ago you said you know we're not meant to be lovers."

"And I told you why. It's because you're way too important to me to have you be something so limited."

"That doesn't make any sense, Penny. Being a lover doesn't put boundaries on things."

"What I mean is if we had fallen into bed when we were teenagers, sex would have been the most important part of our relationship. This way, we have something a million times more important."

"We know each other's worst secrets and can blackmail each other for the rest of our natural lives?" Gail forced herself to try to sound light-hearted.

"We know each other's worst secrets and still care about one another anyway. And we know we love each other enough never to tell anybody what we did in my parents' bedroom on homecoming night, 2007."

"Why tonight? Why after all these years?"

"I'm not sure I know. Maybe it's all part of the housecleaning we've been doing. I moved out all the junk about Roland. You told me about the jerky things kids did to you — to us — back in high school. We've hauled the equivalent of a semi-truck load of garbage out of this house. The possibility of us being lovers has hung between us for years — the invisible orange elephant in the living room. It was time to sweep things out from under all the rugs."

"Was this a huge mistake?"

"No, not at all." She eased over and wrapped her arm around Gail's midsection. "It showed me a new way you're generous and selfless and patient. It's a shame how sex has to be an all or nothing deal." She hugged Gail with both arms. "We've been through a hell of a lot in our time together on this planet. Making love with you tonight is one more special way we're connected to each other."

"Do you think we'll ever do this again?"

"I've learned never to say never, but I'm afraid this would start to seem almost incestuous. You're the sister I never had. With a little bit of time and some decent luck, we can both find other lovers." Penny voice cracked. "But I don't have another lifetime to devote to ginning up a new combination sister and best friend. I've always thought I should call you 'frister,' because you're both friend and sister to me."

Gail felt the sadness creeping into every cell, but used the silence to contemplate what Penny had said.

Penny spoke again. "And you convinced me of something tonight."

"What?"

"I want to find out if there's anything more to this buzz I get whenever Andrea Martinson is around."

"Good. That's good, Penny. You really should."

"Any suggestions?"

"Give her Rita Mae's book of poems."

"*Songs to a Handsome Woman*? Do you think it might work?"

"Yeah, the dedication alone should be enough to flip her switch if she's the tiniest bit interested."

"I don't think I paid any attention to it. What does it say?"

"Slip this book inside your blouse to lie against your heart in innocence."

"Very nice."

"Uh huh." Gail paused. "I'm sorry it didn't work on you."

"Don't kid yourself. If you hadn't noticed, we're pretty much wearing just our birthday suits here, and within the last hour, I've done things with you I've never done with another woman."

"Thanks for letting me — for — uh, for lying here..."

"Don't, Gail. If this was going to happen, it needed to happen right here in Plainfield, Minnesota. For both our sakes, the less we talk about it, the sweeter the memory will be. And I'm really glad we didn't try to do this at Anderson Lake with the gear shift poking me in the butt."

"Remember how we always used to joke about being each other's maid of honor and how we hoped we wouldn't forget ourselves and dance with each other at our wedding receptions?" Penny asked.

"I remember. One of us was probably joking more than the other, though."

"Thanks to tonight, if we ever get the chance to get married, at least we'll know our fears had some basis in fact." Penny stretched and moved toward the side of the bed. "I should drag myself upstairs and try to get an hour or two of sleep."

"Do you have to go?"

Penny hesitated. "No, I guess not."

"I won't do anything inappropriate, I promise. I really want to keep you close to me for a little while."

"Sure. I understand."

Penny folded in snug against Gail's body and laid a gentle kiss on her cheek. "G'night, Mary. I love you."

"Goodnight, Lou. Love you, too."

Chapter
Seven

AS GAIL PASSED the city limit sign on the outskirts of Plainfield, melancholia settled over her like an unexpected autumn snowfall. She and Penny had said their good-bye's, and now she was headed back to her empty cabin in Sweetwater. Would she ever see her hometown again? Would she want to? And what about Penny? Would they be able to maintain their friendship after their experiences homecoming night, or had she lost her last good friend?

As the miles on Interstate 94 rolled by, the empty aching in her heart intensified. First, she'd had the editing project with Connie, and then, the house cleaning venture with Penny. Now what? She had run out of ways to hide from her feelings.

Marissa was dead. Penny—the dream she'd always held in reserve—was no longer a viable possibility. And then there was Connie. How could she be so gullible? Why hadn't she insisted they keep things strictly professional? *And I promised I'd call her when I get home. I get dumber by the day. Damn that Doctor Wilburn. I knew it was a mistake to dredge up all this crap.*

Mixed images of the three most prominent women in her life crowded together inextricably as she (and the cats) drove on. She had survived one painful parting. Did she have the courage to deal with the other two? Gail argued with herself about what was the best course of action all the way to Indiana, where she should have picked up I-65 and headed south. Instead, she turned east, toward Pennsylvania, toward the next farewell she somehow had to find the strength to face.

ONCE SHE HAD made the decision to detour to Pennsylvania, she stopped in South Bend to get maps and to buy some books on tape to distract her on the long drive. To Gail's delight, the cats had become better travelers, happy to sleep away long stretches of time. The west-to-east haul across Pennsylvania seemed to take forever. At last, she left the interstate a few miles south of Berwick and followed Route 11 northeast as it snaked along beside the Susquehanna River.

She was relieved that Marissa's parents weren't Catholic, inasmuch as she saw at least fifty Catholic churches in about as many miles, and signs for as many more, as she drove through the countryside towards Scranton. If Marissa had been buried in a Catholic cemetery, it would have taken forever to find the one with her grave. Fortunately, Gail remembered the name of the church mentioned in the folder from Marissa's funeral. She rolled into the little community of Kingston and soon found the church she was seeking. Perhaps one day, she'd research how it was a place came to be called "Forty Fort, Pennsylvania." For the time being, she was glad Marissa's parents had used the Forty Fort United Presbyterian Church for Marissa's service. It made finding her final resting place much easier.

Brilliant afternoon sunshine reflected off the wooded, rolling hills, which were already wearing their fall colors. The cemetery was situated in a curve along the East Branch of the Susquehanna. Despite its beauty, the bucolic scenery perversely added to Gail's sense of downheartedness.

Gail walked the rows of markers, looking for evidence of a recent interment. She hoped two months had been enough time for Marissa's parents to have her headstone set. She wandered through several more rows, scanning the names on each gravesite.

"Ris, there you are," she said aloud. She dropped to one knee in front of the stone. Tentatively, she touched the granite, expecting it to be cold to the touch, but instead finding it warm from the sun. "I miss you, sweetheart."

That was as much as she could manage to say before the tears blinded her. She let her other knee fall to the ground. Leaning her head against the words, "Marissa Ruth Adler," carved in the polished stone, Gail surrendered to the sorrow she had told herself she'd never acknowledge.

In time, she was able to stanch the flood. She wiped her eyes on her sleeve. She got to her feet and moved a half-pace away from the tombstone.

"If you knew about what I did with Connie down in Atlanta, I'm really sorry." Gail laughed lightly. "And if you didn't know, this is a hell of a time to tell you about it. When I get back to Sweetwater, I'm going to have to call her. I promised I would. I'm going to tell her it was all a big mistake." Gail looked off into the hills across the river. "It was, wasn't it?" She stared at the headstone for a moment before speaking again. "And that stupid night with Penny last week. I don't begin to know what to tell you about that."

Gail felt her heart fall to her feet. "I've mostly made a royal mess of my life, Ris. You were the one thing I almost got right, and then I ruined everything because I didn't protect us with some stupid pieces of paper that wouldn't have taken more than a couple of hours to get drawn up." The tears threatened to start anew; Gail fought them back.

"I hope wherever you are now, you still have the ability to forgive me. I hope you will, baby." Gail spoke more forcefully. "Ris, please forgive me for all the ways I let you down. I loved you more than anything in this world. I can't believe we never got to dance together." Her voice dropped to a whisper. "I can't believe you're gone."

Gail sat on the ground next to Marissa's gravesite. She laid her hand atop the earth and sat quietly. Thoughts of her fourteen happy years with Marissa echoed through her mind. Just as her hip joints were beginning to remind her that she was a little too old to be sitting for long periods of time on unyielding surfaces, a carillon—probably on the nearby Presbyterian Church—commenced to play. It only took five notes for Gail to recognize the melody.

"I'm going to take that as a sign you might be willing to forgive me someday, Ris." Gail rose to her feet as the next bars of "Amazing Grace" sounded from the bells. She noticed a group of four people standing at another grave several yards away. She didn't care if they were watching her or not. With a greater feeling of peace than she'd had in a long time, Gail pictured her beautiful Marissa in her arms as they danced among the gravestones.

"I'VE BEEN TRYING to call you for almost a week. Are you avoiding me?" Penny asked.

"No," Gail replied as she switched to the receiver to her other ear. "I decided to take the long way home."

"Really? Where'd you go?"

"I needed to visit an old friend in Pennsylvania."

"Marissa?"

"Uh huh."

"How did it go?" Penny asked gently.

"It almost killed me, but I know it was the right thing to do."

"Do you want to talk about it?"

"Thanks for asking, but no, I really don't. It's time to look forward, not back."

"Okay, but if you change your mind, you know how to find me."

"I do, and I will."

There was a long pause in the conversation.

"So, how are things in Sweetwater, Tennessee?

"My house has been closed up more than seven weeks. The first order of business was to air it out good. It was almost seventy degrees today, so I had all the windows wide open most of the day. There was a little breeze to help get the stale air out." Gail looked at the mess around her. "I still need to tame some chaos, but I've got a rope around the worst of it. How are things up there in Minnie Hoota?"

"We topped forty-two late this afternoon, so if you discount the weather, things are good. I've already got an offer on dad's house. If it goes through, I can have some peace in my life."

"I'll send some heavy-duty positive energy your way."

"Thanks. How was your extra-long drive home?"

"It took me long enough, but I've figured out the secret to traveling with my cats."

"Yeah?"

"Uh huh. I left the doors on the carriers open. As long as Cubbie and Annette thought they weren't incarcerated, they were perfectly happy to curl up together and snooze for hours on end. I was able to listen to a book on tape for part of the drive. And instead of acting as if I were the pace car at the Indy 500, I took lots of rest breaks. That helped all of us stay mostly mellow. I pulled in here mid-afternoon yesterday. Today, I restocked my cupboards, and tomorrow I'll catch up on my mail and do the laundry, and then Monday, I'll be back on the clock for Outrageous."

"Sounds like you've got it all under control. Hey, Gail, thanks a million for coming up to Plainfield and helping with the house. I'd have been there 'til Christmas if you hadn't done everything you did."

"Don't mention it. It sure will feel strange never to hang out at 331 Vasa Avenue again."

"Not much chance either one of us will forget our last days there, though."

"Not a chance in the world." Gail put up a mental roadblock to keep the rush of memories—including the happier ones which were tinged with melancholy—from detouring the conversation. "Did you go back to work this week? How's Andrea?"

"Work sucks, but Andrea is fine. I gave her the book of poems on Wednesday while we were riding the bus to work." Gail pictured the grin spreading across Penny's face.

"I get the feeling you've got a story to tell."

"Have you got time?"

"I just fixed myself a sandwich. If you don't mind my chewing in your ear while we talk, let's hear it."

"Andrea invited me out to her house after work last night. She left a little bit early, so she gave me directions for finding the place. I had no idea her husband was one of the big enchiladas at the feed and seed company he'd worked for."

"Oh, right, you told me he took an early retirement."

"Complete with a very large golden parachute, it would seem."

"Do tell."

"They live in this enormous house out on Lake Minnetonka in Wayzata. I don't think I've ever seen a bigger, snazzier house except maybe on the celebrity gossip shows on TV."

"How big?"

"Big enough to have an indoor swimming pool, and I don't mean some dinky four-footer, either. This was half a lake. The pool room— carpeted, if you can imagine—has a big-screen entertainment system, a gas barbeque grill, and a wet bar."

"Almost poverty level housing, the poor baby. Did you have any idea Andrea was sucking a silver spoon?"

"Never a clue. I mean, she dresses nicely, and obviously has her nails manicured and her hair done every week, but I was completely in the dark about her being Mrs. Gotrocks."

"Why do you think she works? It can't be for the paycheck to keep groceries on the table."

"She started working right out of college, which was at least a few years before she met Bob. I'm sure Bob wasn't always at the top of the salary heap, so at first, it was probably for the same reason the rest of us do it—to pay the bills. She's told me about how bored she got when she took time off to have her kids. By then, she'd figured out how going to work beat the heck out of dusting the art collection and watching the stock portfolio expand."

"So tell me about the evening."

"After I slapped my jaw back on my face following the grand tour, we talked about going out to a restaurant, but decided we'd have steaks on the grill in the pool room. I offered to run to the store to get the meat and fixings, but Andrea said she'd go. Next thing I knew, it was Bob and me and two bottles of beer in front of the big-screen TV."

"How romantic."

"You know, at first, it wasn't too bad. We talked about his job, my job, the weather in Santa Fe, the weather in Minnesota, what he planned to do with his free time in retirement, their kids. He wasn't nearly the jerk he'd been at the restaurant that night I left you in Plainfield while I went down to my house to pick up the papers I needed for selling Dad's house."

"But?"

"But somewhere in the conversation, Bob hit the remote for the TV. The screen was covered with a half-dozen life-size, living color, gorgeous babes in swimsuits no bigger than gauze patches with dental floss holding them in place. They were cavorting on the simulated beach and rubbing suntan oil all over each other. They draped themselves on their blankets like models on a photo shoot. Bob needed a bib to mop up all the drooling he was doing."

"There you were, enjoying eye candy with Bob?"

"It obviously had an effect on him, if you know what I mean. Now picture the scene. It's barely forty degrees outside, but we're in this room heated to about eighty. He was wearing a robe—a beach cover-up, I guess you'd call it. He shucks that, and underneath, he's wearing a pair of skimpy swim trunks. He must have had them for years, or at least from when he was several pounds lighter. I expected to hear seams ripping loose."

"Couldn't you get up and walk away?"

"Could have and should have, I suppose."

"But you didn't."

"No. And when he used the neck of his beer bottle to point to his—his—"

"Never mind. I can guess where he was pointing. What did you do?"

"What could I do? I laughed and said 'Oh, I see something's come up for you. I really should be going.'"

"What did he say?"

Penny sucked in a loud breath. "His exact words were, 'Actually, you should be coming.'"

"I'd have slapped him."

"I wanted to, but fortunately, I didn't have to."

"Because?"

"Because Andrea came back at that opportune moment. She was very cool and controlled. She walked over to Bob, dropped about five pounds of cold, raw steak in his crotch and said, 'This is the last time I put up with this bullshit from you, Robert Martinson. My lawyer will call you on Monday.' Then she crooked her finger at me and said, 'Let's go.'"

"Where did you go?"

"To my place."

"And, and, and?"

"And we talked all night. Nothing happened. I mean not *the* thing. We sat together on my couch and touched each other a lot, but it wasn't the right time for anything more."

"Is she gay?"

"Not exactly."

"That would be comparable to being sort of pregnant. Either she is or she isn't."

"She told me she's always had her suspicions, but she's never done anything about it."

"Is she still at your place?"

"No, she went back to her house to get some clothes and her checkbook."

"She's not worried about what Bob will do?"

"She's sure he's already out banging some local talent. The marriage has been over for years, but neither one of them was willing to take the first move to end it officially."

"Then along came little Penny Skramstaad and Andrea found a new way to live happily ever after."

"It's a little too soon for me to rush out and buy monogrammed towels."

"Get the 'hers and hers' ones, and then you won't have to worry about returning them." Gail took a deep drink from her iced tea. "Tell me how you feel."

"Excited. Scared. Clumsy. Inept. A kid in a candy shop. What if I screw it up?"

"Impossible. Follow your heart, and everything will be fine."

"I never would have had the nerve to go through with this if we hadn't—you hadn't—we didn't..."

"You were already well on your way, Penny. This is between you and Andrea. I'm just an enthusiastic cheerleader."

"Kim Galloway would be proud."

"Or jealous."

"Not likely. Should I tell Andrea about you and me?"

"About being life-long friends? Absolutely."

"You know I meant should I tell her about homecoming night. She might want to know if I have a checkered past."

"I suppose she might ask you if there have been any other women in your life. My advice is to say something along the lines of, 'there was one, but it was a long time ago.'"

"But it was last week."

"No, last week closed the book on what really happened years and years ago. Leave it in the history books. That's where it belongs."

"You're sure."

"I'm sure, Penny."

"Oh, there's Andrea pulling into my driveway. I should go."

"Good luck, kid. I hope it's all you've ever dreamed of."

"I'll let you know."

"You better. Maybe we'd better skip having me be your maid of honor and make me the flower girl at the commitment ceremony, instead. And don't forget to save the second dance at the reception for me, okay?"

"IT'S CERTAINLY NICE to see you again, Gail. When so much time had passed since your last visit I wondered if I'd ever see you again." Doctor Wilburn used both hands to reseat her glasses on her nose.

"You got the messages I left with your answering service didn't you? The ones canceling my appointments?"

"Oh, yes, but usually when a client cancels two sessions in a row, it means they don't think the therapy is helping them any more."

Marcella Wilburn was wearing the same navy blue ultra suede skirt and off white blouse with the lace collar she'd worn when Gail was last there in July. Gail had seen her in it so many times she thought of it as Wilburn's shrink uniform.

"I'm not sure the therapy is doing me any good, and I told you on the messages I left I was out of town."

"Good for you. Did you take your journal with you? I hope you wrote about your feelings and experiences."

"No, actually, I didn't."

"That's too bad. Many times what someone writes in a journal gives me better insights into what's working and what isn't. Have you made any entries since you were here in July?"

"A couple."

"Why don't we start with them? Read me something from the first entry you made after our last session."

Gail read what she had written while sitting at Tellico Lake Dam on the afternoon of July seventeenth. *"I did something I swore I'd never do. I'm sitting at Tellico Lake. I can see the dock where the EMTs treated Marissa the day of the accident. Dr. W. said I should do things to make me stretch and experience more of life. Right now, this feels more like dying than living, but at least I did it. It's been two years. Marissa's parents still refuse to talk to me when I call. If it weren't for Amy, I wouldn't know Marissa is still alive, if you can call it that. Amy says she's tried to convince her parents to take Marissa off all the life-support machines, but they won't do it. She's only Marissa's little sister after all. It's the cruelest thing I've ever heard of. I wonder if I'll ever stop missing her? I wonder if I'll ever love anyone else?"*

"Good for you, Gail. You've taken an important step."

"I went to Tellico Lake. So what? Pin a rose on me and call me cured."

"Don't minimize it. For the first time, you went back to the place where you experienced one of the biggest losses in your life. It's a very good sign. I want you to realize how significant it is in your healing."

"I guess."

"Tell me how you feel about Marissa."

"You mean now that she's dead?"

"Dead? What do you mean?"

Gail noted the look of shock passing over Doctor Wilburn's usually unperturbed face.

"I mean she's dead. She died on July thirtieth."

"Did you go to the funeral? Is that why you were out of town?"

In an instant, Gail was livid. "Have you *ever* listened to one damn thing I've told you in this office? I didn't find out she was dead until almost the end of August when I got back from Atlanta."

"I'm sorry. I'm confused. You didn't find out she was dead because you were in Atlanta? And why do you think I haven't been listening to you?"

"I've told you a hundred times about how shitty her parents have been. They never told me anything about how she was. Wouldn't let me come to Scranton to see her. Treated me as if I were nothing but a casual friend to her."

"All right, yes, I'm aware of your long-standing anger, but what does her parents' exclusionary stance have to do with Atlanta?"

"The same day I went to Tellico Lake, I got a call from my boss at Outrageous Press. She had a special editing assignment she wanted me to do with an author who lives in Atlanta. You're always pushing me to do things to make me get more involved, so I agreed to take the job.

Because I was going to be gone for at least a couple of weeks, I had the post office hold my mail while I was gone. When I got home, there was an envelope from Marissa's sister with the pamphlet from Marissa's funeral in it."

"Okay, I see the connections now." Doctor Wilburn eased back in her chair and jotted a line in her notebook. "And so because you were in Atlanta on a work assignment, you couldn't go to the funeral."

"No, dammit! I couldn't go to the funeral because no one told me there was a funeral to go to."

"But if you went to Atlanta right after our last session," Doctor Wilburn consulted her notes, "which was on July seventeenth, and Marissa died on the thirtieth, unless Marissa's family knew how to contact you in Atlanta, how do you know they didn't try to notify you?"

Gail stifled the urge to reach across the low table sitting between her and the doctor and slap her face. How many times did she have to tell the moron that Marissa's family acted as if she didn't even exist? Why the hell would anyone call her to tell her Marissa was dead if no one in the family would ever tell her if she was still alive? It wouldn't have mattered if she'd been in Atlanta or the Alaskan wilderness, because nobody left a message to tell her —

It wasn't likely Marissa's parents would have called, but Amy, Marissa's sister, might have. Come to think of it, it was sort of strange there wasn't a line or two from Amy with the funeral folder. What if Amy had tried to call her to tell her Marissa was dead? Of course she'd be upset that Gail hadn't had the courtesy to leave a forwarding number. Then it hit her. No, there weren't any messages. She had turned her answering machine off when she left Sweetwater to go to Atlanta. Penny had complained about it when she talked to her the day after she returned from her surreal experience with Connie Martin's manuscript, not to mention with Connie Martin herself.

Oh God. What if Amy had called to tell her Marissa was dying? To tell her to come see her one last time? To come say goodbye?

Gail felt the blood drain from her head. She thought she might faint.

"Gail? Are you all right? You're pale as a ghost."

"I think I'd better lie down."

"Of course." Doctor Wilburn stepped around the table and helped Gail to the sofa, which was sitting at a right angle to her chair. "Would you like a glass of water?"

"No. I'll be okay in a minute. Just let me be."

Gail lay very still and drew a couple of shaky breaths. Doctor Wilburn hovered nearby, obviously out of her element. *Typical worthless Wilburn. Calls herself a doctor, but only for mental illness. Not worth a damn when I'm really sick.* It felt like nearly a light year before Gail eased into a half-sitting position and wiped her hand over her moist forehead.

"Sorry about that."

"You don't need to apologize. What happened?" Doctor Wilburn returned to her chair.

"I'm not sure. All of I sudden, I felt sick."

"Was it a reaction to realizing Marissa is dead?"

"I doubt it." Gail rubbed her hands together then laid her palms on her cheeks. "I've said all along that, to me, it's as though she died two years ago."

"Yes, but there's a difference between how we tell ourselves something feels in a hypothetical state and how it is in reality."

Gail dropped her hands to her lap. "I let her down again." Gail realized Doctor Wilburn was straining to hear the words. She repeated herself. "I let her down again."

"Let who down? How?"

"Marissa. What if you were right about the Adlers trying to call me? I know her parents wouldn't have tried, but her sister might have. I might have missed a call from Amy. What if I might have gotten there in time to hold Marissa one last time? What if she came out of her coma and asked for me?" For the first time in the ten months she had been seeing Doctor Wilburn, Gail couldn't fight back her tears.

"Don't punish yourself with irrational thoughts, Gail. From what you've told me about the degree of Marissa's brain damage, there's absolutely no chance she regained consciousness and asked for you."

"But I'll never know for sure."

"You could ask Marissa's family."

"I don't think I want to know."

"You can't have it both ways. Either you want to know, or you don't."

"It wouldn't change anything anyway. She's dead, and I wasn't there to hold her while she died." Gail slumped down on the sofa. "And where was I? In Atlanta whoring it up with Connie."

"Pardon?" For the second time in the session, Gail watched Doctor Wilburn labor to maintain her composure.

"Never mind. It's one more thing I can feel guilty about for the rest of my life."

"The whole point of your time with me is to help you come to terms with your feelings. Maybe you should tell me a little more about this." The doctor leaned over to retrieve her notebook from the table. The friction of the ultra suede skirt against the leather produced another encore of the Wilburn Sonata in F-Flat.

"What's to tell? I had an affair with some woman I barely knew and didn't particularly like." Gail crossed her arms across her chest. No way would she tell Wilburn about what happened between her and Penny. One shock treatment per session was enough. "There. Have a field day analyzing that little nugget of information."

"It's probably more important for you to analyze it."

"I'm a depressed, lonely, sex-starved woman who ruined her

lover's life because I was too freaking lazy to get a lawyer to do a couple of stupid pieces of paper. I fell into bed with the first person who asked me to, and I was probably cramming my tongue down her throat at the very moment Marissa died. Let me know if I missed any important details in my analysis."

"How about taking a look at how you feel?"

"How the hell should I feel?"

"You know there isn't a rule book for emotions."

Gail lurched to the front edge of her seat. "Oh, Christ on a crutch! I've had enough of your psycho-babble bullshit. If you can't see I'm mad as fire, then you've got no business being a therapist."

"Of course I can see you're angry. But why are you angry?"

"Because the woman I loved more than life itself is gone forever, and no one is ever going to love me again."

"I see. And when you say those words, what's going on inside of you? Take a moment and give me an honest answer."

Gail squinted as she thought. "I feel like a little kid who can't find her mommy."

"And your feelings surrounding that?"

Gail eased back in her chair and counted to ten before she answered. "Scared. Alone. Lost. Frightened. Petrified. Terrified."

"I'm sure I've mentioned this to you before. Sometimes, anger is a mask for fear."

The tears rolled down Gail's cheeks. *Maybe Wilburn isn't totally worthless after all.*

"CONNIE? HI, IT'S Gail Larsen." Gail switched the phone to her other hand and cuffed Cubbie, who was batting at the pens and pencils lying on the end table. He knocked two of them to the floor before she managed to stop him. "Stinker."

"That's one way to describe you."

"Sorry. My cat is making a pest of himself. In my next life, I'm going to stick with goldfish."

"How are the kids?

"The kitty carriers are out of sight, so they're fine. Cubbie and Annette have had about as much time away from home as they can stand. First, it was a month with you in Atlanta, and then another three weeks up in my old hometown, followed by an extra long-trip to get back to Sweetwater."

"I'm glad they're okay. More importantly, how are you? I'd almost given up ever hearing from you."

"I know. I got back from Minnesota week before last, but things have been nuts. The house was a mess, and I had tons of laundry to do. Plus, I had some appointments I needed to take care of, and Lydia had a pile of work she wanted me to jump on. I've been meaning to call you, but I couldn't seem to find the time."

"I'm glad you did."

"So what's going on with you? Got any new books in the works?"

"Happy as I am to talk about my books, I'd rather we discuss some meatier subjects. I hope we're not going to just dodge the issue with small talk."

"It's not small talk. I want to know what you've been doing."

"Exactly what I told you I was doing the last time we talked."

"Oh."

"You remember what I told you, don't you?"

"More or less."

"Have you thought about what I said?"

"A little."

"I really want to see you. If you don't want to come to Atlanta, I'll come up there."

"I don't think that's a good idea."

"There's someone else, isn't there?"

"No, that's not it."

"If you're not involved with someone, then it's got to be you're not at all interested in me." Connie cleared her throat. "I don't want to believe that. I can't believe that. In fact, I won't believe that, especially when I remember how it felt every time I held you in my arms. I can still hear the way you'd say my name. It made me feel almost...almost attractive."

Gail tried to fight down the reaction she was feeling. "It's really kind of complicated." Gail hoped her voice didn't betray her rising libido.

"As best I can tell, nothing in this life is simple, not once you get beyond about second grade anyway," Connie said.

"This is well beyond second grade."

"So what? Something being complicated doesn't mean it isn't worth pursuing."

"I just don't think I'm ready to... for..."

"Just go ahead and tell me you find me as appealing as a sack of potatoes."

"Connie, don't run yourself down like that."

"There's no other explanation. Maybe you've been able to forget what it felt like to lie in each other's arms, but I haven't." Connie's voice broke. "I'm sorry you find me so ugly."

"That's not true." Gail was at a loss for anything more to say.

"I've had six weeks to get over you, and it hasn't happened. If anything, it's worse than ever. Please, Gail. Give me one more chance. You can call all the shots. If you want to date, we'll date. If you want chaperones, we'll hire chaperones. If you want love sonnets and flowers and strolling minstrels, consider it done. If you want to rub me down with Crisco and slap me with kitchen spatulas, I'll buy rubber sheets and swing by the Kroger's. But don't make me go through the rest of my life wondering if your eyes are really as blue as I remember them."

"All right, Connie. When do you want to get together?" Gail willed herself to think about the Rockwell picture on the calendar hanging on the wall beside her—anything to get her mind off how she'd felt about herself for betraying Marissa with Connie.

"Today."

"You're kidding, right?"

"Serious as a shark attack. You've told me you'll see me. I sure don't want to give you time to change your mind."

"Are you saying you don't trust me?" Gail asked.

"I do trust you, but I know you've got your doubts about us. Maybe I don't trust myself."

"I don't follow."

"Let me borrow a line you used earlier. Things are kind of complicated for me, too."

"Does that mean you're seeing someone?"

"No," Connie said, then stopped. "No, my complications have nothing to do with anyone else. How about we save the hard topics to talk about face to face? I've never been very good at phone confessions."

Gail absent-mindedly scratched Cubbie's ear. "Okay. So when should we meet?"

"I told you. Today. It's only a little after one. I need less than an hour to get organized and hit the road. It's about two hours to Sweetwater from here, so I should see you around four."

"Let me give you some directions."

"Don't need them. Remember I told you when I called you in Minnesota that I'd been up there trying to find you when you didn't answer my e-mails. That was before I badgered Lydia into telling me you'd taken a leave of absence to go help your friend. I used the Internet to get maps to find your house."

"George Orwell warned us big brother would be watching."

"I bet he didn't have a clue how right he was."

"Probably not."

"So, I'll see you in a couple of hours."

"I won't have time to do much to the house. It's a disaster."

"I'm not coming to see your house, Gail. Don't worry about it."

"Okay. Drive safely."

"I will. Thanks for calling. I can't wait to see you."

Gail hung up the phone and looked around the main room of the cabin. The tabletops needed a swipe with a dust cloth. Tumbleweeds of cat hair were visible in the corners. Rat stacks of magazines and newspapers adorned a number of surfaces. She knew at least two days' worth of dishes were still soaking in the kitchen sink and the bathroom vanity probably had enough crud on it to cause dysentery.

Oh, screw it. I'm not going to knock myself out trying to impress a woman I don't even like.

Then, one more time making a liar of herself in regards to Connie Martin, Gail launched into her impersonation of the white tornado.

Chapter
Eight

GAIL MET CONNIE as she pulled up next to the cabin. Connie stepped out of her Toyota Camry into the cool October afternoon.

"It's so gorgeous up here."

"Yeah, the leaves put on a nice show this time of year."

"When I was up here a few weeks ago, they hadn't started to change. I can see why you enjoy living here."

Connie opened her arms as if to ask for a hug. Gail obliged.

"You smell exactly like I remember, Gail." The tone in Connie's voice made Gail shudder as she struggled to control the reaction Connie's words brought forth. She wasn't sure if it was arousal or trepidation.

"I guess I'm still wearing the same old cheap perfume."

"I'll buy it for you by the tanker truck full if you promise to wear it forever. What's it called?"

"Golden Autumn."

Gail's memory catapulted back to the homecoming dance when Penny Skramstaad had commented on the very same fragrance. The flashback messed with her mind. Two women — one she now knew she would never have and one she was sure she didn't want — both thought she smelled divine. *Maybe I should switch to Aqua Velva.*

"I guess since you're here right on time you didn't have any problems on the drive up." Gail pulled free from Connie's embrace.

"Nope. We'll need to remember Thursday afternoon is a good time to make the drive between our places. I got out of Atlanta before the downtown traffic had a chance to clog up I-75. That made a big difference."

"Come on inside. You can say hi to the cats and see the house."

"I looked in the front windows when I was up here before," Connie said.

Gail cast a sideways look at Connie.

"I wasn't stalking you or playing peeping Tom. I was afraid you might have fallen or were sick or something. Besides, if I could still see furniture and other belongings, it meant you hadn't moved away without leaving me a forwarding address."

"Oh, okay." Gail led the way to the front door and said nothing about the ramp they were walking up. To Gail's relief, Connie didn't comment about the fact the cabin was handicapped-accessible.

Cubbie raced to the door to see if the visitor — a rarity at Sweetwater Cabin — had brought him something good to eat or fun to play with.

"Hi, Annette," Connie said as she leaned over and scratched the long, lithe orange tabby gingerly behind the ear.

"No, that's Cubbie. Annette is the brunette, remember?" Gail pointed across the room to a dark gray — so gray she was almost black — compact cat lounging on a carpeted cat tree in the far corner.

"Apparently not. Sorry, fella." Connie pulled her hand back just in time to catch her sneeze.

"Bless you," Gail said.

"Thanks." Connie sneezed again.

"Is the cat dander getting to you?"

"I'm afraid so."

Gail thought Connie was already sounding congested.

"I brought my allergy pills. I'll pop a couple quick, and I'll be fine in a minute." Connie rummaged in her shoulder bag for a bottle and shook two capsules into her hand.

"I'll get you some water. You seemed to do okay when we were at the Magnolia Suites working on your book. The cats were there the whole time." Gail headed for the kitchen.

"I never know when this is going to hit. Might be because the cats live here and there's more of their hair around. Might be there's mold in the leaves that have fallen, and I reacted to that walking in from the car. My prescription is broad spectrum. It'll do the trick." She took the glass from Gail. "Thanks." She sounded as if she were speaking from inside an empty oil drum.

"I am really sorry. Should I lock the cats in one of the bedrooms?" Gail looked to the closed doors on the far left side of the room.

"No, once the drugs take effect, it'll be all right. I'm allergic to all sorts of things. I should have been smart enough to take my meds before I got here. Give me twenty minutes, and I'll be good to go." Connie sat down on a wooden rocking chair and extracted an inhaler from her bag. She took two quick sucks on it and put it away. She struggled with a breath or two, but soon was breathing more freely.

"There, good as new," she said as she stood up.

"We probably shouldn't spend much time here. I mean, the cats have been absolutely everywhere in this house. The act of sitting on the sofa might kill you." Gail laughed sardonically.

"Really, it's fine. I've dealt with this for years. I can tell if I'm going to have a really bad attack, and this isn't going to be one."

Gail wished Connie's affectionate smile didn't unnerve her so thoroughly.

Connie continued. "And I probably told a little fib a minute ago. I shouldn't blame the cats or the leaf mold for bringing this on. I often have flair ups when I get really excited. I was almost hyperventilating most of the last ten miles."

"Why?"

"As if you don't know." Connie moved closer. "I've missed you so much."

To Gail's relief, Connie's attempt to plant a kiss on her was derailed by four sneezes in rapid succession.

"Uhhh," Connie groaned as she tried to clear her sinuses. "This certainly isn't going to help me score any points with you, is it?" Connie helped herself to some tissues from the box sitting on the lower shelf of the end table by the sofa.

"Or me with you. By the looks of things, your first visit to my place will be your last."

Connie blew her nose. "Technically, it's my second visit, and I hope to high heaven it's not my last." She dabbed at her runny eyes.

"I hadn't pictured you as the masochist type."

"The subject of that old joke, huh?"

"Which old joke?"

"A masochist and a sadist are making love. The masochist says, 'beat me,' and the sadist says, 'absolutely not.'"

"Very funny," Gail said. "But I guess if you're able to tell jokes, you're maybe not doing too badly."

"Hang with me for a few more minutes. I can feel the drugs starting to do their thing. And if I could stop my impersonation of a teenager on her first prom date, I'd do myself a world of good."

Gail chose to let the comment pass. "So what have you been doing since we finished your book? What did you decide to call it?"

"I went with 'Rings and Things.' It felt right for it. And thank you again for being such a trouper in getting it ready so quickly and for sticking to your guns on that scene with the boss."

"You're welcome on both counts. And I like the title you picked. Have you started on a new one?"

"No, but if I had I suppose I'd have to call it 'A Tale of Gail.'"

"I'm hoping that's t-a-l-e- and not t-a-i-l, but given the amount of weight I put on over the summer, I could see how you might choose the latter."

Connie rolled her eyes back in their sockets. "C'mon, Gail. For starters, you look fine. Better than fine, actually. Perfect, in fact. Are you going to keep side-stepping my efforts to get you to talk to me about what's going on between us?"

Gail opened her mouth, but closed it again without speaking. They stood rooted to the spots they'd been in for several minutes.

"Say something. Anything," Connie urged.

"I was going to say there's nothing going on between us, but that's not true, is it?"

"Not if I can have my way."

"Connie, I think I gave you the wrong impression."

"Look, I know I came on too strong with you." Connie eased a half step toward Gail. "It's not something I typically do. I apologize. You've made it real clear you're not comfortable picking up where we left off in Atlanta, but I'm still hoping you feel about me as I feel about you."

Gail offered no discernable reaction, so Connie went on. "How about this? Let's for tonight behave as though all we did at the Magnolia Suites was work on my book. Let's say we liked each other as work associates and found out maybe we could be friends. Now, here it is a month and a half later, and we've managed to get together for an evening of conversation and catching up. I won't rip your clothes off, or put my hands on your body, or say all the things I practiced saying to you on the drive up here. We're two new friends, still getting to know each other. Deal?"

Gail raised her hands slightly, palms up. "I guess. Are you feeling better? Do you want to see the rest of the place?"

"Yeah, I'm a walking example of better living through chemistry. The anvil is off my chest. I'd love the grand tour."

"Nickel tour is a better description, and you've already spent more than two cents." Gail took a few steps to her right toward the kitchen. "We've been lingering here in the near foyer of the primary ballroom. As you can see, it also serves as the parlor," she waved majestically to the sofa, rocking chair, and recliner, "den, study, and library annex." She gave another wave, this time toward the bookcase, television stand, and small desk she used for household affairs and what few snail mail letters she wrote. "And, obviously, the feline gymnasium." She took four steps to the cat tree in front of a large window, where Annette was still situated. The cat rolled over; Gail rubbed her upturned belly. Connie followed, but settled for blowing a kiss in Annette's direction.

"Now, through this soaring archway, you enter the gourmet kitchen where we have, as you see, strictly state-of-the-art food preparation accoutrements, provided your state is Tennessee circa 1985 and your taste in art leans toward paint-by-number scenes of deer grazing in the forest." The kitchen was long and narrow, running the length of the cabin, front to back. A small table with two chairs sat at the near end surrounded by windows, overlooking the trees.

"Does that door go outside?" Connie asked. She indicated a door on the end opposite the table.

"Huh uh. It's the laundry room. The litter boxes are out there, and I store the cat food, extra litter, kitty carriers, and lord knows what all else in the closet in there. You can get to the side yard from there, but I almost never go out that way."

"I saw the little flap in the door and figured it was how the cats let themselves out."

"Strictly indoor kids. Supposedly, it doubles their life expectancy because it protects them from illnesses and injuries. And up here in the woods, they'd be fox fodder or hawk snacks or target practice for poisonous snakes."

"Oh, right. I hadn't considered the consequences."

"Why would you have? From what I saw earlier, cats are nothing but histamine triggers for you."

As if on cue, Cubbie appeared out of nowhere and began his solo conga line dance around Connie's feet.

"Let me put him some place where he can't rub his scent glands all over you." Gail snatched him up and draped him over her arm.

"Scent glands?"

"Uh huh. Cats have glands all over themselves, in their face, lips, tail, toes—and they leave their particular smell on things and people they want to claim as their own. That little maneuver he used on you got you with almost every gun in his arsenal."

"Annette, you big flirt." Connie wagged a finger at the cat hanging boa-like over Gail's arm.

"One more time, this is Cubbie. You're good with words, Connie. Remember Annette's the brunette."

"You said that to me before, didn't you?"

"Right before your immune system went into hyperwarp after we came through the front door."

"I've got it now. I won't mix them up again." She laid her hand on Gail's arm, near Cubbie but not touching him. He tried to inch out of Gail's grasp to slide his chin over Connie's fingers. As he did so, he pulled his lips back and opened his mouth slightly.

"Is he going to bite me?" Connie yanked her hand away, just in case.

"No, that's called the Flehman reaction. On the roof of their mouths, way at the back, cats have something called a Jacobson's organ. It's kind of a cross between a nose and a tongue—it registers both smell and taste. When he does that, he's trying to decide if he recognizes what he's sensing."

"Did he?"

"Beats me. These guys don't ever tell me what they've figured out except if I've forgotten to fill their food bowls or if the litter box needs changing."

"He's really kind of cute."

"I certainly think so." Gail snuggled the tabby to her chest. "How 'bout it, handsome?" She dropped him to the floor, and he scampered to the living room to join his sister on the cat tree.

"Why did you name them Cubbie and Annette?"

"I didn't. Mar—a friend of mine did. I'll tell you about that later. Let's finish what's left of the tour before we run out of daylight."

Gail led the way from the kitchen across the living room. "Okay, this is my office." She swung the leftmost door back. Connie stepped into the doorway. The three interior walls were lined with bookshelves stuffed to overflowing with hard covers, trade paperbacks, reference books, style manuals, and sheaves of papers banded in bundles. In the corner of the room to the far left was a workstation with a computer, printer, and twenty-two inch monitor. "Do you think a big monitor makes a difference?" Connie asked.

"As much time as I spend looking at manuscripts from Outrageous, I'd be blind in a week if I didn't have it."

Connie wandered over to inspect the monitor more closely. She glanced out the window and saw her car. "Oh, I see. This is the front corner of the house. I get turned around so easily once I'm inside." She scanned contents on the bookshelves as she walked back to the door. "You sure have a lot of English literature text books."

Two years earlier, as Mrs. Adler had instructed her to do, Gail had loaded most of Marissa's personal effects into Marissa's car for her father to collect and take to Pennsylvania. She had chosen to keep all of Marissa's course materials and had crammed them onto her bookcases. No matter how hard she tried, she hadn't been able to take them back to the University or to donate them to a library or book sale. They were still sitting on the shelf, gathering dust.

"Never know when you might want to check out a literary reference or verify an old master's point of view," Gail said.

"And look. A string of books by someone named Connie Martin." The fading sunlight couldn't fully mask the crimson hue flushing Connie's cheeks.

"Yes, she's all the rage in the world of lesbian love stories. I'll loan them to you if you want to page through them sometime."

"Oh, no. I never sully my mind with cheap Harlequin trash. I only read the classics." Connie flung her head in mock disdain, her long hair swaying from side to side.

"Yeah, me too, except for the ten hours a day I spend working on books for Outrageous. C'mon let's make the last stop on our excursion."

As they stepped back into the living room, Gail pulled the door shut. "I only let the cats in there if I'm at my desk. Otherwise, they think it's their responsibility to rearrange everything. It's a miracle they haven't killed themselves, given the number of times they've brought a whole shelf of books crashing down."

"Maybe they have, and they're already on number seven or eight of their nine lives."

"Could be. This is the bathroom," Gail said as she passed the middle of the three doors to their left. "Help yourself. I'm sorry. I didn't ask if you wanted to use it when you got here."

"I'll need it in a little while. My allergy pills not only help my lungs, but they're a diuretic, too."

"And here's my bedroom." She pushed open the door to the room and stood back, letting Connie go in first.

"Ohmygosh!" Connie rushed to the sliding glass door on the opposite wall. "I had no idea."

"The way the house sits on the lot, from out front you can't tell this is back here. From the other side of the house, it appears to be just forest."

Connie stared at the view in front of her. The cabin backed to the rim of a ravine between two ridges of the foothills of the Great Smokies. A deck wrapped around the corner of the bedroom, giving a panoramic vista across the valley below. Several smaller folds of hills rolled down either side of the main channel.

"It's so gorgeous it almost looks artificial." Connie drank in the panoply. "And the colors. I didn't think there were so many ways to do red and orange and yellow."

The sun hung above the top edge of the far border of the valley. The light played and danced off the painted leaves on the hardwoods; the pine trees were so green they looked like brushed verdant velvet, providing contrast to the autumn hues.

"Look." Connie pointed to six or eight large birds soaring in the distance. "Are those eagles?"

"I doubt it. They might be hawks, but from the wingspan and shape, I'd say they're ugly old turkey vultures. If you're lucky enough to see an eagle at all, it would more likely be around lakes and rivers. They're fish eaters, so hanging out here in the woods wouldn't make much sense."

"Oh. Who knew? But anyway, those birds don't look ugly to me."

"When they're riding the wind currents, you're right, they're graceful, but once you've seen one of them pulling the innards out of a dead possum on the road, you never feel quite the same about them."

Gail walked over next to Connie and stared out over the chasm. It used to be her favorite way to start and end the day. She and Marissa would steal a few minutes on weekday mornings or take as long as they pleased on the weekends to sit out on the deck. Sometimes in the winter, they saw snow flurries struggling on the swirling winds. In the spring, they'd look for the first signs of the trees budding. In the summer, they watched the shadows pull back from the floor of the chasm as the sun seemed to race into the sky from the horizon to the east. The endless changes in the colors gave them the world's biggest kaleidoscope in the fall. In the evenings, they'd sit together on the swing suspended from the rafters and sway and talk, grateful for the time to be together.

"Can we go out?" Connie reached for the handle on the sliding glass door.

"Sure. We need to close the door before the cats try to join us. I'd hate to watch one of them think they knew how to fly when they leaped off the railing trying to get a bird or a squirrel."

Connie slid the door along its track and felt the bite of the autumnal air. Gail eased out behind her and dragged the screen door over to block the opening. She heard two pleading feline voices as she latched it in place. "No, you guys have to stay in the house. Sit there and smell the evening breezes." Cubby and Annette butted their heads against the screen a time or two, then gave up and sat on their haunches, tails wrapped around their feet.

"What a terrific place." Connie leaned out over the railing and looked in every direction. "What ever made a girl from Minnesota decide to move to the woods of southeastern Tennessee?"

Gail hesitated and was relieved when Connie opted not to press the matter. They stood side by side, the sun about to drop from sight.

"I love how the last shafts of light are flowing between those low clouds and the run of trees along the crest of the hills." Gail looked where Connie was pointing. "I've always called that a God sky."

Hearing the exact words Marissa had used so often in the very place she often spoke them hit Gail like a slap to the face. She burst into tears. The emotional outburst surprised them both. Gail folded herself into Connie's arms. "Hold me."

Connie pulled her close and whispered, "Tonight and always, my love."

GAIL FELT CONNIE shiver. "You're getting cold. We should go inside." She disentangled from Connie's arms and dug in her pocket for a tissue but came up empty handed. She squatted down to keep the cats from bolting onto the deck as she pushed the screen back. After Connie cleared the door, Gail yanked the glass door shut.

"I'm sorry about raining on the parade." Gail grabbed a tissue from the box beside the bed. "Must be my hormones." Gail turned on the lamp on the nightstand. "I will be so glad when I'm done with menopause."

"Don't worry about a few tears. Did I say something to upset you?"

"Not really. An old memory snuck up on me."

Connie's eyes adjusted to the dim light in the bedroom. "What are those?" She pointed to something in the corner by the dresser.

"Leg braces. For someone with polio."

"Yours?"

"No, they belonged to the woman who used to live here."

"And she left them behind when she moved out?"

"That's one way to put it."

Connie reflected on Gail's comment for a moment. "And another way to put it?"

"This was all bound to come out sooner or later. It might as well be tonight. Let's go inside where we can sit down." Gail moved across the bedroom and out into the living room. Connie followed. "Do you want something to drink? Tea? Or wine or something stronger, maybe?" Gail offered.

"I'd better stick with tea or Coke because of my allergy medicine."

"Okay. Have a seat. I'll be right back." Gail flipped on a couple of lamps as she went. She was back shortly with two glasses of sweet tea. Connie sat on the wooden rocker.

"No sense tempting the Fates," she said as she took the glass from Gail. "You're probably right about the cat hairs in here, so this chair seemed my best bet."

"It's probably not too comfortable."

"It's fine." Connie put her tea glass on the coaster on the small table next to the rocker.

Gail sat on the end of the sofa at a right angle to Connie. She took a sip of her tea, set it down, then picked it up and drank again and stared into the glass.

"Having trouble deciding where to start, Gail?"

"Yeah, everything I start to say feels like it's in the middle of the story."

Connie adjusted her glasses and used both hands to push her hair back behind her shoulders. She leaned forward, nearer to Gail.

"I have the same problem when I'm starting a new book. I finally figured out the best thing to do is just put something down on the page. Sometimes it proves to be exactly the right opening line, but if it's not, my editor will help me come up with a better one." She smiled at Gail. "So go ahead and give me an opening line, and if we have to, we'll come back and edit it later."

Gail struggled. Connie waited. "She's dead," Gail finally managed to say.

"The person with polio the leg braces belonged to?"

"Right. Her name was Marissa. She was my partner."

"I didn't think people died of polio any more. Wasn't that all but cured in the early sixties?"

"She didn't really die of polio."

"What then?" Connie asked gently.

"Complications."

"Complications from polio?"

"No, she was in an accident—a boating accident. She and I were in a canoe up on Tellico Lake. A powerboat came by and capsized us, and she hit her head and got trapped under the canoe. She couldn't get any air, and her brain was severely damaged."

"Oh, Gail. I'm so sorry. How long ago did she die?"

"July thirtieth."

"Last year?"

"This year. Not quite three months ago."

Connie's face clouded. "How can that be? You couldn't have been in a canoe on Tellico Lake on July thirtieth because you were with me in Atlanta on July thirtieth."

"The accident happened in July of 2005, but Marissa died this July thirtieth."

"She lived for two years after the accident? Where was she? Down at Emory, or Shepherd, or one of the other Atlanta care centers?"

"Scranton, Pennsylvania."

"Why there?"

"Her parents live there."

"So you and her parents decided to put her in a place up there?"

"I didn't have anything to do with it."

"But why not? You were her partner."

"Her parents didn't see it that way." Gail sighed from the bottom of her soul. "It's such a long story."

"Maybe you could tell me about the day on the lake."

Gail started with the morning of the accident and told all the details of the day. Then she recounted for Connie how she and Marissa had failed to complete durable powers of attorney and living wills, leaving her without recourse in directing Marissa's care. She told about Mrs. Adler banning her from Marissa's room at the hospital in Knoxville and taking Marissa away, and how, for two years, she had heard next to nothing about Marissa's condition, except for the occasional note from Marissa's sister, Amy. Through clenched teeth, she told about the funeral pamphlet waiting for her when she returned from her time in Atlanta with Connie.

"Her parents ignored all of Marissa's wishes about wanting a death with dignity. Every single thing about her funeral service was all wrong. It made me sick."

Connie took it all in with an occasional nod of her head or a comforting pat on Gail's knee.

"All the literature texts you saw on the bookcases were Marissa's. She taught at the University of Tennessee in Chattanooga. Those books and her leg braces are all I have left after sixteen years together. We had fourteen years of absolute heaven and two years of indescribable hell while she was kept alive like a creature from a horror film. Instead of coming straight back here after I was in Minnesota, I went to Pennsylvania to see her grave. I had to do that to make it real—make myself believe she's truly gone."

"I'm so sorry, Gail." Connie paused momentarily. "Tell me how you met."

And so Gail rewound the tape of her life. She told Connie everything from her early days on the farm outside Plainfield, Minnesota, to her wanderings from coast to coast trying to come to terms with her sexual orientation. She named her lovers—or at least those she remembered—and related the tale of her first lover, Jill, leaving her to join a convent. She told how she and Sandy had started out to cover the Appalachian Trail, only to abort the hike and, her spur of the moment decision to move to Chattanooga, where she met Marissa when she took one of her classes. If she had stopped to think about what she was saying, she might have censored some of the details she shared with Connie, but for the first time since Marissa had slipped into the coma, Gail let herself remember and feel all of the ways in which she and Marissa had belonged to one another and all of the ways she'd stopped participating in life while Marissa hung to the edge of existence with the help of the machines. Doctor Marcella Wilburn might have made a lot more headway as Gail's psychologist if she had been given the benefit of the details Gail told Connie that night in Sweetwater Cabin.

"Back in January of this year, after I'd had another stretch of three or four days where I didn't get out of bed except to feed the cats and go to the bathroom, I decided I'd better get some help. I started seeing a therapist in town, but I don't know if it's doing any good."

"Many times, we don't know until much later whether or not something helped."

"It's my therapist's fault I was in Atlanta with you this summer."

"Lydia LaGrange would be surprised to hear that."

"You're right. What I should have said is I had been to see Doctor Wilburn—my therapist—and she told me I needed to do things to get more engaged in life. I went straight from my appointment with her that day up to the public access place on Tellico Lake where the paramedics had worked on Marissa. I hadn't been able to make myself go there since the day it happened. When I got back here to the cabin, there was a message from Lydia. If I hadn't been so turned inside out from going to the lake, I'm sure I'd have told her I wouldn't take the editing job to do your book." Gail looked around the room as though she'd never laid eyes on it before. "Seeing where it happened brought all the ghosts back to life. I couldn't sit in this cabin aching for Marissa any longer."

"So you came down to Atlanta to edit *Rings and Things* because the spirits pushed you out of your own house."

"Uh huh. And the next thing I knew, I was breaking every vow I ever made to Marissa Adler. I don't think I've ever hated myself more than I did right after we made love the second time."

"The second time?"

"The first time, which, as you may recall, was on the third day we were together, everything happened so fast I didn't think about what I was doing. I went on autopilot and zoned out and let my hormones neutralize my brain. But the second time, I knew better. I could have stopped it. I should have. But I didn't. I cheated on Marissa over and over again. I hated myself for that, and I hated myself for not telling you about her. And then when I got home and found out she was dead, I really hated myself."

"Was there any chance she was going to come out of the coma?"

"That doesn't change anything."

"Okay. Let me ask it this way. If it were the other way around and you were the one in the coma and Marissa had the chance to fall in love and have a shot at a happy life, would you have wanted her to waste her life while you lay on life support?"

"Don't try to trick me with rhetorical questions."

"It's not a trick. I really want to know how you'd feel if the situation were reversed. Assuming you could feel anything at all. You're brain dead, remember? Would you ask Marissa to sit and wait, God knows how many years, while you die a quarter of an inch at a time?"

"Are you trying to rationalize away what we did at the Magnolia Suites?"

"Not really. But I do want you to try to think about all this from a different point of view."

"And that would be?"

"On a day when your therapist suggests you need to do more about getting back into life, you go to a place that upsets you so badly you describe it as waking up all the old ghosts. Then on the very same day, a highly unusual opportunity comes your way — one you said you'd never have agreed to if all the preceding events hadn't happened exactly as they did."

"So what?"

"Maybe you really did exactly what you said. You woke up an old ghost. And that ghost told you it was time to move on with your life."

"It was just an expression."

"I know. And when we drop our guard and say exactly what we feel, it's almost always the thing we most need to understand."

"Now you're trying to tell me Marissa — in some altered state of being — played paper dolls with Lydia LaGrange and your regular editor and ginned up some circumstance to push you and me together?"

"That makes it sound kind of macabre." She gave Gail a reassuring look. "I see a loving, benevolent soul from another realm nudging things along a little on your behalf."

"Or a convenient way for me to wiggle off the hook for being such a cheating whore."

"Maybe it isn't all about you, Gail."

"What's that supposed to mean?"

"What if Marissa needed to know you were ready to accept what the rest of your life might offer before she could let go and do whatever she needed to experience next?"

Gail wanted to argue, but she couldn't find the words to do so.

"Not every sign has to be a biblical burning bush, you know." Gail tried to look away, but Connie laid a hand along side her face, forcing Gail to meet her gaze.

"I'm glad you used the modifier, otherwise I might have thought you were talking smut." Gail let a small smile shine.

"So what was it I said out on the deck earlier that made you cry?"

"You took me off guard when you used one of Marissa's favorite expressions."

"Which expression?"

"You called the way the light was coming through the trees a 'God sky.'"

"See? Marissa was good enough to give me the right opening line."

WHEN GAIL EXTENDED the offer, Connie decided to stay the night at Sweetwater Cabin. The long, soulful conversations they'd had about Marissa and the vagaries of the circumstances that had brought Gail and Connie together left them both feeling pensive. The sofa in the living room made out into a bed, but not a very comfortable one, so they lay side by side on the queen-sized bed in Gail's bedroom.

"Now you know every last detail about me. It's your turn to spill a few beans about your history." Gail rolled onto her side and faced Connie's still-supine body.

"I wanted to be a gynecologist, but I couldn't hack it, so instead, I write lesbian fiction. I had an affair with one of my therapists, who happened to be a man, and I live in Atlanta."

"Well, you've certainly filled in the blanks. Come on, Connie. You told me all that when we were working on your book."

"At least I'm consistent."

"And secretive and perhaps the teeniest bit annoying."

"Perhaps boring is the precise word you're seeking."

"Hey, I'm an editor. I'll decide the right word. Might be dull or tedious or monotonous or uninteresting or dreary or unexciting or lackluster or bland or uninspiring."

"Stop it. You're giving me a complex — not that I needed any help in that regard."

"Or a hang-up, psychosis, neurosis, phobia, or obsession."

"Since you insist on being a human thesaurus, let me remind you of something — reference books are never taken out."

"Yuk, yuk, yuk. The first time I heard that one, I laughed so hard I kicked the slats out of my cradle." Gail laid a playful slap on Connie's thigh. "And don't think I haven't noticed you still haven't answered my question."

"There's really not much to tell."

"Oh for the love of Pete. You're an author. You can make a story out of the ingredients list on a bag of cat food and the wad of cotton from an aspirin bottle."

"I do okay with made up stories, but real life stumps me."

"I'll hand you back what you told me in the living room tonight. Put the opening line out there. We can go back and edit it if we need to. What's the opening line to your life's story?"

"How about if I tell you how I wish my life had been?"

"All right. Go ahead."

"I was born on a farm in south Georgia, down around Waycross."

"Where all those awful fires burned this spring?"

"Uh huh. Once I left there, though, I didn't go back much, but I still hate to think how badly the fires ravaged the area."

"Some of the smoke made it all the way up here when the fires were at their worst and the winds blew just right. I can't imagine how bad it must have been living down there."

"I know what you mean. Life was already tough for average folks in that part of the state without having to contend with a major natural disaster."

"I'm sorry I interrupted your story. Tell me about your childhood in Waycross."

"That's okay. Since I'm making it up as I go along, we can jump right back into it." Connie resumed her tale. "So, in my make-believe youth down in Waycross, Georgia, my daddy was a peanut farmer, and my mother was a music teacher. I had one older brother and two older sisters and one little brother and a baby sister named Sarah."

"Didn't the rest of your sisters and brothers have names?"

"Since this is make believe, I won't remember them unless I write them down. It doesn't matter what their names are, anyway."

"Okay. What else?"

"We lived in a nice house with a big porch all the way around it, and in the summer, we'd all sit out there at night and watch the lightning bugs. I was an average student, but my parents didn't care because I was so gifted musically. They knew I'd be a music teacher and follow in my mother's footsteps — possibly become a well-known performer someday."

"Did you go to college?"

"Oh, yes, on a music scholarship to Mercer University. And I did graduate work at Georgia State University, too."

"And your love life?"

"Please, we were a fine Southern family. I had a social life. Love lives are for the lower classes."

"Excuse me. Do tell." Gail squelched a giggle and rolled from her side onto her back.

"Of course there was my coming out party at sixteen."

"I love that expression, don't you?" Gail laughed out loud.

"I don't mean your trashy announcement about being a lesbian sort of coming out." Connie swatted at Gail's arm. "A cotillion with a frilly hoop dress and long white gloves and young gentlemen with only honorable intentions swarming around me."

"Good thing I know this is fiction, or I'd be feeling sick about now."

"And at college, I was pinned by a boy from the best fraternity on campus."

"I bet you were. Pinned in the backseat of his daddy's Chrysler."

"More of your filth and perversion. He gave me his fraternity pin and pledged his love and gave me his fidelity."

"I don't think I've ever heard that euphemism applied to that particular male body part before."

"Climb on up out of the gutter, Gail. Come sit here on the curb with me while I finish my life's story."

"Sorry, but you have such a way with words, Ms. Martin."

"Smooth talking flatterer. Anyway, I found I wasn't able to devote myself both to my music and to running Majestic Oaks Manor, which was the house on the estate Edward and I inherited from his family, so, I gave up my life in the lap of luxury and became a bohemian. I moved to New York and gave concerts anywhere someone would let me play."

"You dragged your piano around with you?"

"Who said anything about a piano? And you call yourself an editor. I'm a violin virtuoso. I make callous men weep and women relinquish their virtue."

"Right. You didn't mention the instrument. My mistake."

"Never assume facts not in evidence."

"I'm sorry. I won't let it happen again. Okay, you're in New York playing the violin with such fervor it causes people to change their personalities. Then what happened?"

"That brings us up to present day. My life is good, but I feel a yearning for something—someone—to complete me."

"And?"

"And blessedly, I meet the woman I was meant to spend my life with."

"The end," Gail supplied.

"No, the beginning," Connie corrected.

"Oh, sorry. Another mistake on my part."

Connie groped under the covers until she found Gail's hand. She laced their fingers together.

"That's okay. But please don't make the mistake of ever leaving me."

CONNIE'S TOUCH STIRRED a feeling in Gail akin to the one that preceded all of their physical encounters in Atlanta, but she wasn't ready to endure the guilt she was sure would follow if she surrendered to it.

"Was any of what you told me true?"

"Some of it."

"What parts of it?"

"I was born on a farm near Waycross, Georgia and my father did work on a peanut farm."

"And your mother, the musician?"

"She worked on the peanut farm, too. I only heard her sing a few times. She had a beautiful voice."

"Why didn't she sing more often?"

"Because if my father heard her singing, he'd beat her."

"Good lord, why?"

"He didn't need reasons."

"And your brothers and sisters?"

"I didn't have any. It was only me."

"But you said you had a baby sister named Sarah."

"I had a doll named Sarah. I always pretended she was really my sister and it was up to me to protect her from my father. I wished I'd had siblings because maybe we could have ganged up on my father and made him stop beating my mother."

"Did he beat you, too?" Gail caressed Connie's arm, then held her hand again.

"No, my mother took it all."

"So what you said about porches and lightning bugs and music and school..."

"Stories I used to make up in my head to make the bad thoughts go away. We lived in a beat up trailer. It was hotter than Hades in the summer and cold enough to freeze to death in if we had a run of bad weather in the winter. The wooden steps leading to the door were so rotted you had to walk way to the outside edges to keep from punching right through and scraping all the skin off your legs. My mother always told me the only way out of there was to do well in school and make something of myself. So, I tried. I was lucky. I had some good teachers, and they looked out for me and gave me extra help with my school work."

"We should find them and thank them."

"I'm not sure they'd want to know about having played a part in producing a lesbian author. Anyway, the special attention made the other kids call me 'teacher's pet' and pick on me, but I didn't care. Once I figured out that my teachers approved of my extra-credit stories, all I wanted to do was learn as many words as there were in the world and find new ways to put them together in stories."

"Which means you always knew you wanted to write."

"I always knew it was a good way to avoid reality. For much of my life, hiding out from what was going on around me has been my highest priority."

"What about the swarms of suitors and college and fraternity pins?"

"Lies, lies, and more lies."

"You never went to college?"

"Actually, I did, but there's a whole 'nother chapter I need to give you."

Gail squeezed Connie's hand, which she was still clasping tightly.

"We've got all night."

"I was still in high school. My father had stomped the living daylights out of my mother for the millionth time and then gone off to drink with his bad-ass buddies. While I was helping her put salve on some of her bruises and cuts, I worked up the courage to ask her how she ever managed to have sex with a man who was so cruel. She told me part of the reason he was always so angry was because he was impotent. Of course she didn't know that word, but I knew what she meant. He'd been a limp noodle for most of their married life.

"I'd spent fifteen years feeling I was to blame for how awful life in that household was, so I started to cry, and told her I was sorry she had ever gotten pregnant with me. If she hadn't been saddled with taking care of me, she might have left Earl, that lowlife husband of hers, and made a better life for herself."

Gail edged closer to Connie and brought their upper arms and outer thighs into contact.

"That night, she absolutely blew my circuits. She told me I wasn't to blame for anything that had happened because I was adopted."

"You were adopted? Are you sure she didn't tell you that to try to persuade you it wasn't your fault everything was so awful at home?"

"No, it was true. She told me my real mother—my birth mother—had died in childbirth. She said she convinced Earl they should take me in, since there wasn't much hope he'd ever be able to keep the flag pole up long enough to get the job done on his own. I'm sure you can guess those are my words, not hers, but you get the idea."

"I know. Tell me the rest of it."

"She said my real mother was one of the women she worked with on the farm, and she had gotten involved with the son of a man who owned lots of land in Ware County—that's where Waycross is. Of course, it wouldn't look too good for someone who owned thousands of acres of peanuts to have an illegitimate grandchild.

"The way my mother told it, my birth father made the mother of his child deliver me in the back of one of the farm wagons hidden way out in one of the fields. The woman I knew as my mother, Sudie Rae, was there to help her friend with the delivery. Something went wrong, and she bled to death. Sudie Rae felt so awful that she took me and kept me as her own."

"So instead of being part of the landed gentry, you ended up being raised by—"

"Call it what it is, Gail. Trailer trash. According to the woman who raised me, I was supposed to have been..."

Connie's voice faltered, and Gail finished the thought. "The beautiful young woman who had a coming out party and a cotillion and eager suitors looking to claim her hand and a share of granddad's peanut plantation."

"The beautiful part is still a stretch of fiction, but the rest of it is fairly close to accurate."

Gail dropped Connie's hand and eased up on her side, then laid an arm across Connie's midsection.

"We really need to work on the misconception you have about your looks, but first, I want you to finish telling me the real story."

"Sudie Rae never told me who my father was, but I figured it out. Sudie Rae and Earl both worked on the same peanut farm. The owner of the operation had a son who would have been about the right age to think he was entitled to help himself to the hired hands if he wanted to. He was being groomed to take over his father's peanut business, and he was engaged to the daughter from a family with one of the other big farming operations down there. The details Sudie Rae had given me let me piece it all together. I told Sudie Rae I was going to confront him, and I was sure there was no way he could deny he was really my daddy."

"Did you?"

"I didn't have to."

"Why not?"

"I spent the better part of a year checking up on him. In Waycross, all you had to do was mention the name, and people would tell you every bit of gossip they'd heard. He was probably the most miserable human being on the face of the earth. Deep down, he was probably a decent guy, but all his life, he'd been told he was destined for great things. He'd been handed the usual bullshit rich people shovel on their kids."

"Such as?"

"Go to the right schools, marry the right girl, be in the right pew at church every Sunday, and stay away from the poor folks, except to hire them at poverty wage, so you can keep your rightful place at the top of the social order." Connie drew a breath. "But he was a hollow man."

"Why do you say that?"

"There was talk about how something bad had happened to him. The local gossip said whatever it was made him go dead inside. He did everything he was supposed to do—married a local girl from the right side of the tracks and did his daddy's bidding, but whatever was eating him from the inside out turned out to be more than he could face. He lost his mind. His rich family covered for him, of course, and he was never institutionalized, but he was just a blathering fool."

"And you think you know what that awful something was."

"Uh huh. My guess is he really cared about my mother, but he couldn't bear the wrath from his father."

Gail gave Connie a squeeze and rolled to her side. "Did you ever find out for sure?"

"It took a lot of wheedling, but I got Sudie Rae to confirm what I'd managed to dig up from the blabbermouths around town. The father—the man who was technically my grandfather—had discovered his son was seeing my mother—my real mother—and told him she wasn't someone who would ever be part of their circle. Then the father threatened to disown him if he ever saw her again."

"So when it was a choice between a fortune and a girl he's knocked up, there really was no contest."

"Sudie Rae told me he swore he didn't know his girlfriend—her name was Constance—was pregnant until shortly before I was born. He wanted to give her money to go away to Albany or Savannah or Atlanta or somewhere out of state to have the baby and start a new life, but she didn't want to go. Everybody she knew was in Waycross. Who could blame her? And how could anybody know she'd die when I was born?"

"You said your father was insane?"

"Yes, according to the word on the street in Waycross. My guess is he was totally consumed with guilt. All his life, he'd done whatever his father wanted him to do, and he sold his soul and then his mind in the bargain. So what if Edward Barrington—that was his name—had a huge house and a trophy wife and a bank account with a balance so big it looked like a social security number? He didn't know he had it. He didn't have happiness, and he didn't have peace of mind. A woman he probably loved had died giving birth to a child he never knew, and nothing he did would ever change that."

"What finally happened?"

"I had it all plotted out in my head. I was going to demand I be given my birthright and be acknowledged for who I really was, but what I learned about him convinced me I could have been just as unhappy on Barrington Farms as I was with Earl and Sudie Rae in their decrepit trailer. I'd have been unhappy for different reasons, but somehow I knew all the money in God's creation didn't make unhappiness any easier to deal with."

"But still..."

"It was obvious this man was paying a price way beyond anything that could be measured in dollars. What difference would it make what name I went by? No, I didn't live in a fancy house, but Sudie Rae did her best for me. She protected me from Earl, and that counts for a lot. My real mother was long since dead, and Edward Barrington was trapped in a hell worse than anything I could have wished on him.

"In coming to terms with what I found out about the man who made up half of my genetic code, I had an epiphany. I decided I wanted to be a gynecologist. I saw it as a way to make things right for Constance, my birth mother. If she'd been able to get birth control, if there'd been a doctor to help her deliver, if poor women had more choices about having babies—"

Gail waited to see what Connie would say next.

Connie exhaled loudly. "I was a senior in high school. I still thought you could up and decide something, and miraculously, things would fall into place."

"You just walked away?"

"I walked away." Connie paused. "I walked away with a college education."

"How did that happen?"

"Sudie Rae never confessed to all the details, but before Edward Barrington lost his mind, she must have threatened to reveal his dirty little secret, and somehow, she persuaded him to do right by his bastard daughter. All of a sudden, there was a big, fat juicy savings account in my name at the Waycross bank."

"Didn't you want to talk to him — get to know him?"

"What would it have accomplished? Even if he could somehow be made to understand who I was, I wasn't going to be welcomed into the family with open arms. All I wanted was to get out of Waycross and never look back."

Gail let her hand slide aimlessly up and down Connie's torso. "Please promise me what you've told me tonight isn't another one of your fantastic cranial creations."

"If I were going to give you a load of horse feathers about my past, I'd have stuck with the first version with the porch and the fireflies and the cotillion. Why would I make up a story describing me as a refugee from tobacco row?"

"Good point. One thing about what you told me still puzzles me, though."

"If it's only one, you're lucky. Almost everything about it still ties me in knots every time I let myself think about it. What bothers you?"

"You never said what happened to Constance. If she died in a farm wagon on the night you were born, there was a body that needed to be buried. And what about her family? Or her friends and the other people in Waycross? They'd have known she was pregnant, and then one day, she just was gone."

A long silence hung between them.

"There was one little detail I lied about."

I knew it. Connie Martin is nothing but a manipulative, duplicitous pretender. Isn't that what I told Penny? Gail stopped her caress of Connie's body and waited for Connie to reveal the "little detail" she had misrepresented.

"I told you her name was 'Constance.'"

"Yes, and I figured your adoptive mother called you 'Connie' in her honor."

"I can see where you'd think so." Connie drew away from Gail's touch, her reluctance to say more, evident.

"Tell me, Connie. I want you to tell me the rest."

"Her real name was Consuelo. Consuelo Martinez."

Chapter
Nine

AS THE SUN came up the next morning, Connie left to return to Atlanta. They had talked all night. By the time Connie left Sweetwater, Gail felt as though she knew the circumstances of Connie Martin's life almost better than she knew her own. Connie had told her that Earl, her adoptive father, had been killed in a freak accident on the peanut farm the summer after she graduated from high school. No one ever said as much, but Connie suspected he was drunk and misjudged operation of one of the pieces of equipment on the farm and was largely responsible for his own demise.

Not long after, her adoptive mother, Sudie Rae, was diagnosed with Parkinson's disease. Connie blamed her illness on all of the blows Earl had landed on her head, but what was the difference? The only mother Connie had ever known had lived out the last years of her life in a nursing home in Waycross.

While growing up in Waycross, Connie had been known as Cassandra Ridgeway—Ridgeway being Earl's last name. She didn't become Connie Martin until a year after she graduated from high school. Sudie Rae was already declining rapidly from the Parkinson's, so Connie used some of the money her birth father, Edward Barrington, had given her for her education to get Sudie Rae set up in a care facility. Then Cassandra Ridgeway legally changed her name to Connie Martin. With her high school transcripts as Cassandra Ridgeway, a court order showing her name change to Connie Martin, and a letter of recommendation from one of Ware County's most respected citizens—something else Sudie Rae had managed to extract from Edward Barrington—Connie gained admittance to Agnes Scott, an all-women's college outside Atlanta.

Agnes Scott offered a degree in pre-med, but it was in her undergraduate biology labs there that Connie deduced she would never make it in the pre-med program. As she had told Gail when they were working on her book at the Magnolia Suites back in July, every time she had to cut a frog open or look at cells under a microscope, she'd pass out. Sometimes just reading about a surgical procedure or talking in class about the physiological components of human illness made her woozy.

The English program at Agnes Scott gave Connie the perfect alternative haven to torturing herself in science classes. When the required reading for her courses didn't satiate her, she devoured every novel in the school's library, and then worked her way through the offerings in the DeKalb County public library. She excelled in all of her literature courses from medieval to contemporary, British/Irish to American to African-American. In her junior year, in the Advanced Creative Writing Seminar she was taking, her favorite professor, Lucretia Murray, picked up on the struggles Connie was having with failing to follow through on her promise to become a gynecologist. Professor Murray urged Connie to use the school's counselor to help her find an objective professional to work with. The therapist convinced Connie to employ writing as a road to healing, and so Connie followed her natural inclination of painting pictures with words and honed her skills.

After she got her bachelor's degree, she decided to stay at Agnes Scott and pursue a Master of Arts in Teaching Secondary English. She continued to see the therapist and to use her writing to deal with her pain and insecurities. Soon, her short stories were picked up by various magazines. She thought she had succeeded in finding a path and a purpose to her life.

In the first year of her master's program, Connie met Blanca Juarez, another grad student. Blanca made every Agnes Scott gringa who had ever had a passing thought of kissing a woman want lips tasting of salsa. Connie fell head over heels for Blanca. They had a torrid affair, which Connie presumed marked the start of their life together. It lasted only a few months. To Connie's devastation, Blanca dropped her like a rotten tamale when Connie confessed to being Chicana. Blanca was from Paraguay and clung to her prejudices about purity of bloodlines and the evils of miscegenation.

Badly distressed, Connie left Agnes Scott without finishing her master's degree. She rented an apartment in Decatur, not far from the campus. She started writing lesbian fiction in earnest, but shied away from anything more than casual encounters with other women. Thanks to Blanca's treatment of her, she was convinced she was anything but a desirable commodity. One painful rejection followed by a broken heart was enough.

When the female therapist whom she'd been seeing since her junior year moved away from Atlanta, Connie began seeing Doug, the therapist she had told Gail about when they were working on her book. After his rebuff, Connie had concluded she'd never be attractive to either sex; her best bet was to live her life through the characters she created in her books. And until Gail Larsen entered her life, other than a few casual flings, which Connie ended after two or three dates, that was exactly what she had done.

Gail went through the motions of her morning routine. She made the bed, fed the cats, ran a load of laundry, showered and dressed, turned on the computer to work on her editing jobs, but the only thought occupying her mind was Connie Martin.

Some of the jigsaw picture was coming together. The soft, compact body. The short stature. The hair and eyes and face shape. Now that she knew Connie's heritage, she couldn't believe she had failed to see her Hispanic features.

The stories from Connie's (or should she think of her as Cassandra?) childhood were haunting. What a start in life: adopted by a loving but cowed mother who was married to an abusive man, and a spineless birth father who let her mother die and vanish without a moment's remembrance for her life. Gail thought back to the droves of migrant Mexicans who had come to northern Minnesota to harvest the sugar beets every year. She pictured the horrid huts that dotted the edge of the flat, black fields and the hollow, haunting eyes of the men, women, and children who spilled out of them. It wasn't hard to imagine truckloads of Mexican workers showing up on the peanut farms in south Georgia and faring no better there than they had in her home state. One of the women on the peanut farm in Waycross, Georgia, had caught the eye of the boss man's son. Did Edward Barrington really have feelings for Consuelo Martinez, or was he still trying to buy a soothed conscience by forking over college funds for an illegitimate daughter who might turn his already tortured life into a bigger knot? And so what if he did love her? Consuelo Martinez was still little more than expendable chattel. It wouldn't have been too hard to obscure the death of a migrant worker. Gail felt a shudder of revulsion as she struggled with thoughts of how grueling Consuelo's final hours on the planet probably had been.

Connie had said Edward Barrington was miserable. His life was at first a sham, and then total shambles. He had paid for Connie's education, making at least one respectable action he'd taken.

Small wonder Connie was so consumed with writing her books. Gail used words as a hideaway, too, especially in the two years since Marissa's accident. How many times had she immersed herself in the pages of whatever manuscript she was editing to blunt the pain? Gail could see that Connie had been through no fewer than six levels of hell. Knowing what she knew now, Gail saw Connie's behavior in Atlanta when they were working on *Rings and Things* in a new light.

Time and again in their discussion the night before, Gail had asked Connie why, after all those years of shunning emotional involvements, she had made such an immediate play for Gail at the Magnolia Suites. All Connie would say was, "I loved you the minute I saw you. When you touched my face where it was bruised, I hoped you might be the woman who would heal all of my bruises."

It still didn't make sense — at least not intellectual sense — but the mere wisp of the memory of Connie Martin lying next to her, telling

Gail she made her feel whole and healed—made rational thought as impossible as pouring rain back into a cloud.

She had pressed Connie about her aggressive, domineering, sometimes dismissive conduct while they were working on her book. Connie's reply had been, "I'd never felt about anyone the way I was feeling about you. I didn't know how to act. I wanted you so much, but I was afraid wanting you would only lead to another devastation."

"Why didn't you just tell me you had feelings for me?" Gail had asked.

"Twice before in my life, I'd told people I cared for them. Both Blanca and Doug found me lacking. I knew I was still the same woman. Why would I expect it to turn out differently this time?"

"But when you called me in Minnesota..."

"It was better to know—better to have you tell me no once and for all—than to agonize over the possibility, wondering for the rest of my life if you were the one."

Gail ran and reran her memories of the night's conversations. She kicked the thoughts around in her head until she feared her brain would disintegrate. She decided not to think about it any more, but when she acknowledged the feelings inside her—feelings refusing to be ignored—it didn't matter if any of her dealings with (and feelings for) Connie made sense or not.

Damn. She was falling in love with Connie Martin. But before she could fall in love with Connie (or anyone), there was a lingering piece of old business she needed to attend to.

"AMY? IT'S GAIL Larson, calling from Tennessee."

"Gail? It's nice to hear from you."

"I was afraid you might not want to talk to me. Thanks for taking my call."

"You're welcome. Is there something I can help you with?"

"It's overdue, but I wanted to express my sympathy on Marissa's death."

"That's kind of you, Gail. Losing my only sister was a real blow for me, but I know her death is a big loss for you, too."

Gail had to wait for the flash of unexpected sorrow to pass before replying. "It was. One of the biggest in my life, in fact."

"I'm sure it was."

"Do you mind if I ask you a few questions about Marissa?"

"Not at all. What would you like to know?"

"It's not that I want to know, more like I feel I need to know."

"I understand."

"My first question isn't really about Marissa, but I'll ask anyway. Why do your parents hate me so much?"

"It wasn't you, Gail, it's what you represented. Marissa told them—

told me, too—that she was gay when she was in junior high school. They always hoped she'd come to her senses, as they used to say. They couldn't bring themselves to hate their own daughter, so they shifted their focus to the women my sister loved."

"What about you? Do you hate me, too?"

"No, not in the least. Marissa wasn't just my big sister, she was my best friend when we were kids. I didn't care who she loved or who she slept with. All I wanted was that she be happy."

"Do you think she was happy with me?" Gail held her breath, waiting for Amy's answer.

"I know she was. I'm sorry you and I didn't get better acquainted, Gail. I only met you that one time when I came for a visit, but Marissa and I talked and emailed at least a couple of times a week. She always had the sweetest things to say about you. Thanks for taking such good care of her."

Gail frowned as she spoke. "Not good enough. I let her die in a way she'd have hated."

"I tried to tell my parents that Marissa wouldn't want to be on life support, but there was no changing their minds."

"How bad was it?" Gail braced for the worst.

"I'll tell you how it seemed to me. I don't think Marissa was there at all. Sure, her body was tied to all those machines, but the real Marissa was long gone. In my opinion, she died in the accident, and it just took two agonizing years for my parents to realize it."

"This always seems like such a stupid question, but was it peaceful? Her last little bit of time, I mean."

"Yes, I think so. Her heart and lungs got weaker and weaker. Her other organs started shutting down. It was sort of like she slipped a little farther away each day until she was finally gone."

"She never woke up? Never asked for me?"

"Oh, no, Gail. From the minute my parents brought her to Scranton and put her in the care facility, she was in a coma. There wasn't any sign of brain activity at all."

"I'm sorry it was so awful."

"I'm sorry, too. I don't think Marissa knew, though, so that helped somewhat—at least in my opinion."

"Thank you for telling me all this, Amy. And again, please accept my sympathy."

"I'm glad we had a chance to talk. It's quite a coincidence that you called today."

"Oh? Why do you say that?"

"Last night, I was helping my folks sort through the box of her personal papers my dad brought back when he picked up Marissa's car from you. I found a handwritten note Marissa had clipped to one of the piles of things in the stack."

Gail wasn't sure she wanted to know, but she asked anyway. "What did it say?"

"I've got it right here. I was planning to drop it in the mail to you later this morning. It says, 'Gail, if you're going through these papers, it means I checked out first. I hope I didn't make a big scene on my way out. More importantly, I hope you'll remember lots of songs from our time together. When you distill them to their essence, all of them had the same two verses. The first was that I loved you with my whole heart, and the second verse: keep dancing.'"

"HI, CONNIE. I'VE been thinking about you. Did your drive back to Atlanta go okay?" Gail had snatched up the phone on the first ring.

"I should have left either earlier or later. I hit some heavy inbound traffic on I-75, but since it's Friday, it wasn't as bad as it might have been. It only cost me about twenty minutes."

"Good. You told me you needed to get back this morning so you could keep a doctor's appointment. I was so caught up thinking about all the things we talked about I forgot to ask why you were seeing a doctor."

"I've been so tired lately. Menopause is looming on the horizon, and I've been having really heavy periods, so I'm probably anemic. He drew some blood to check my hematocrit levels, and I turned white as a sheet and fell over. You know, my usual performance any time I have a simple medical procedure done. And I needed to get my allergy prescription renewed, too."

"That's something else I was going to ask you about. When you first got here yesterday, you clogged up faster than a Los Angeles freeway at rush hour, but when we were in bed last night, both of the cats were right there with us, and you seemed fine. How long do your allergy pills usually work?"

"Four to six hours, but by the time we were lying in bed, I had calmed down a lot. I told you, I'm often my own worst enemy. I had gotten myself so worked up on the drive to your place the air sacs in my lungs didn't stand a chance."

"But wouldn't what we were talking about stress you out, too?"

"Good question." Connie pondered a moment before continuing. "I was really grateful you felt close enough to me to tell me about you and Marissa. That helped me take my mind off being so excited about getting to see you again. And I was so relieved to be able to tell you the truth about me. You were so sweet and gentle about everything, I didn't feel anxious any more. Now that I think about it, I suppose I should have been nervous as a virgin at a prison rodeo. The only other time I'd told a lover about my background, she tossed me out on my Mexican *pollino*."

"From what you told me about Blanca, I'd say your Mexican ass was probably the least of her problems."

"And is my Mexican ass a problem for you, Gail?"

"Only when it's too far away for me." Gail didn't believe she had actually spoken those words. Her chagrin was evident. "Sorry, how crude of me."

"Not at all. You can talk that way to me any time." Connie laughed from a place deep in her throat. "What are you doing next weekend?"

"You mean I have to wait a whole week to see you again?"

"I hope not, but I want to ask you to do something for me, or more accurately, *with* me."

"What?"

"Next Saturday is the Southern Women's Writers' Association awards banquet. I want you to come down to Atlanta for it."

"Oh, I couldn't."

"Why not?"

"It's not the sort of event writers bring their editors to."

"I don't want you to go as my editor, I want you to go as my date — my escort — my girlfriend."

The affection in Connie's voice melted Gail's heart. "Are you sure? I mean, it's not exactly a lesbian occasion."

"Honey girl, the people who put this little shindig on know what kinds of books I write. Supposedly, that's what makes this award such a big stinking deal. Our corner of the world is for once going to get a pat on the back from the people who think they own all the words in the dictionary. Seems to me we owe it to lesbians all over the planet to show up as the happiest couple to ever stroll arm in arm."

"I don't know, Connie."

"Are you ashamed to be seen in public with me?"

"No, not in the least. It's just that —"

"That what?"

"People will think we're — um — together."

"And you don't want us to be?"

"No, that's not it."

"So what is it, then?"

Gail stammered three times before getting the words out. "Are we together? A couple, I mean."

"Why, Gail Larsen, that almost sounds like a proposal."

It took a minute for Gail to realize it. Yes, that was exactly what she was doing. "Let me do it right." She steeled herself as though she were about to ask for a queen's ransom. "Cassandra Connie Ridgeway Martin, will you be my life partner?"

When Connie said "yes," Gail thought she might spontaneously combust.

"YOU GUYS WILL be okay for a day." Even though she had already committed to be in Atlanta the coming weekend for the awards banquet, after her phone call with Connie the previous morning, Gail decided to make the drive down to spend the day with Connie that Saturday as well. She sat on the floor of the living room at Sweetwater Cabin while she flapped a long plastic stick with a shoelace tied to one end. Cubbie pounced on the shoelace and rolled on his back with the string between his front paws. Annette lay tight against Gail's thigh. Gail petted the cat from head to tail in a smooth, sweeping motion. "You'll be happier here with all your toys. You can sit on your tree and look at the birds through the window. I'll miss you, but I'll be home tomorrow night."

When Marissa was still alive, they used to leave the cats alone on an occasional weekend to take in a concert or a play in Knoxville or camp overnight in the woods on the far side of Tellico Lake. A cat food dispenser with a timer burped out dry food twice a day, and an electric water bowl with a fountain and reservoir provided more than enough water to get them through a weekend. As long as the litter boxes were completely clean when they left, Cubbie and Annette could make do for two days until their people got back home to scoop and refill them.

Gail hadn't left the cats alone in more than two years. Her conscience was nagging her big time, but her eagerness to see Connie was overriding her concern for her furry kids. Her call to Marissa's sister the previous day had left her feeling gratified and freed. She'd taken a few moments to write in her journal, and in doing so, had realized her worst fears about Marissa's true death were unfounded and that her grieving period was, at long last, drawing to a close.

After her late morning call with Connie on Friday where she had surrendered to the beckoning of her heart, she had spent the rest of the day hastening through an edit job she had promised the author she'd have finished by Monday. Saturday morning, she dashed around the cabin pulling things together so she could get down to Atlanta to spend most of Saturday and much of Sunday there with Connie.

The second thoughts didn't catch up with her until she crossed the Georgia line. What if Connie wanted to continue to live in Atlanta? Gail wouldn't ever be happy living in a major city again. She'd never seen Connie's house. *What if she's a slob with dirty clothes on the floor and a year's worth of newspapers piled on the table and empty pizza boxes under the bed?* Worse yet, what if she lived in a fancy house with numbered prints on the walls and Faberge eggs and Lladro statues in lighted glass cases?

After two more heartfelt good-byes with the cats, Gail climbed into her pick-up and was on her way to Connie's house. The colorful autumn scenery in the mountains of Tennessee only added to her euphoria. She felt young and happy and light and excited — a kid again on a ride at the carnival or reveling in the first day of summer vacation.

For that matter, did saying they were a couple mean they would live together? What if Connie wanted them to each keep her own place and commute on alternate weekends? Or both of them live in one house one week and in the other house the next week? *Roses won't last, violets will die, you're schizophrenic and so am I. Oh, gawd, what am I getting myself into?*

What did she really know about Connie Martin? She'd had a maniacal month with her at the Magnolia Suites, during which she'd decided Connie was a self-consumed fraud. Then there was the middle of the night phone conversation with her while Gail was in Plainfield helping Penny with her father's house. Gail's summation then was to tell Penny the best she could muster was feeling sorry for Connie. And third, she had night before last's revelations, which could have gotten Connie a spot in an episode of *Ripley's Believe it or Not.*

Gail felt her mouth parch and her stomach somersault. She pulled off the road at the next exit and swung into the first fast food joint she saw. She parked the truck and walked inside. "Large Coke, extra ice," she said to the youngster behind the counter.

She walked around the parking lot while sipping her drink and chomping ice chips. Should she run for cover back to Sweetwater? Should she go see Connie to apologize and pull out before they got in any deeper? Why couldn't she have kept her trap shut? Why did she have to go and ask Connie to be her life partner before she truly knew the woman? Hell, she'd had longer and (if you discounted the sex) more intense relationships with people she'd stood on-line with at the Department of Motor Vehicles.

Gail looped the lot three times, arguing with herself every step of the way.

"Hey, are you lost or sick or something?" Gail looked up to see who was speaking to her. Two soft butch females were sitting on the dropped tailgate of a shiny black Ford F-150. They were eating burgers and sharing a milkshake. The afternoon sun glinted off their Ray-Bans. "We've watched you for a few minutes, and we wondered if we could help."

"I'm okay. I suppose you might say I'm lost in thought and sick of making stupid decisions." Gail stopped behind the truck. "But thanks for asking."

"Pull up a tailgate and have seat." The two women moved closer together to one side to make a spot for Gail. "Which way you headed? Big A or Choo-Choo?"

"Good question," Gail said as she perched on the edge of the tailgate. "I'm supposed to be on my way to Atlanta, but I'm thinking about changing my mind and going back home. Home, by the way, is Sweetwater, Tennessee." She offered her hand to the woman nearer to her. "I'm Gail."

"Hi, Gail. I'm Marilyn, and this is my much better half, Evan." Gail reached across Marilyn and shook Evan's hand.

"Nice to meet you both. How about you guys? Are you from Atlanta?"

"More or less. We live in Avondale Estates on the east side of town.

We were up doing some leaf looking and apple picking. All the fresh air made us hungry, so we thought we'd better make sure we had our daily dose of saturated fat." Marilyn popped the last bite into her mouth and crumpled the wrapper from her burger.

"Great weather for getting out of the city." Gail set her drink cup on the tailgate between her legs.

"Yeah, most folks are headed to the mountains. What brings you out of the hills of Tennessee?" Evan took a gulp from the milkshake and offered the cup to Marilyn.

"You wouldn't believe me if I told you. I'm not sure I believe it myself."

"Lady trouble?"

"Am I that transparent?" Gail picked up her cup, shook some ice chips into her mouth, and ground them between her teeth.

Marilyn swirled the milkshake in its cup. "We saw the rainbow flag on the back window of your truck when you pulled in. When you started wearing a path in the asphalt here at Mickey D's, Evan said, 'She either just got dumped, or she's trying to work up her courage to dump her honey.' I said if you'd been dumped, you'd have red eyes from crying, so you must be the dumper, not the dumpee." Marilyn used a straw to slurp the last of the shake from the cup. "Plus, if you're on your way to Atlanta on a sunny Saturday afternoon when everyone else is making tracks for the woods, I'd have to vote for you trying to decide how to tell your big city girlfriend 'so long.'"

"Not exactly, but you're darn close. If you guys aren't detectives or shrinks, let me tell you, you've missed your calling."

"I write advertising copy and do an occasional story for *Creative Loafing,* and Evan is a scheduler for one of the delivery services, but it's nice to know you think we could make a living doing something else."

"Creative Loafing? The weekly newspaper that covers all of the musical performances and independent theatre shows and so on?"

"Right. We're the largest alternative weekly publication in Atlanta. We've been around since 1972, and our circulation is up to over a hundred and thirty thousand a week."

"I've seen it a few times. I don't get down to Atlanta much." Gail tapped the last ice chip from her cup into her mouth. "Can I ask you two a kind of personal question?"

"Why not?" Evan laid her hand on Marilyn's forearm. "After all, the two of us have been playing twenty questions with your personal life."

"How long after you met did you move in together?"

Marilyn and Evan chuckled. "Let's see," Evan said. "We went to a concert on a Friday night. Then we saw a movie on Saturday afternoon, had dinner together Saturday night..."

"Then it was brunch on Sunday, a walk through Piedmont Park Sunday afternoon, and Sunday night we discussed whether to sleep at your place or mine," Marilyn added.

"Tuesday, I took the day off from work and rented a U-Haul and dragged all my furniture and books to Marilyn's apartment."

"So, start to finish, that works out to nearly four full days. Possibly a record for the longest it's ever taken two lesbians to decide to cohabitate." Marilyn looked at Evan in a way that made Gail remember how Marissa used to smile at her when they both knew nothing else merited mention. "And *for* the record, next month, we'll have been together for seven years. You know what? I still regret wasting those first three days."

"You never wondered if you'd done the right thing?"

"Oh, please," Marilyn sighed. "We had been together about two weeks when I found out she was a Catholic—a *practicing* Catholic. Imagine the shock to this lapsed Baptist's heart."

"And our first Christmas, you told me—didn't ask me, told me—we were going to spend the holidays with your family in Florida, but we couldn't sleep together while we were there."

"We fought about that 'til Easter."

"Yeah," Evan agreed. "I wanted to kill you, but I was afraid it would mean way too much time in purgatory."

"Some rather big differences, huh?" Gail pulled her left leg up and clasped it to her chest.

"The big problems turned out to be the easy problems. It's the little ones that drive us crazy. I like to sleep with the windows open, but Marilyn says it makes her head stuffy. I like to sleep late on weekends; she wants to get up at dawn and go on mini-adventures all over the state."

"What about you and your no-underwear-in-the-dryer rule?" Marilyn said.

"It ruins the elastic."

"So? For three bucks you can get five new pairs at the Wal-Mart."

"And for no bucks, you can hang them on a drying rack and they last for two years." Evan stuck her tongue out at Marilyn for emphasis.

Again, the two women exchanged a glance that left no doubt about their feelings for one another.

"The deal is, at the end of the day, I know I'm still lots better off with her in my life than I ever could be without her. So we keep working things out. When you find the right one, nothing matters except being together." Marilyn wrapped her arm affectionately around Evan's shoulder.

"You're only saying that because you know you'd never find anybody else who will put up with all your BS." Evan leaned into Marilyn's embrace.

Gail eased off the tailgate and stretched. "Thanks for the conversation." Gail glanced at her watch. "I'd better get going."

"North or south? Have you decided?" Marilyn asked.

"South, but not to say 'good-bye.'"

"So you're going to give it another shot?" Marilyn hopped off the tailgate to stand beside Gail.

"Yeah. I think it's worth it."

"How long have you and — "

"Connie," Gail supplied.

"How long have you and Connie been together?"

"Let's see." Gail made a show of counting on her fingers. "Only six years, eleven months, three weeks and six days less than you two."

"Huh?" Evan asked as she gathered the lunch trash.

"Today would really be the first day of thinking of ourselves as a couple."

"Good for you, Gail!" Marilyn said as she punched her lightly in the arm. She pulled her wallet out of her hip pocket and handed Gail her business card. "Here, take my card. Give me a call and let us know how you're doing. Maybe the four of us can get together for dinner sometime."

"Sure. That would be fun."

"I hope things work out for you and Connie." Evan extended her hand to Gail.

"Thanks again. See ya." Gail released Evan's hand and laid her index finger on her forehead as she tipped her imaginary cap. She walked to her truck and backed out of her parking spot. She circled the lot and pulled up behind the black F-150. Gail leaned over to speak to Marilyn and Evan out the open passenger window. "Watch your backs. It's only six years, eleven months, three weeks, and six days 'til Connie and I catch you guys."

Marilyn flashed Gail a thumbs up. "Remember, the only route to forever is one day at a time."

GAIL WAS RELIEVED to find Connie's house was neither a pigsty nor a palace. As Connie ushered Gail on a tour of the house, she told her she'd purchased the smallish house in Decatur about ten years earlier. Connie explained she had become familiar with the area during her time at Agnes Scott College and saw no need to cast a wider net when the time was right for her to become a homeowner.

Connie's house was a two-bedroom brick rambler, the exterior indistinguishable from all the other houses on the blocks surrounding it in any direction. The kitchen was small, and the dining room could, at best, seat six. Connie had painted the wall behind her small dining table a deep aqua. The hue was perfect to pick up the accent tone in the area rug under the table and the matting in the four Southwestern-themed prints hanging on the walls.

The perimeter of the living room was ringed with bookcases. Gail was struck by the absence of Connie's own titles on them. In the center of the room, a rust-colored upholstered love seat sat opposite two butter yellow leather chairs with footstools. *Mama bear chairs. They look comfortable.*

A coffee table sat between the chairs and the love seat. A square border rug lay under the coffee table on the beige wall-to-wall carpet. The outer border was the rust of the love seat, the second band the yellow of the chairs, and the middle a warm cocoa brown, making the room feel very cozy.

Off the right rear of the living room, a short hallway led to the bathroom, the den, and two undersized bedrooms. A small deck overlooked the back yard.

The smaller of the two bedrooms was Connie's writing studio. Open books were visible on every surface. A well-worn glider rocker sat in one corner with a two-tiered table on either side of it. Both tiers of both tables were heaped with writers' magazines and book review periodicals. Her desk sat along the long interior wall. The desktop was a hodgepodge of papers, water bottles, computer disc storage boxes, calculator, tape dispenser, a calendar (two months out of date), a ceramic mug overflowing with pens and pencils, file folders, dictionary, thesaurus, paper clips, earphones, loose change, colored markers, and computer devices — monitor, printer, keyboard, CPU, laptop, and docking station. Copies of all of Connie's books from Outrageous Press were lined up on a shelf affixed to the wall over the desk.

After their quick tour of the house, Gail sensed Connie was on edge, but for that matter, so was she. Connie had kept up a rapid fire running commentary since the moment Gail came through the door. All Gail had been able to do was murmur an occasional "uh huh" or "that's pretty" as Connie ratchet-jawed her way from room to room. The tour over, they were standing in the hallway area off the living room. Connie seemed to have suddenly run out of things to say, and Gail couldn't figure out how to fill the conversational void either.

They looked anywhere but at one another.

After what felt to be ten minutes later, they both decided to speak at exactly the same second.

"I like your house," Gail said.

"Can I get you something to drink?" Connie asked

"Thanks," Connie answered.

"No, thanks," Gail replied, once again right on top of Connie's words.

They each gave a nervous half laugh.

Connie took a step toward the living room. Gail caught her by the arm and turned her so that they were facing. She laid a finger across Connie's lips. "I really do think you've done a great job of decorating. It feels very homey." She let her hand drop by her side.

Connie returned the favor and placed her pinkie on Gail's lips. "I'm glad you think so. Would you like to go in the other room and sit down?

How about a Coke or some wine?"

Gail reached up and took Connie's hand, drew it to her lips and kissed it. "Maybe in a minute, but first..."

Connie closed the gap between them and wrapped her arms around Gail's torso. They kissed, tentatively at first, then more feverishly, and soon, ardently.

"Ohhh, that was worth waiting for," Connie moaned softly. "I've dreamed of this since I watched you leave the Magnolia Suites."

"Then we'd better make sure it was exactly what you wanted it to be." Gail let her lips find Connie's again.

Connie drew her hands down Gail's face. "Come with me." She led them to the bedroom and half pushed, half helped Gail onto the bed.

Gail looked up at Connie standing over her by the side of the bed. Her long hair hung down in front of her shoulders. Gail grasped a handful of Connie's thick, auburn mane in each hand and tugged gently. "I need you." Her voice was hoarse and evocative.

Connie fell face forward onto the bed and flung her leg over Gail's pelvic region. "Not half as much as I need you."

"DO YOU KNOW where we'll be one week from right now?" Connie looked at the clock on the nightstand. It said nine-fifteen.

"Having a repeat performance of what we just did?" Gail felt a happy shudder course through her as she spoke. She and Connie were bundled together like puppies in a playpen in Connie's bed.

"That would make quite a headline. 'Lesbian Author and Lover Shock Crowd at Writers' Association Banquet.'"

"Oh, gosh, I forgot all about that."

Gail and Connie had spent nearly four hours getting reacquainted. It had been every bit as all-consuming as their first encounter at the Magnolia Suites in July. In many ways, it was sweeter because Gail was free of the recurring remorse that had plagued her in their earlier times together. The afterglow was a welcoming, secure place for them both.

"You are going to go with me next Saturday, aren't you? You said you would."

"I'll go, but I'll be an onion in a petunia patch."

"Why?"

"Because I'm such a dork in a dress."

"So don't wear a dress."

"It's a formal affair. I've seen the write-ups on these Southern Women's Writers' galas. The women are always dressed to the nines. It's mink stoles and pearl chokers and long white gloves."

"Yes, but their escorts don't wear high heels and pantyhose."

"Are you suggesting I show up in drag?"

"I prefer to think of it as you being appropriately attired as the arm candy of one of the award recipients."

Connie saw it in her mind's eye so clearly. Gail's five foot seven frame was lean and angular. She'd look so good in a tuxedo with a crisp, white shirt with an azure blue bowtie and a matching cummerbund. It would make her blue eyes look even deeper and more mysterious. Gail never wore make-up. She didn't need to. Her skin was firm and unblemished, and somehow, she still had her farm girl rosy cheeks. Her eyelashes were long and thick and several shades darker than her hair color. Her hair was still mostly blonde, but a little bit of gray was starting to show at the temples. If she got it trimmed a fraction of an inch early in the week and then used some mousse to keep it in the soft waves that played along the sides of her head, she'd be a shorter, butchy-femme version of a young Paul Newman. Maybe Connie could talk her into a wearing a showy pair of diamond stud earrings instead of the usual small hoops she wore in her pierced ears. She'd look way better than any of the paunchy guys who were going to be there, putting on supportive acts of what they no doubt thought of as their wives' "writing hobby."

"Isn't that playing into the stereotype we lesbos try so hard to shatter?" Gail asked.

"Who gives a flying Wallenda? Most of these dames have already got it in their minds we're lesser creatures. Giving me an award is somebody's stab at being politically correct for one evening and getting some ink for the sake of their own publicity." Connie stretched her arms over her head then looped them back around Gail's warm body. "Besides, there's a dance after the banquet. How would it look if you and I were floating around the ballroom looking like high school sophomores who couldn't get dates for homecoming?"

"Funny you should pick that analogy."

"Why?"

"Because last month when I was back in my old hometown, I went to the homecoming dance with my friend, Penny."

"No joke?"

"Gospel truth." Gail told Connie an abbreviated version of homecoming night with Penny Skramstaad. She glossed over the details of Penny's childhood abuse at the hands of Roland Dekeman and pointedly left out the particulars of her "Lou Grant and Mary Richards" experience with Penny in Carl and Lillian Skramstaad's old bedroom. The toilet papering of Kim Galloway's house, however, got thorough coverage. She hoped the diversionary tactic of telling tales on how she and Penny had reverted to juvenile pranks might throw Connie off the scent of a quarry she'd rather they not hunt. No such luck.

"Were you and Penny lovers in high school?"

"No, Penny wasn't that kind of girl back then." Gail swallowed the knot in her throat. "But I suppose I should confess it would have been okay with me if Penny wanted to eat crackers in my bed."

"Is she gay now?"

"Not quite."

"Come again?"

"One of the thousands of things she and I talked about while we were clearing out her dad's house was her long-standing but mostly-ignored attraction to women. She called me a couple of days after I got back from Minnesota and told me about this woman at work who's left her husband. At long last, Penny admitted her attraction to her—her name is Andrea. I'm sure the next time I hear from her, she'll tell me they've been sweating up the sheets."

"How does that make you feel?"

"She's been my friend since Moses wore diapers. I hope she can find someone who makes her happy."

"Since it can't be you, you mean."

How the hell can she have seen right through me? Gail lay very still and listened to the lub-dub of Connie's heart as blood pumped through the vein in her neck.

Connie shifted Gail's head so that it rested on her upper chest.

"I can see where you'd want to hook up with somebody who feels safe and familiar," Connie used her index finger to draw circles on Gail's back while she searched for the right words, "now that Marissa is gone."

"I guess you think I'm about a half a step above pond scum in the evolutionary chain."

"Why would I think that?"

"Because of the way I treated Marissa." She didn't bother to add her thoughts about still harboring feelings for a lover she would never have...or at least never have again.

"From what you told me at your house Thursday night, you and Marissa treated each other with a lot of love and respect."

"Yeah, right up until I fell into bed with you shortly after we met."

"Gail. Sweet, sweet Gail. By everyone's measure—everyone's except your own, I suppose—you waited two years beyond when you lost her to let yourself feel one little bit of joy. You told me she never would have wanted to be kept alive with those machines. If you and she had done the living wills you talked about, without the life support, she wouldn't have hung on more than a few days after the accident. Have you given any thought to what I said? About maybe your being with me is what Marissa needed?"

Gail pulled back from Connie's embrace. "But what if our being together is what made her quit trying—quit wanting to get well. If she had some kind of sixth sense or special power telling her about us, it might have broken her heart."

"Is that the kind of thing Marissa would have done? Died to spite you? Died for the purpose of making you feel worse yet about everything that happened?" Connie pulled her close again.

Gail didn't answer, but deep inside she knew Marissa was too decent, too kind to ever want to hurt her. She remembered what Amy had told her about Marissa's condition. She had been gone in spirit for a long time. Her physical death in July was only the period behind a sentence that had been written more than two years earlier.

"Look at my situation, Gail. I was supposed to have been a little rich bitch in south Georgia. Instead, I spent my childhood with a drunk and a woman who felt sorry for me. If Sudie Rae hadn't had the guts to face my real dad, I never could have gone to college, and if I'd never gone to Agnes Scott, I wouldn't have met Blanca. If she hadn't treated me so badly, I wouldn't have stayed in therapy and wouldn't have taken all those tumbles in the sack with Doug. If he hadn't tossed me out faster than three-day-old fish, I wouldn't have sunk myself into my books, and without that, I probably wouldn't have done well enough to have been invited to the Southern Women's Writers' Association banquet to get my award. If the banquet hadn't come up at exactly the time it did with my regular editor out of the country, Lydia LaGrange would never have assigned you to work with me on getting *Rings and Things* ready to hit the shelves to coincide with the award. No award, no Rhonda Helmstad out of the country, and viola, no Magnolia Suites, and without the Magnolia Suites, we wouldn't be here, together, right now."

Gail lay stock-still and silent on Connie's chest.

Connie continued. "Nothing happens in a vacuum, love. If you change any one thing in either of our lives, this exact moment never would have come about. Whether Marissa had anything to do with it, either as a loving spirit who wanted you to find new happiness so she could finally be free, or as a life force simply incapable of hanging on any longer, we *are* together now." Connie drew in a breath. "If you want to be, that is."

Gail sidestepped the indirectly asked question. "Doctor Wilburn told me in one of our sessions if you want to change one thing, you have to change everything."

"Yep, I agree. I used slightly different words, but that's the sentiment I was trying to express."

"I told her I wanted what I couldn't have."

"What did she say to that?"

"She said I should learn to want something else."

"Like maybe wanting your old high school friend, Penny." Gail heard the hint of envy in Connie's voice.

"What I felt for Penny is ancient history. She and I both know if we had been lovers back in our youth in Plainfield, Minnesota, we probably wouldn't still be friends today. It turned out exactly as it was supposed to."

"Nice try, Gail."

"I mean it. It's a closed chapter—a part of my life that was really part of some other life. So different, it's like I wasn't the one who lived it."

"You could say the same about Blanca and me."

"Except Penny and I are friends and probably will be 'til the day we die."

"But in both cases, we were people wanting something we couldn't have."

"Okay, I'll grant you that." Gail eased a little higher up Connie's body. Connie rolled from her back to her side. They were lying face to face. Gail laid her hand on Connie's face.

"I'm damaged goods, Connie. I wasted a lot of years aching for a woman who thought of me as the sister she never had. My first real lover tossed me over for God himself. After that, I left a trail of angry, hurt women from one coast to the other. My only semi-success was with Marissa, and you know how our relationship ended up."

"You don't have a corner on the market. Do you think I'd want my record posted anywhere? You pointed it out yourself when you said the bio sketches in my books never say anything about having a partner."

"So what should we do?"

"We probably should follow the advice of Doctor Wilburn and learn to want something else."

"Do you think we can?"

"Absolutely. In fact, I've already started." Connie's voice dropped half an octave. "I want you."

Chapter
Ten

CONNIE AND GAIL slept late on Sunday morning. It was after ten before they dragged themselves out of bed. Connie suggested brunch at a place called The Flaming Biscuit on the other side of Decatur. It was a trendy place, and by the time they got there, the line of people waiting for tables stretched out the door and snaked most of the way down the block. Wooden benches lined the sidewalk for patrons to lounge on while they waited for their names to be called. An employee of The Flaming Biscuit walked up and down the line of patrons doling out small Styrofoam cups and filling them with coffee.

The place was obviously popular with the gay and lesbian crowd. Gail noted any number of couples making no effort to hide that that's exactly what they were. Gail saw it as one good thing about being in a metropolitan area. Being lesbian didn't automatically mean you were regarded with disgust by ninety-eight percent of the locals. There weren't exactly scores of establishments flying their rainbow flags up in Sweetwater, Tennessee, so she and Marissa had always been very discreet when they were out in public. She was sure at least some of the denizens of Sweetwater knew the truth about them, but most were perfectly happy to think of them as "that nice college professor with the leg braces and the outdoorsy woman who lives with her."

The mid-October air was warm, easily twelve or fifteen degrees warmer than it would have been up at the cabin, Gail surmised. Gail was delighted to sit side by side with Connie on the bench and people watch. The sun shining on her face felt good, and the warmth of Connie's thigh next to hers felt better still.

Every little while, a group would leave the restaurant, a new group would be called to get seated, and they'd pick up and move to the next location on the benches. She knew she should be starving since she and Connie hadn't made it out of the house for dinner last night, and now it was pushing noon. It might have been the deep discourses; it might have been the avid lovemaking; it might have been the buzz of feeling all the energized people around them, but Gail hadn't given a thought to food since breakfast at Sweetwater Cabin almost twenty-four hours earlier.

They eventually moved far enough up in the line to get inside the door of the eatery and take seats on individual chairs that reminded Gail of the ones at the Bridgeman's Ice Cream Parlor back in Plainfield. The main room was cavernous, with a fourteen-foot high ceiling. All of the heating and air conditioning ductwork was visible overhead and was painted with a dull-finish black paint. Hammered black tin covered the visible flat surfaces around the ductwork. Gail looked around at the eclectic decorating scheme. Assorted tapestries, African war masks, pictures, collages, ceramics, and art made of everything from broken glass pieces to scraps of fabric adorned every wall. Some was primitive, some was modern, some abstract, some so pointedly concrete it could hang unnoticed in a home furnishings rental center.

Off to the left, up a short run of stairs, Gail saw another dining room, smaller she thought, but hard to tell, since she couldn't tell how far toward the back of the building it ran. She saw more of the varying art forms festooning those walls, too. The din from the throng of people enjoying their Sunday morning fare at The Flaming Biscuit was disorienting. Gail guessed there were at least eighty people in the main room and half again that many in the second room. Waiters and waitresses, bus boys and girls, and two hostesses added their particular contributions to the cacophony.

"We've got a table for eight that's only got four at it. They've said they won't mind the company if you don't mind sharing a table." It was all Gail could do to make out what the hostess was saying, but Connie seemed to be able to isolate her voice from all the background noise.

"Sure. Never know when you might make a new friend." Connie leaned in near the hostess's ear to be heard.

"Great. Come with me." The hostess grabbed two menus from the stack on her podium and led them on a winding course among the tables dotting the terra cotta floor. "Ladies," she said loudly to the foursome at a table most of the way to the rear of the room, "say hello to your dining companions." She handed the menus to Gail and Connie and hurried back to her station.

Gail had occupied herself trying to get a better look at some of the more unusual art pieces on the walls and so had barely paid attention to where they were going.

"Gail? Oh my gosh, what are the odds?"

Gail spun to look at the woman speaking. "Marilyn? I don't believe it!"

Marilyn pushed back from the table and wrapped Gail in a quick hug. "You remember Evan," she said as she pointed to the woman with whom Gail had shared a pick-up truck tailgate at an exit on I-75 the previous afternoon. "And these are our friends, Margarita—she goes by 'Mickie'—and Darlene." The two women on the far side of the table stopped eating and smiled. "This is Gail," Marilyn continued as she laid a hand on Gail's shoulder, "and unless I miss my guess, Connie."

"How do they know my name?" Connie stared at Marilyn in disbelief.

"Your girlfriend told us all about you." Marilyn laughed with abandon. "Sit down, and we'll tell you the whole sordid tale."

Gail and Connie claimed seats opposite from one another, Gail next to Evan on her and Marilyn's side of the table and Connie next to Mickie.

The waiter sashayed to the table. "What are y'all having to drink? Mimosa? Long Island iced tea?"

"Orange juice for me, please," Connie said.

"Me, too, and a large glass of water."

"Got it. Back in two shakes of a lamb's tail." The waiter wiggled his rear end twice as he pranced off.

Connie and Gail studied their menus for a minute or two. "What's good?" Gail mouthed at Connie across the table.

"Everything. Brunch special number two is tasty, and the biscuits and gravy are out of this world."

The waiter appeared with their drinks and then stood poised by the table with his pen and order pad. "Your selections, my lovelies?"

Gail had never acquired a taste for buttermilk biscuits drowning in chicken-flavored cream gravy. Worse yet, The Flaming Biscuit's version was gravy with chunks of pork sausage in it, so she opted for the eggs Benedict with the hollandaise on the side. Connie ordered biscuits and gravy with hash browns and a rasher of bacon.

"One traitor, yellow goop corralled. One set of drowned biscuits, tossed taters, half a hog coming up." The waiter slid his pen behind his ear with a flourish and flounced toward the kitchen.

"Quite a crowd," Gail observed to no one in particular.

"Believe it or not, it's worse on Saturdays," Evan answered. "Thank goodness some people go to church. If today is like most Sundays, we'll get a lull in the action here in about ten minutes. Then we'll have about an hour 'til the after-church-bunch starts showing up."

"From what Marilyn said about you being a practicing Catholic, I might have thought you'd be part of the church bunch, too."

"We Catholics got smart years ago. I go on Saturday night. Leaves Sunday wide open for more entertaining pursuits." She looked at Marilyn in a way that left no doubt what they had done in the privacy of their own home before heading to the Flaming Biscuit for brunch.

"You know these women's religious preferences? The curiosity is killing me. How do you guys know each other?" Connie gestured from Gail to Evan and Marilyn, then turned her hands palm up to demonstrate her confusion.

Marilyn provided a circumspect reiteration of their conversation from yesterday afternoon while soaking up the sun in the parking lot of a McDonald's restaurant off I-75 in northwest Georgia. She carefully avoided any reference to Gail's bout of cold feet and described it as nothing more than three women — whose gaydar picked one another out — having a friendly, get-acquainted chat while taking a break from driving. Her story was perfectly believable, inasmuch as it was pure coincidence that they'd all shown up at the Flaming Biscuit. The waiter arrived with Gail and Connie's orders just as Marilyn finished her recap. The sight of food in front of her turned Gail into a nutrition-starved eating machine. Connie followed suit. Darlene, Mickie, Evan, and Marilyn took advantage of the waiter's presence to order refills on their coffee.

Evan's prediction proved accurate. About the time Gail and Connie laid their forks down and eased back in their chairs with sated sighs, there was a marked out-flux of diners, and no matching influx to replace them. The Flaming Biscuit's tin ceiling and tiled floor became less of an echo chamber and more of a comfy eatery. Conversation at normal voice levels was, at last, possible.

"I'm sorry. Hunger apparently made me forget my manners," Connie said as she turned slightly in her chair and looked at Mickie. "Thank you for letting us crash your table and horn in on the four of you."

"De nada. No hay problema, amiga," Mickie replied

"Como te llamas?" Connie asked.

"Margarita Izaguirre. Pero, casi todos me llaman 'Mickie.'"

"Gusto en conocerte, Mickie Izaguirre."

"Igualmente, Connie..."

"Consuelo Martinez, pero todos me conocen como 'Connie Martin.'"

Darlene set her coffee mug down with a clunk. "Connie Martin? Not *the* Connie Martin?"

"Depends on which Connie Martin you have in mind." Connie's cheeks flushed.

"The one who's written a couple of dozen books every lesbian in our circle has read."

Connie's face glowed — from the compliment and from the blush. "I guess I'd be the same one," she said softly.

"Oh, wow. I had no idea we were having brunch with a celebrity," Darlene gushed as she grabbed Mickie's arm. "Mickie, did you know?" Without waiting for an answer, Darlene looked across the table at Evan and Marilyn. "What about you guys?"

"Not a clue," Evan assured her. "We've known Gail for almost a whole day now. Believe me when I tell you we had no idea she was hooked up with the leading lady of lesbian fiction." Evan tried not to look awestruck, but failed.

"Do you think you might autograph some books for us? I mean, if we're not being too pushy. We've got some friends who would positively die of delight if we put an autographed copy of your book in their hands." Darlene leaned around her partner and caught

Connie's eye.

"Not at all. I'd be glad to do it for you. Think of it as repayment for sharing your table with us this morning."

"You know, if you guys wait a week, you can get the newest Connie Martin release," Gail whispered conspiratorially. "I have it on good authority that *Rings and Things* will hit the shelves a week from today."

"Really? Next Sunday?" Darlene's eyes grew big. "What do we have to do?"

"Everything's set up with Charis Bookstore, isn't it Connie?" Gail asked.

"Uh huh. I talked to the publicity person earlier this week. They've got a shipment coming in on Friday, and I'll be there Sunday afternoon from two to four to do a reading and sign autographs."

"Sometimes I am the biggest cretin on the planet," Marilyn sighed. "I did the full-page lay-out in *Creative Loafing* announcing that event. Wasn't there something else in there? Something about an award?"

"Right," Gail replied. "Connie will be honored at the Southern Women's Writers' Association ceremony this coming Saturday."

"That is so cool," Mickie said. "Felicitaciones, nos haces orgullosas, Consuelo."

"No es para tanto," Connie replied.

"Outstanding! Double whammy," Darlene concurred. "Hispanic lesbian. Now, there's a one-two punch." She swung one fist and then the other.

"Gail is going to the banquet with me," Connie said. "Don't you think she'd look great in a tux?"

The six women had a long discussion of what Gail and Connie needed to do to pop the eyeballs out of the sockets of everyone at the banquet. In the ensuing half hour, Connie agreed to have her hair cut—probably by half—and styled into a cut that framed her face more softly. The next morning, which happened to be Mickie's day off, she'd accompany Connie to a one-hour eyeglasses store and help her pick some frames better suited to her and then take her to a salon where Javier would work his magic on her tresses. If there was still time in the day, they'd visit some dress shops.

"I guess this is sort of a belated la quincenera party for me." Connie seemed ill at ease with all the attention being showered on her.

"My family had a big celebration for me and both of my sisters when each of us turned fifteen. My mother and aunts must have spent a month cooking to get ready for them," Mickie said.

"I'll be fifty-five this fall—I suppose our theme could be 'better forty years late than never." Connie blushed a little more.

Yes, you'll be a mujer mas madura, but I'll make it my personal mission to see to it you're the prettiest one at the banquet," Mickie grinned broadly.

"'More mature woman' is putting it mildly." Connie was blushing from her neck to her scalp.

"What about me?" Gail asked, hoping to give Connie a reprieve from her discomfort at being fawned over.

"You can rent a tuxedo from the formal wear shop on Monroe Street. That's where I got mine when I served as an usher at a coworker's commitment ceremony a couple of months ago," Marilyn said. "Mickie could drop you by there tomorrow when she's out with Connie." Marilyn turned to her friend. "Right, Mick?"

"Sure. We'll go right by it on our way to Javier's."

The cats will be fine. I'll be back to Sweetwater by early afternoon. Gail tried to push her guilty thoughts aside.

"We probably should get our checks and let someone else have this table. Looks like the second wave is about to hit." Evan nodded her head to the mass of people near the hostess station. "And if I don't do something about the gallon of coffee I've had, my kidneys will never forgive me."

"I'll pay the bill and meet you out front." Marilyn pulled her blazer from the back of her chair. She stood and fished in her pocket for her credit card.

Connie, Gail, Marilyn, Darlene, and Mickie worked their way to the cash register and then out the front door of The Flaming Biscuit, where they waited for Evan.

"Let me ask you something, Connie," Mickie posed. "I've got a good friend on the staff of the Georgia Hispanic Chamber of Commerce. If she could arrange it, would you consider doing an interview for their newsletter?"

"I don't usually do that sort of thing."

"I wish you would. They're always looking for ways to promote economic advancement for Hispanics and to build bridges to the non-Hispanic community. Your story would be a four-lane expressway."

"When you put it that way, how can I say no?"

"Good. I'll talk to her on Tuesday and we'll see when we can arrange for you two to meet."

Evan emerged from the restaurant and joined the quintet. "There, much better. I can probably ride all the way home without having to find a gas station restroom now."

Marilyn started the round robin of hugs among the women.

"Nice to meet you."

"You, too."

"This was fun. Let's do it again."

"You all should come up to Sweetwater sometime."

"Really looking forward to the book signing at Charis next week."

"Can't wait to hear all about the awards banquet."

"See you in the morning, Mickie."

"Thanks for sharing your table."

Connie and Gail set off in one direction; the other four went another.

"We had brunch with Connie Martin." Darlene's voice, edged with incredulity, carried far enough to reach Connie and Gail.

"What she doesn't realize is she's had brunch with me at least ten times. I see those four women almost every time I eat there." Connie shook her head as she spoke. "I probably could have gone another ten years and never been recognized in public. Now, thanks to you, Gail Larsen, mistress of the inexplicable coincidence, my cover of anonymity is blown." Connie pushed the remote unlock button on her key fob as they reached her car.

"I expect next week's award ceremony would have about taken care of that anyway." Gail eased into the passenger seat. "The *Atlanta Journal Constitution* will do a big write-up and knock the last pin out of the hinges of your closet door." Gail looked at the clock in the car's dash as Connie started the engine. It was almost exactly twenty-four hours since she had pulled up at Connie's house. "There, that makes one."

"One what?"

"One day closer to our having been together forever."

GAIL WAS GLAD she let herself be talked into wearing a tuxedo to the banquet. She had never given in to anything so profoundly butch. Oh sure, she'd worn a lot of corduroy jeans and flannel shirts, and she had some steel-toed, lace-up work boots she wore when she was out in the woods up at Sweetwater. She always said they were to protect her from snakebites, but Marissa had teased her mercilessly about the way she swaggered and strutted whenever she wore them.

The tuxedo made her feel she was a totally new person. It gave her a bravado and a confidence that allowed her to almost glide through the evening without so much as moment's self-consciousness.

Why, yes, I was Ms. Martin's editor for her latest book. No, her publisher and I are still in negotiations for her future offerings.

As you know, many states don't permit gay and lesbian people to marry, so we think of ourselves as a monogamous, committed couple, but tonight is about Ms. Martin's contributions to the literary world, not our personal politics. (So what if they'd been committed for all of a week? They were one week closer to forever.)

Questions which ordinarily would have left her groping for a coherent response were merely curious inquiries by Connie's sister authors. When Connie was called up on stage to receive the plaque proclaiming her "One of Georgia's Most Influential Writers" and Connie had Gail stand to take a bow as "a member of her wonderfully supportive team at Outrageous Press," Gail stood tall and waved to the room full of people as though it were the sort of thing she did nearly every Saturday night. If she had been in an evening gown or a dressy woman's pantsuit, she'd have turned as red as the carnation pinned to her lapel and barely been able to lift her butt a quarter inch off her chair before trying to shrivel into a wad half her normal height. Powerful talismans, those bowties and cummerbunds.

And holy frijoles, had Mickie done a job on Connie. The lines of the dress they picked made Connie look six inches taller. It was a floor-length, long-sleeved, deep mauve sheath with deep kick vents on both sides. Pencil-lead-thin glimmering strands of bronze and gold silk ran through the fabric and were the perfect color to accentuate the almost imperceptible bronze glow of Connie's skin — skin which peeked ever so alluringly from the revealing décolletage.

The cut and styling Javier had done let the natural body in Connie's hair come out. The long, loose look she had worn before had the effect of pulling her face down. This new cut left her face full and open and expressive.

Mickie and Connie had practiced all week on getting Connie's make-up just right. A hint of eye shadow to complement the dress color, subtle mascara, a touch of rouge. A lot of heads swiveled when Connie Martin walked into the banquet room at the Atlanta Hilton. And if Gail Larsen hadn't been escorting her, she knew she would have been one of the many who stopped dead in their tracks and asked, "Who is that beauty?"

Open bar cocktail mixer. Seven course meal. Speeches. Awards. Applause. Thank you's and acknowledgements. More awards. More applause.

It was nearly eleven o'clock when the formal part of the evening was over and the band began to play in the adjoining room. *Thank goodness it's a band and not an orchestra.* Gail and Connie stood with several other couples inside the doorway to the ballroom. *Anything other than a box-step waltz, and I'm a dead duck.* Gail surreptitiously wiped her damp palms on her pants legs.

Two by two, the women and their husbands began to drift onto the dance floor.

"You realize we've never danced, don't you?" Gail whispered in Connie's ear.

"I know, but I've always heard you can tell how good a dancer someone will be by the way they make love." Connie pressed in close against Gail's ear so her words wouldn't be overheard. "I figure that makes you the Ginger Rogers of lesbians."

"Have I told you how incredibly beautiful you are, Ms. Martin?"

"Not in the last hour or two."

"You are. You're an absolute knock-out. I tried to tell you when we were still at your house, but you said I was ruining your hairdo."

"The evening's almost over. Very soon I'll let you do whatever you want to — with both of my hairdos."

Gail heard herself gasp as she caught Connie's meaning. "We better do something to burn off some of this energy you're generating." Gail grabbed Connie's hand and moved toward the dance floor.

"That's no way to ask a lady to dance." Connie pulled away in mock disgust.

"I'm sorry." Gail bowed deeply from the waist, one hand in front of her, one hand behind her back. "Ms. Martin, could I have this dance?" The music the band was playing was nothing like the Anne Murray song, but Gail felt the power of the words as she spoke them. They reminded her of both Marissa and Penny; for a fleeting moment Connie, Marissa, and Penny blended into an ethereal amalgam of the three women Gail had loved the most.

Connie folded into Gail's arms, and they joined the other couples. The band played only slow, contemporary songs—nice smooth tunes with steady backbeats, so they had no problem finding a rhythm.

"I'm glad you wore your Golden Autumn perfume like I asked you to." Connie's whisper made Gail almost forget to keep moving to the music. She couldn't help but remember the last time she had held a woman in her arms while music filled the room and heard her dance partner comment on that same fragrance.

Funny how life turns out. She should have felt so at home in Plainfield, Minnesota, with Penny Skramstaad, but it had been graceless and ungainly. No fewer pairs of eyes were boring holes into her and Connie now than had been on the dance floor in Plainfield, but she honest to goddess didn't care. *This* was a homecoming—coming home to her heart.

"How long do we need to stay?"

"I don't think anyone would notice if we left now. Why?" Connie pulled back and regarded Gail's face.

"I propose we call it a night." Gail drew Connie against her chest. "Just so you know, I'm thinking of wearing only one thing to bed tonight."

"Oh? And what will it be?"

"Golden Autumn."

SUNDAY AFTERNOON, GAIL and Connie were lying fully clothed on Connie's bed, both wishing they had the energy to do something about the urges they were finding difficult to ignore.

"What a weekend." Gail wedged her hands behind her head.

"You said a mouthful. I hated to leave the bookstore with so many women still in line, but once we ran out of copies of *Rings and Things*, there really wasn't much point in making them wait."

"It was nice of you to offer to go back next month to do another signing."

"Not much of a sacrifice on my part. I know Lydia thought she had ordered plenty of copies to get me through today."

"It probably would have been if Mickie hadn't rounded up every lesbian with a teaspoon of Hispanic blood in her body to be there this afternoon."

"I had no idea there were that many women like me in Atlanta."

"Are you sorry you took yourself off the market before they had a chance to make an offer?"

Connie eased into a sitting position against the headboard. "You know better than that." She kissed Gail softly as she joined her against the headboard. "I have to admit it's kind of a funny feeling, though. I haven't ever thought of myself as being Hispanic, really. I always told myself I took the name Connie Martin to honor my mother, but by anglicizing it, I sort of dishonored her at the same time."

"But you've learned to speak Spanish. Wouldn't that show that you had some pride about your background?"

"Or show I was determined to make Blanca Juarez think of me as a worthy mate when we were at Agnes Scott. I learned enough to get by and pass as Hispanic when it suited me, but it wasn't necessarily because I felt a connection to my maternal heritage."

"When you spoke Spanish to the women at the bookstore this afternoon, I thought we were going to have a Selena incident on our hands. They went crazy."

"There were hardly enough people there to storm the stage and cause a human stampede, but quick, name me two popular contemporary Hispanic authors in any genre, and then name me one lesbian author who either is Hispanic herself or writes about Hispanic characters."

"Good point."

"I'm a little surprised you know Selena."

"It got so much coverage in the news it would have been hard to miss."

"Sorry to say a lot of people didn't have much problem tuning out news of the death of a young Hispanic singer." Connie tipped her head back and stared at the ceiling. "Selena Quintanilla-Perez."

"I don't think I ever knew anything more than 'Selena.' How long ago was that?"

"I don't remember exactly. I think it was 1994 or 1995." Connie seemed lost in thought for a moment, then turned to look at Gail. "I've been doing this so long I've lost count of how many readers have told me how finding books by, for, and about lesbians saved their lives. You remember how it felt to think you were the *only* person in the world who had those feelings for other women."

Gail only had to recall her trip to Plainfield and the feelings she'd had while at the homecoming dance to resurrect exactly the emotions Connie was talking about.

"Think how much worse it must be when you can't find any characters who eat the foods you eat, speak the language you think and dream in, dress and look like you do."

"You're right, Connie."

"I've been thinking—"

"You've been thinking maybe you should write a book—maybe a series of books—featuring Hispanic women."

"Exactly!" Connie's face lit up. "The research would be fascinating. Think how much I might learn about what it means to be Hispanic in America, not to mention what I'd learn about myself. Look at these business cards the women at the book signing gave me today." She reached over to the nightstand and picked up a small stack. "Of course there are Mickie's friends from the Georgia Hispanic Chamber of Commerce. This one is from La Raza. Here's one from the Georgia Association of Latin American Journalists. Mexican American Business Chamber. Georgia Hispanic Network. This one says Georgia Association of Latino Elected Officials." Connie thumbed through the cards. "There are some saying their business supports the Hispanic community. But all of these women—and the ones who didn't give me business cards—probably those women especially—have stories to be told. And there have to be lots of women like me. Women who have some Hispanic connections, but never knew much about that part of their legacy. The possibilities are endless. Main characters, supporting characters, and plot lines running the whole gamut of combinations—think of it."

"It would certainly give you something to do after lunch for a few days." Gail felt herself catching Connie's enthusiasm.

"Would you help me?"

"Help how?"

"Working leads, gathering background, following up with people on their suggestions, surfing the net, proofing, all sorts of thing. I bet Mickie knows a million people who are treasure troves of information. Oh, and of course editing the final product. "

"Won't Lydia want to decide who edits your books?"

"I'm sure I can convince her you're the one for the job." Connie looked at Gail lovingly. "Besides, I have far more important tasks for you, and neither Lydia LaGrange nor anyone else will ever convince me you're not the perfect one." She kissed her deeply.

"Tempting as it is to let this go where I'd like it to, I really need to make tracks for Sweetwater. The cats have been alone since Friday, and they were alone all last weekend, too. I hate it, but I'd better go. I've already let all the daylight get away from me, and Sunday nights are always pure hell on I-75."

"I know. I guess I should be glad the cats are sort of self-sufficient for even a day or two. I hate that they'll get to sleep with you tonight and I won't." Connie burrowed in for a long hug. "We maybe need to talk about what we're going to do about living arrangements."

"Yeah, but let's do it when we have time to give it the attention it deserves." Gail clung to Connie's embrace.

"Maybe it can be the first thing on the agenda for next weekend."

"You're still planning to come up to Sweetwater, right?" Gail asked.

"If the invitation still stands." Connie let her arms drop from around Gail. "I've got an appearance at Outwrite Books on Thursday night, and then I'll be up early Friday morning. Is that all right?"

"It's too many days away, but I'm all right with it." Gail laid a kiss on top of Connie's head.

"Thanks for being here this weekend." Connie tugged Gail's ear playfully.

"Thanks for asking me. I'm really glad you got the award. You deserved it."

"I bet you say that to all the authors."

"Only the ones I'm in love with." Gail stood and reached her hand toward Connie. "So there's exactly one."

Connie rose to accept Gail's embrace. "Call me when you get home."

"I will."

Chapter
Eleven

THE GREAT SMOKIES blessed them with another superbly gorgeous day. Connie arrived at Gail's cabin shortly before noon, Friday, complaining of a nagging headache. Gail suggested they take a walk down the lane leading to her cabin in hopes the fresh mountain air might help Connie's head. Tall, arching trees lined both sides of the narrow lane. Gail's cabin was one of only three houses on the quarter-mile dead-end road.

"Connie, be careful!" Gail grabbed for Connie's arm, but it was too late to catch her. Connie fell to the ground and landed with a thud. Gail dropped to one knee beside her. "Are you all right?"

Connie rolled to a sitting position and flexed her wrists and arms. "I don't think I broke anything. Help me get up, will you? I'm not usually this clumsy."

Gail took both of Connie's outstretched hands and pulled her to her feet. "How about your knees and ankles? Better see how they feel."

Connie tentatively bent each joint of her lower extremities. "All systems go, as best I can tell." She brushed the dust off the fronts of her pants legs. "Now I've fallen for you twice — once when your cat surprised me at the Magnolia Suites in July and again here, today."

"I hope you've fallen for me in less physically painful ways, too."

"Absolutely, but I can't show you those out here on the road." Connie dusted her hands together to dislodge the grit. She blinked hard. "Are both of the lenses still in my glasses? My right eye seems real blurry."

"Let me see." Gail checked Connie's eyewear. "Yep, they look fine. Maybe you bumped your head when you landed."

"Maybe." Connie sucked in a breath. "Would it be okay if we headed back to the house? I'm feeling kind of funny." She took two steps and nearly fell again.

Gail reached for Connie's arm again. This time she caught her elbow and stopped her from collapsing to the ground. "What's wrong, babe? Tell me how you feel."

"I'm not sure. The right side of my body almost seems to be missing."

"Why don't you sit here by the road, and I'll run get my truck and drive you back to the cabin."

"No, if we go slow, I'll be fine." Connie stood very still, her head tilted slightly to the right.

Gail kept her grip on Connie's elbow but eased around to be directly in front of her and studied her face. "Squeeze this as hard as you can," she directed as she placed her hand in Connie's left hand. "Now do it with this hand." She moved her hand to Connie's right hand. "How many fingers am I holding up?" She put three fingers in front of Connie's right eye.

"Three. Why are you doing this?" Gail heard the edge of fear in Connie's voice.

"Just to be safe. Now how many?" Gail held two fingers in front of Connie's left eye.

"Two."

"Good. Now, follow the movement of my finger. Don't move your head, only your eyes."

Connie did as Gail told her. "Okay, tell me your name and give me your street address and phone number."

Connie complied.

"Who am I?"

"Gail Larsen."

"What day of the week is it?"

"Friday. Why are you doing this, Gail? You think something awful is going on, don't you?"

"I'm not sure, sweetheart. Let's see what happens when you try to walk. I'm going to hold on to you, okay?" Gail moved to Connie's left side, keeping her hand tightly on Connie's upper arm.

Connie walked a little ways.

"Does one leg feel weaker than the other?"

"No, but I'm fuzzy. A little disoriented—not quite here."

"It's probably nothing, but I think we should get you checked out at a hospital." Gail tried to sound calm, but her concern showed through.

"Is it a stroke? Oh, God, please say you don't think I'm having a stroke." Connie clutched at Gail.

"You know I don't have any medical training, but I'd rather we go to the emergency room and get sent home for being alarmists than take a chance on this being something needing attention." Gail laid her hand over Connie's. "It's most likely a silly, simple something." The words rang hollow.

"Did I get the number of fingers wrong? Did I give you the wrong address for my house or mispronounce your name?"

"No, you did fine."

"What then? Why do you think we need to go to the hospital?"

Gail debated hedging the facts with Connie, but then decided truth was her ally. "The right corner of your mouth is pulled a little to the side and your right eyelid is drooping."

"It *is* a stroke, isn't it?"

"Try not to jump to the worst possible conclusion. You don't seem to have any difference in strength between your left and right sides. You can answer questions. I read somewhere those are two of the best tests for stroke.

"If it's not a stroke, what is it?"

"As I said a little while ago, my medical training is non-existent, but when I was a court reporter, something similar happened to a judge one day. Every time he'd try to walk, he'd gravitate to one side, and his face did the same thing yours is doing."

"What was wrong with him?"

"He was diagnosed with Bell's Palsy."

"I've never heard of it. Will I still be able to write books?"

"Connie, listen to me." Gail's voice was gentle. "Let's not stand here on the side of the road and speculate on what might be happening and what long-term consequences might come with it. Let's let someone who does medical diagnoses for a living look you over. Then we can deal with whatever we need to, okay?"

Connie started to shake.

"Are you cold? Do you feel faint?"

"No, I'm super nervous. You know how bad I am with medical tests. Is it all right to be scared?"

"Of course it is. But don't be. I'll be right beside you the whole time." Gail took her hand from Connie's arm where it had been for many minutes. She wrapped her arm around Connie's shoulder. "Now, let me help you sit down, and I'll go for the truck."

"Huh uh. I want to walk back."

Gail didn't argue. She got a firm grip on Connie's waist, and they set off for the cabin, two hundred yards away. Every fifth or sixth step, she'd have to correct their course, because Connie drifted a little farther to her right with each footfall.

Back at the cabin, Gail helped Connie into the truck, then hurried inside to get her keys, wallet, and two bottles of water.

"How are you feeling?" Gail asked as she started the truck.

"Kind of wrung out."

"What about your headache?"

"Not as bad, but it's still there."

"Can you stand an hour on the road? I'd say Knoxville is our best option." Gail turned onto U.S. Route 11, headed for Interstate 75.

"Whatever you say. I don't want to talk, though, okay?"

"Lean back and think calm thoughts. I'll try not to make any sudden stops or take the curves too fast."

"You're a good driver. I know I'm safe with you. Get me there as fast as you can so they can tell us nothing is wrong and we can come home." Connie closed her eyes and put her head on the headrest.

Gail's mind leapt back to another fast drive up the interstate to Knoxville General Hospital to learn the fate of a woman she loved. She would have rather driven directly into the jaws of hell.

"IT'S BEEN ALMOST five hours. What's taking so long?" Gail leaned aggressively over the desk in the emergency room and glowered at the receptionist.

"I checked on your friend twenty minutes ago. She's still in the MRI lab. As soon as there's any word, I'm sure one of the ER doctors or a nurse will come talk to you. Maybe you'd like to go to the cafeteria and get a cup of coffee or a bite to eat."

"I'll wait right here, thanks." Gail huffed off and flopped onto the vinyl bench along the wall. She lasted there all of three minutes—a full minute longer than she had the last time she tried to sit down—and resumed her tiger-in-a-cage walk in the cramped waiting room.

It was all too reminiscent of that Sunday afternoon in July two years ago—an absolute dearth of information from the hospital's medical personnel and her imagination painting one dire picture after another.

Maybe it was a stroke. Connie had been under tremendous pressure—first to get the new book out on a compressed timeline, and then with getting ready for the awards dinner. The book signings in Atlanta had been mob scenes, albeit happy and exciting mob scenes, but tension-producing, all the same. Lydia LaGrange was already making noises about putting Connie on a promotional tour of *Rings and Things* at the major feminist bookstores all around the country. The spotlight on Connie was much brighter than it had ever been.

The last few weeks had helped Gail come to understand Connie's shaky self-image. Knowing more about Connie's history and all her questions about her true persona, it wasn't hard for Gail to see how recent events could have strained Connie to a breaking point. And then there was the possibility Gail's arrival in Connie's life as more than a one-time-only-good-deal stand-in editor was a contributing factor as well. Whether distress or pleasant stress, stress is stress, and if someone is vulnerable—

But Connie wasn't showing classic stroke symptoms. Bell's Palsy. Maybe that's what it is.

And then Gail was off again on another mental goose chase about what if and what next.

IT WAS NEARLY six o'clock when a nurse came to the door of the waiting room and called Gail's name.

"Right here." Gail sprinted the distance to reach her. "How is she?

Is she all right? Can I see her?"

"She's in one of the exam rooms, waiting for one of our on-call doctors. She asked if I'd bring you back to hear what the tests we've run show." The nurse pushed the swinging door behind her open with her butt. "This way."

She led Gail down a hallway of curtained-off rooms. "Here we are." She grabbed the edge of the curtain and pulled it back for Gail to enter. "The doctor should be here in a minute."

"Hi." Gail hurried to the side of the bed. Connie was dressed and sitting up, but her color wasn't good and her face was still pulling to the right. "How'd it go?" She rubbed Connie's back briefly.

Connie offered a wan smile. "I only passed out twice. Once for the blood work and again when they injected me with dye."

"Why the dye?"

Before Connie answered, the doctor arrived. Gail couldn't believe her eyes. It was Doctor Ayinala, the doctor who had told her Marissa was brain dead and that she wasn't going to come out of her coma. She waited to see if he would give any indication he remembered her. He didn't seem to. She was oddly relieved and not at all surprised. Why would he remember one conversation with someone he regarded as an unauthorized intruder? At least in the current situation, Connie was able to speak for herself. Since she had asked for Gail to be there, he couldn't push her aside, an unwelcome non-entity.

"Hello. I'm Doctor Ayinala. I'm one of the neurologists on staff here. The ER doctor who ordered up your tests wanted me to come in and look over the test results to confirm his diagnosis. I agreed to meet with you and tell you what we've found." He flipped through a sheaf of notes in his hand. "I've got your MRI films on the light board down the hall. Let's go take a look at them, shall we?"

He held the curtain back and made a sweeping motion with the papers he was holding.

"Can you walk, Connie?" Gail asked.

"I think so. Let me lean on you just in case, okay?"

Connie eased off the bed and gingerly took a few steps. Gail had Connie's elbow firmly in hand. They both were pleased when she seemed steadier on her feet than she had been earlier in the day. The threesome made their way down the hall.

"All right, then." The doctor flipped the switch to illuminate Connie's films. "You had two MRI's of your brain done, one with contrast dye and one without. The one without is unremarkable, but the one with dye is showing an abnormality right here." He used the tip of his pen to point to a specific spot. "It has the characteristics of a metastasized cancerous tumor."

Gail wanted to slap the man. No prelude. No cushioning the blow. No consideration whatsoever for the impact of his words on the two women staring dumbstruck at the undecipherable blobs on the screen in front of them. Two years ago, she had suspected him of being nine parts ego, one part arrogance, with the bedside manner of a viper. His current conduct left no doubt.

She knew he was still talking. She saw his lips moving, and occasionally, a word would find its way through the fog growing ever-thicker in her brain and strike a familiar chord. She also knew Connie was standing by her side crying, but her presence seemed as surreal as the blathering of the doctor.

Gail forced herself to focus on each moment and concentrate on each separate word.

"My recommendation is to find a good oncologist. I can recommend someone with privileges here at the hospital, if you wish. You need to find the primary cancer source and deal with that first. Once you know what kind of cancer this is, then we'll know if we've got treatment options for this secondary growth. I can also make a recommendation on an excellent neurosurgeon, when the time comes."

The doctor stopped talking to the screen and turned to look at Connie and Gail. "Any questions?"

Gail struggled to retain her composure. "As a matter of fact, I do have a question. Do you keep your head crammed up your ass every minute of every day, or do you sometimes pull it out and take a look at the carnage you've left in your wake?"

In a quick, fluid motion, Gail snatched the two MRI films from the lighted screen and yanked the pages of paper from the doctor's hand. "Go to hell. And while you're there, let the devil himself teach you some manners. You're the sorriest excuse for a doctor I've ever seen." She felt the bile rising in her throat. "No, correction. You're the sorriest excuse for a human being I've ever seen."

Gail took Connie by the hand. "Come on. Let's go." She and Connie started up the hall.

"You can't walk out of here with those films and our reports." Doctor Ayinala caught up with them and blocked their path.

"A piece of advice. Unless you want to spend the rest of your life singing soprano with the Vienna Boys' Choir, get out of my way."

"Have a nice evening, *ladies.*" The sarcasm in Doctor Ayinala's voice was almost too much for Gail. Connie tugged at Gail's hand and said in a voice so soft it was barely audible, "He's not worth it, Gail. Take me home." But for Connie's request, she'd have decked him.

THE WEEKEND LOOMED before them, an infinity of unanswered questions and immobilizing fear. It was nearly eight o'clock Friday evening when they got back to Sweetwater—much too late to call doctors' offices to arrange appointments. All they could do was wait for two interminable days. Wait and worry.

They decided the available pool of doctors was much better in

Atlanta than in eastern Tennessee, so at daybreak Saturday, they set off in both vehicles for Connie's house. Since she had no idea how long she'd be in Atlanta, Gail brought the cats along. Despite seeming to sense Gail's anxiety, Cubbie and Annette behaved themselves perfectly for the drive.

"Do you want to go out and get some dinner?" Gail asked after they'd brought things inside and gotten the cats situated with a litter box in the bathroom and their food bowls in a corner of the dining room.

"No, it would be a waste of time and money. I'm too upset to eat." Connie was pale as a ghost. The corner of her mouth wasn't quite as drawn as it had been the day before. Gail hoped it was a good sign.

"Do you want to go to a movie? It might be a good way to pass a couple of hours."

"I don't think so. Just a different way to waste time and money."

"A walk, maybe? Or we could listen to music and read." Gail's knew her mind was every bit as overloaded as Connie's was, but she felt obliged to at least make an attempt at diversion.

Connie shook her head. "I know what you're trying to do, sweetheart, but it's no use. If we agree not to talk about it, we won't say a word all weekend. We might as well give in to the inevitable." Connie dropped into one of the leather chairs in the living room. Gail sat on the love seat across from her so she could watch Connie's face.

"You know one of the first things the doctors will ask me is if there's a history of any kind of cancer in my family. Since I never knew either of my parents, I won't be able to tell them. They'll have to test for everything. Do you think they could knock me out? I won't be able to stand seeing all the needles and smelling the rubbing alcohol."

"It might not be so bad. I'll bet they can do a full body CT scan to check for almost everything. If so, needles won't be required. And they might have to do some chest x-rays to look for lung cancer. And probably a mammogram. You'll get through all of those without too much trouble. If they want to look for skin cancer, that should be easy, too."

"What do you think they'll find?" Connie's voice cracked and tears splashed down her cheeks.

Gail stepped across to the chair where Connie was sitting and knelt beside her. "There's no way for us to know, babe. I guess breast cancer is a possibility, but I don't know what kind of cancer is likely to spread to the brain."

"We could look on-line."

"We could, but I don't think we should. Right now, we're better off to believe ignorance is bliss. The more we read, the more confused and crazy we'll get. Let's let a doctor guide us through this."

"But all the magazines say you have to be an informed and participative partner in your own health care."

"And we will be — when we know what we're dealing with." Gail rubbed Connie's arm. "Why torture ourselves with information about lung cancer or ovarian cancer or whatever other kind of cancer when it might not be the type you've got."

"Oh, God, Gail. I have cancer." Connie dissolved into hysterical sobs. Gail did her best to fight it, but the emotion was too great. They clung to one another and cried until they were hoarse. And then they cried some more.

CONNIE'S PRIMARY PHYSICIAN, Doctor Anthony Lohman, agreed to see her first thing Monday. With Connie and Gail waiting outside the door to his office when his receptionist arrived to unlock it, he'd have been hard pressed to turn her away. Unlike Doctor Ayinala at Knoxville General, he demonstrated compassion for the situation. He sat with Connie on the settee in his office and patted her consolingly on the shoulder as Connie and Gail told him about Connie's difficulties with falling down when they were in Sweetwater and showed him the MRI films and lab reports from Knoxville General. Then they talked at length about which of the many oncologists in the city she should be referred to.

Doctor Lohman had his receptionist set up Connie's intake appointment with a woman he described as "the best cancer doctor in Georgia." They would meet with her at three o'clock, only a few hours hence. Gail suspected he had made a personal call to Doctor Edna McIntyre the moment they left his private office to ensure things happened expeditiously. She had heard horror stories of thirty-day waits to get on busy oncologist's schedules. Thank goodness Connie would be seen right away.

After seeing Doctor McIntyre, they set about arranging appointments for all the tests she prescribed. By day's end, Connie was scheduled for a mammogram, a colonoscopy, a full body CT scan, an examination by a dermatologist, chest x-rays, and every other cancer screening test in modern medicine's arsenal. The week was a blur of trips to various medical facilities. To her relief, Connie didn't pass out when they drew her blood to check for leukemia. The tests took all week. Then there was another endless weekend to endure before they would see Doctor McIntyre to get the results.

Monday morning, they left Decatur two hours before their nine o'clock appointment to be sure they'd make their way through traffic and get to the doctor's office near Piedmont Hospital in downtown Atlanta on time. They were plenty early. They spent forty minutes roaming the hallways of the multi-building office park to fill the extra time. The final ten minutes in the waiting room of Doctor McIntyre's office seemed to take almost as long as the previous ten days had. They sat silent as statues, side by side, holding hands in the brightly-colored chairs.

At long last, they were called in to the doctor's consultation room.

"Good morning, ladies." Doctor McIntyre smiled warmly. Gail feared the doctor's big smile meant the worst possible news. "I'm sure you've had an agonizing weekend."

Cut to the chase. Neither one of us can take this much longer.

"Sit down and try to relax." The doctor gestured to two chairs, then picked up a fat file folder from her desk and leaned against the front edge.

"What kind of cancer do I have?" Connie stood up from the chair she'd barely sat down in.

Doctor McIntyre scanned the contents of the file. "I have very good news for you this morning."

"Skin cancer?" Connie guessed.

"No," the doctor replied.

Gail took a stab. "Early stage breast cancer?"

"No, not breast cancer, either." The doctor closed the file folder and looked directly at Connie. "In fact, I don't believe you have any kind of cancer at all."

"How can that be? The doctor in Knoxville said I've got a tumor in my brain, and it's cancer that spread from somewhere else." Connie folded her hands beneath her chin and grabbed the collar of her blouse.

"The brain is a very complex organ. We've really only begun to understand even the most basic things about how it works and how to diagnose what's wrong with it when something goes awry."

"But we saw the MRI films. There was a big shadow on one side. It's got to be something." Gail leaned forward in her chair.

"I've looked at those films, and yes, there is evidence you've had some sort of brain episode, but based on the results of all your tests last week, there's nothing here to suggest what showed up on your MRI is a cancerous growth." Doctor McIntyre placed the file folder on the desk behind her.

"Did she have a stroke, doctor?" Gail asked.

"I'm not a specialist in brain treatment, but no, this doesn't look to be a stroke, either."

"What wrong with me, then?" Connie was still standing in front of her chair, grasping and releasing her collar in a nervous tic.

"I have a suspicion, but want to refer you to a neurologist and let him tell you the most likely reason for your difficulties walking and the distortion of your mouth week before last."

"Will I have to have more tests?"

"Probably a few, but I'm fairly sure the ultimate news you get will be much less devastating than metastasized brain cancer. I'll have the staff at the front desk get you set up to see Doctor Phil Wentworth. He's a great guy. I think you'll like him."

CONNIE COULDN'T GET an appointment with Doctor Wentworth until Thursday. With the specter of cancer not looming as large, the wait was a little easier. Gail drove them to the doctor's office at the Atlanta Center for Neurological Disorders early Thursday afternoon. Connie filled out the five-page questionnaire the receptionist handed her, then, a few minutes later, they were taken back to an exam room.

"Hello, I'm Phil Wentworth." A short, round, balding man wearing running shoes, cotton twill slacks, cardigan sweater, white shirt, and bowtie, entered the room where Gail and Connie sat on straight-backed chairs. "Which one of you is Connie Martin?"

Gail thought she must be looking at the prototype for the Fisher-Price "Weebles" collection. He looked to her to be the sort of fellow who would bob right back up on his feet if someone gave him a push to try to topple him over. *Weebles wobble, but they won't fall down.* Gail couldn't keep the jingle from the television commercials she'd seen at least forty years earlier out of her mind.

"I am." Connie offered her hand. She and Gail remained seated on the chairs along the wall.

"Nice to meet you." Doctor Wentworth clasped her hand in both of his. "And you are?" he asked, looking at Gail.

"Gail Larsen. I'm Connie's...uh..."

"Partner. Yes, it's good you came with her. I'm always glad to have a family member along when I meet with a patient." He shook Gail's hand, then sat on a small four-legged stool on wheels in front of the two women. Gail was impressed with his adroit manner. How he so quickly discerned the nature of her relationship to Connie was a mystery, but one she was happy to let go unsolved.

"I've seen your test results, including the MRI films Doctor Lohman said you'd brought him from your visit to the hospital in Knoxville." Once again, Gail was impressed with the man. He knew the name of Connie's doctor without having to read it from a file and knew where Connie had gone for emergency treatment.

"I understand Edna McIntyre has told you the tests you were put through might have been unnecessary. You know, we use the expression 'practicing medicine' for a reason." He chuckled in a way Gail found endearing.

He looked intently at Connie. "I concur with Doctor McIntyre's assessment. What showed up on the pictures of your noggin isn't a brain tumor." He clapped his hands several times rapidly. "And I applaud that good news."

"But there still is something wrong, isn't there?" Connie asked.

"Yes, the MRI does show an anomaly." Doctor Wentworth paused for a few seconds. "I'm sorry to tell you, in my professional opinion, you have MS—multiple sclerosis."

"Are you sure?" Connie slipped her hand into Gail's.

"Not absolutely. I want to have some additional tests done, but I look at a lot of brain scans, and this looks to be a classic MS plaque deposit."

"What kind of tests? When? Will I have to be poked with more needles?" Connie's skyrocketing apprehension level made her voice pinched and tight.

"I want you to have what we call a VER and a BAER. The letters stand for 'visual evoked response' and 'brain-stem auditory evoked response.' They're easy tests. We'll put a helmet on you with electrode sensors and track what your eyes and brain do in response to some stimuli. We've got a testing center right here in this building. I can probably get you in down there before you leave today."

"Okay, that sounds all right." Connie sighed in relief.

"I also want to do a test to measure if there's any breakdown in the myelin sheath surrounding your spinal cord. It's actually the most definitive test we have to diagnose MS."

"How do you do that?" Connie gripped Gail's hand more tightly.

"It's a quick procedure called a lumbar puncture."

"You mean spinal tap, right?" Gail used the now-passé descriptive phrase.

"Yes. I'll draw out a small amount of spinal fluid and have it analyzed."

"I'll faint." Connie turned white.

"You might think you will, but I bet you'll come through with flying colors. I've done a lot of them, so I'm quite good at it. And since I know you're nervous about it, I'll make sure you never have to see the n-e-e-d-l-e." He spelled the word slowly, smiling at Connie while he did so.

"When will you do that?" Gail noted the brave expression Connie coaxed to her face.

"I'd like to do it today. The sooner we know for sure if this is MS, the sooner we can get you in a treatment program."

"What sorts of treatments do you recommend?" Gail asked.

"If it's all right with you two, I'd rather do the tests and be sure it's MS we're dealing with before I load you up on all the information you'll need."

"Can I be with her while she has the tests?"

"No, I'm sorry, you can't. We need her to be free of distractions while she does the evoked response tests, which means you can't be in the room for those. And the lumbar puncture is done in a sterile environment. I'll be performing it in our surgery pavilion on the top floor."

"How long will it take to do everything?"

"Maybe an hour at the evoked response lab and twenty minutes for the LP."

"I better do the ones with the helmet first. If I pass out from the other one, I won't be able to do them today."

"Actually, I'm going to take you right up to the surgery pavilion now. I know you'll surprise yourself at how well you hold up, and if we get it behind you right away, you can do the easy evoked response tests without the anxiety over this other one distracting you."

"So we'll know before we leave here today if Connie has MS?"

"Probably not. It will take a day to have the spinal fluid analyzed, but I can call you tomorrow when the report comes in. Then I'll get you back in here, and we'll talk about next steps." Doctor Wentworth rose from the stool where he'd been sitting since the conversation began. "Climb up on this exam table, Connie, and I'll check your reflexes."

He spent the next several minutes having Connie perform simple acts, such as pushing against his palms with her fists and resisting pressure from his hands with her arms straight out from her shoulders. He tapped her knees, ankles, and elbows with his triangular rubber mallet and had her touch various places on her face with her fingertip while her eyes were closed. Gail watched as he put Connie through her paces. It was fairly easy to tell when Connie couldn't do something as well as she ought to.

Multiple sclerosis, Gail mused. *I don't know the first thing about MS.*

"All right, lovely lady," Doctor Wentworth said to Connie when he was finished, "may I escort you upstairs?" He offered Connie his hand to help her off the table, then offered her his arm as though she were his date for the dance. "Gail, come with us. I'll show you where you can wait while I get to know a little more about our Miss Connie."

GAIL HAD TWO hours to fill until she'd see Connie again. She used the time to browse the literature on the racks in the waiting room. She found herself wishing she hadn't.

There were more than twenty-five separate brochures from the National Multiple Sclerosis Society, none of which Gail would describe as "uplifting." The titles alone were enough to make her recoil. "Controlling Stress to Help Manage Your MS;" "Coping with Emotional Changes brought on by MS;" Essential Nutrition for MS Patients;" "Adjusting Intimacy Levels due to MS;" "Controlling Spasticity in MS Patients;" "Facts and Myths about Longevity for MS Sufferers;" "Financial Planning for a Life with MS."

But the one that smacked her right between the eyes was entitled, "A Guide for Caregivers—Helping a Loved One with MS." It was broken into three main parts: managing major changes, managing specific issues, and taking care of the caregiver. The opening sentence in the booklet pulled the air right out of her lungs. "Caring for someone with MS is likely to be physically, mentally, and emotionally exhausting. Since MS is different for everyone afflicted by the disease, a caregiver's role is to hope for the best but plan for the worst. This may include converting a house for handicapped-accessibility, protecting assets and making long-range financial contingency plans, and finding appropriate medical professionals and support groups to assist when the ravages of the illness strike your loved one."

Gail was having her own version of an evoked response test. Her feelings were a mix of rekindled grief, new-found terror, and at least a little resentment. How could it be that she was going to live her life with yet another woman who had a daily battle with a life-changing disease? The pictures in the brochures conjured memories of Marissa and all of the ways they had had to adapt to her polio. The information with the pictures left Gail reeling from what appeared to be an endless list of unpleasant possibilities which might surface in Connie's future. And why was it she had to be the one who got another turn in the barrel with a lover affected by an ugly infirmity? Hadn't she paid her dues with Marissa?

Suddenly, she felt very much as she had felt on her first day at the Magnolia Suites with Connie. Her instinct was to flee the building, climb in her truck, and make tracks for Sweetwater as fast as the wheels would carry her.

I can't face anything this awful again. I just can't.

Gail turned her back on the rack of MS leaflets and walked to a chair as far away from it as possible. She picked up a two-year-old copy of National Geographic and thumbed through the pages without comprehending a word of what she read.

"Hi. Sorry it took so long." Connie dropped into the chair next to Gail.

Gail had been so distracted by her mental wanderings she hadn't seen Connie enter the room.

"How did it go?"

"Doctor Wentworth was right. I was fine with the lumbar puncture. He really knows how to make a patient feel important and safe. The hold-up was in the evoked response lab. There were three other patients ahead of me before I got my turn in the helmet."

"Did they tell you how you did?"

"No, the doctor will give me all the results when we see him one day next week or the week after. He asked me if I wanted him to call me tomorrow with the lumbar puncture results, but I said I'd rather wait to see him face to face to talk about everything."

"Oh, okay. Are you ready to head for the house?"

"More than ready."

They left the waiting room and walked down the busy hall to the elevator filled with people. Connie waited until they were outside to speak. "You seem upset. Did something happen while I was having my tests?"

"I think the pressure of the last two weeks was the only force holding me together. Now that we sort of know what's going on, I realize I've been wrapped tighter than a top, and I'm tired to the bone.

Nothing's wrong. I need to get some rest, that's all." Gail hoped her words were more convincing to Connie than they sounded to her ears.

"I know what you mean. A ten-ton load has been taken off my shoulders, but I'm still so exhausted, I could drop right here on the pavement."

"Don't. I'm too tired to drag you to the truck." Gail briefly embraced Connie's shoulder. They walked slowly to the parking lot.

"I'd never have thought being told I have MS would be good news, but compared to what I thought I was facing, we probably should throw a party to celebrate."

Gail unlocked the truck and held the door for Connie as she got in. "Maybe, but not this weekend, though. All I want to do is sleep."

"With me, I hope." Connie reached out from the cab and touched Gail's face gently. "I haven't been too good in the bedroom since — gosh, since the night of the awards banquet, really, when I stop to think about it."

"You had good reason, love." Gail closed the door and walked around to the driver's side. She was surprised — and pleased — to find she was having pulse-quickening thoughts about what she and Connie might do to, for, and with one another at the little house in Decatur.

Later that evening, they were both delighted when passion trumped fatigue. As Connie brought Gail to yet another climax, she thanked her lucky stars she hadn't allowed her fears to make her run away to Sweetwater. The slumber granted to them after making love was a balm from the gods.

Chapter
Twelve

ON FRIDAY, THE receptionist from Doctor Wentworth's office called to set up Connie's appointment to discuss her test results. He would meet with them a week from the following Tuesday at nine. Saturday, Connie and Gail had what felt like the first normal day they'd been granted in two weeks. They took in a movie, had an early, leisurely dinner, went for a stroll around Connie's neighborhood, and took advantage of every opportunity to glory in their love for one another. Connie didn't bring up the topic of MS, and Gail was more than willing to let it lie undisturbed.

Sunday night, before Gail left to drive up to Sweetwater, she and Connie sat in the living room in the mama bear chairs, each lost in her own thoughts. At last, Gail spoke.

"You're sure you don't mind taking care of the cats for a week or so? I really need to winterize the cabin. A cold snap might hit any time. And I've got a doctor's appointment on Friday, too. I can cancel it, if you want."

"No, you should go take care of things in Sweetwater. We'll be fine. I know the cats' routines now, and they both seem to like me, so your conscience should be clear." Connie hesitated a moment before continuing. "Promise me you'll come back. I hate to think what they might do if I became their only mother." Connie bridged the gap between the two chairs and caressed Gail's arm.

Gail forced a tinny laugh. "Hey, they're my furry children. How can you remotely suggest I'd abandon them?" She rose from her chair. "I guess I should hit the road. Sunday night traffic is always a bitch." She scooped up Cubby who had been snoozing by her feet. "Behave yourself, mister." She gave him a squeeze and let him drop lightly to the floor. "Tell your sister to mind her manners, too."

"Any advice for me?" Connie asked as she lowered the footrest and left her chair to stand beside Gail.

"Try not to worry about what the doctor might say. Get some rest. Call me if anything happens."

With a hug and a kiss, Gail walked out the front door of Connie's house.

GAIL WASN'T EAGER to keep her monthly session with her therapist, but she did need to make sure her house was ready if the mercury plunged. She was a little taken aback to discover how relieved she felt to be driving away from Atlanta—and it wasn't only the city itself she was glad to be leaving behind. How much longer would Connie leave sealed the topic of her likely diagnosis of MS? And what would Connie think of Gail's feelings on the subject? She and her mental demons argued all the way to Sweetwater.

As she walked up the ramp to the front door at her cabin, the fears that had assailed her at Doctor Wentworth's office roared back with a vengeance. She had chickened out before reading all the worst case scenarios in the MS literature, but she had seen enough to know wrist and ankle braces were typical MS apparatus. Wheel chairs, electric scooters, canes—oh, God, how could she do it all again?

Sunday night was anything but the usual hallowed peace she had always found at Sweetwater Cabin. Seeing Marissa's leg braces in the corner of her bedroom when she opened her eyes Monday morning made her want to run again—but where? All her secure sanctuaries had been corrupted. No place felt safe any more. She spent the next four days putting up storm windows and wrapping water pipes. She brought in the hoses and put insulated covers over the outdoor faucets. She drained the water heater and checked the seals before refilling it. She changed the furnace filter and the filter on the well pump. She raked leaves and pruned bushes and did anything and everything to busy herself—except think about what might lay ahead for Connie. Maybe talking to Doctor Wilburn would be a good thing after all. Someone was going to have to help her figure out how to back out of the promises she'd made to Connie. No way in hell was she going to spend the next however long being dragged backwards through another emotional wringer. She'd done that with Marissa, and once was more than enough.

"TELL ME ABOUT the past month, Gail." Doctor Wilburn reached for her bottle of water, generating the opening notes of the F-Flat Sonata.

Gail did her best to explain about her intensified involvement with Connie, Connie's revelations about her early years, the awards banquet, the scare over Connie's health, the battery of tests, and her probable MS.

"When I suggested you find a way to become more involved in life, you certainly took it to heart, didn't you?" Doctor Wilburn's smile left Gail thinking, *Holy cow, the woman is human. Who knew?*

"I might not have, if I'd have known how it would make me feel."

"Tell me more about that."

Gail ummed and urred and stalled for as long as she dared. Doctor

Wilburn cleared her throat as if to say, "I'm waiting."

"I'm not sure I want to spend the rest of my life with someone who's got a serious illness," Gail blurted out.

"I see."

"You think I'm a selfish little shit, don't you?"

"More important is what you think of yourself, Gail."

"I think I'm a selfish little shit."

"All right. What else?"

Gail looked everywhere except at her therapist and wondered why she had thought meeting with her would be a good idea. "I don't care if I'm being selfish. I deserve a chance at a happy, easy time of things, not another situation where every aspect of my life is complicated by my partner's illness."

"Anything more you want to say?"

I hate you, and I hate myself for ever thinking you could help me with this.

"I spent almost half my adult life with Marissa, and almost every minute of our time together was consumed with worrying about her when she coughed too much, wondering if I was making her do more than what she should because of her legs, dreading she might have the late-in-life set-backs so many polio patients have. All of my concern was wasted. I lost her anyway. I don't want to go through that sort of anguish again."

"You can't. Marissa and Connie aren't the same person. Each relationship is unique."

Hello? Are you listening? I don't care how many ways Connie is different from Marissa. I'm worried about the horrible way they're alike.

"Doesn't feel that way to me. If I stay with Connie, it might end up being the same thing all over. I'd rather be alone."

"You have the right to make your choices."

"Gee, thanks." Gail's sarcasm hung in the air.

"And how does Connie feel about this?"

"About what?"

"About having MS, about how it affects you as her partner, or more to the point, about your preference to be alone instead of being with her."

"We haven't talked about it."

"I see."

More squirming and deep sighs from Gail before she spoke. "I guess you think I should."

"Wouldn't you want that courtesy if the situation were reversed?"

"I suppose."

Gail fought every step of the way, but the therapist put her through one of the most intense sessions she'd ever endured. It was clear to Gail Doctor Wilburn wasn't going to validate her hesitancies about setting herself up for what might be a string of potentially all-but-insurmountable hurdles, but Gail still wished she would. She gagged down her anger and frustration as best she was able, but as the hour drew to a close, she couldn't contain it any longer.

"Aren't you supposed to give me advice?" She slapped the palms of her hands on the table between them.

"I see my role as helping you seek your own internal advice."

"I can promise you, that didn't happen today. This was a complete waste of time." Gail pushed her back against her chair and crossed her arms defiantly.

"I'm sorry to hear you say so. Is there something I can do in our last few minutes together to help?"

Gail squinted at the therapist. "You're the shrink. You tell me."

Doctor Wilburn folded her hands in her lap briefly and then tapped her lips with her index finger before returning her hands to their original position. "Do you listen to country music?"

"Sometimes."

"Then you might know a song called 'The Dance.'"

"Sure. Garth Brooks."

"Think about the lyrics, Gail. There's some very good advice there, in my opinion." Doctor Wilburn unclasped her hands. "You can opt out of life's difficulties, but in doing so, you probably miss out on the sweetest dances, too. And sometimes, it takes until the second verse for you to find your true rhythm. Maybe you should let yourself listen to the whole song instead of sitting down too soon."

Gail willed herself not to cry until she was safely out of Wilburn's office and in her truck. She let the words from the song Doctor Wilburn mentioned play in her head. She hadn't gotten to dance with Marissa, and the aching disappointment was a relentless claw that still tore at her heart. According to Amy, the last words Marissa had thought to leave for Gail encouraged her to keep dancing.

Marissa. Sweet Marissa. What if she were given the chance to trade everything she had had with Marissa for the one thing they didn't have—a dance in one another's arms. Would she make the swap?

Of course not.

She sat behind the wheel and mulled over her years with Marissa Adler. Without a doubt, they had shared a satisfying, meaningful life. She didn't remember ever telling Doctor Wilburn about the fantasy she and Marissa had about Marissa's legs one day being healed so they could dance, yet it was the exact analogy Doctor Wilburn had drawn when suggesting she reflect on the words from "The Dance." Then it dawned on her: there are lots of ways to dance. Come to think of it, she and Marissa *had* danced in all of the ways that really mattered.

I'll be darned. Marcella Wilburn really didn't waste her parents' money when she went to therapist training.

A second revelation worked its way into Gail's conscious thought. There might be some pain along the way, but dancing with Connie Martin—with or without music—was exactly what she wanted to do.

GAIL DROVE TO her cabin. As she walked up the ramp, she thought to herself, "If it is MS and it gets really bad, at least Connie will be able to get around here."

She went inside and used the bathroom. Before they moved in, she and Marissa had rails installed on either side of the commode and in the bathtub to help Marissa more easily pull herself up from sitting positions. The rails had been there for so long Gail had become oblivious to them. Now they made her realize how perfectly normal they were — a useful fixture in a happy home.

She walked through the cabin and tried to look at everything with fresh eyes. Even though Marissa hadn't lived there for more than two years, the cabin was still basically as it had been when she was there. There were no rugs on any of the floors — Marissa had a tendency to trip on them. All the faucets were single-lever controlled, allowing Marissa to use one hand to steady herself if she needed to while washing up or getting a drink of water. Door fixtures were likewise flat and easily grasped, not round. To the extent possible, everything in the kitchen was stored in the upper cabinets rather than under the counter because it kept Marissa from having to bend down to reach something she needed. The bed was a raised platform style, giving Marissa a shorter distance to negotiate in lying down and getting up. The swing suspended from the ceiling on the deck off the bedroom was hung a little higher than usual because it was more accessible for Marissa.

Gail stepped out onto the deck. She stood in the chill air of the early November forenoon and looked out over the valley behind the cabin. So much had happened to her in less than half a year. She remembered what Connie had said to her the first time they had been on this deck, gazing into the distance: "Maybe Marissa needed to know you're ready to accept what the rest of your life might bring before she could finally let go and move on herself."

I hope Connie was right.

The sky had been low and gray all morning, but was showing signs of brightening. As Gail was about to go inside, the sun broke through the clouds and sent shafts of light shimmering off the lingering clouds. Gail smiled through her tears at the "God sky."

"Okay, Ris. I get the message. We're both ready for whatever comes next. The music is still playing. It's up to me to keep dancing."

On her way through the bedroom, Gail collected the leg braces from the place they'd stood for two-and-a-half years and carried them out to her truck. She knew of an organization that would retrofit them for someone else to use.

GAIL HAD THE key in the lock, on her way out the door for Atlanta when the phone rang. She assumed it would be Connie wondering when to expect her.

"Hi, sweetheart."

"I'm fond of you, too, but I hope you won't mind if I stick with calling you 'Gail.'"

"Penny Jean Skramstaad."

"In the flesh."

"How long have you been trying to reach me?"

"This is my first try. Why?"

"Never mind. I haven't been here much lately. Maybe you should play the lottery today. Your luck seems to be running high. By the way, shouldn't you be at work? I hope nothing's wrong."

"Everything's fine — better than fine, in fact. I'm taking a couple of days off while I move."

"Does this mean what I hope it does?"

"What do you hope it means?"

"You climbed on the train for Andreaville."

"All aboard. Woo, woo."

"Good for you, kid. I'm proud of you." Gail swallowed hard to make the lump in her throat go away.

"Thanks. Now I guess we really can think of ourselves as sisters."

"Sisters twice over. So, you and Andrea decided you wanted to set up housekeeping in a new place?"

"Actually, I'm moving to her house."

"The mansion on Lake Minnetonka?"

"Uh huh."

"What about Bob, that piece of work also known as Andrea's soon-to-be former husband?"

"He's already gone back to Santa Fe. Andrea suspected he'd had a long-term affair with some woman down there. She was right. He's decided to rumple the sheets with her again. He's basically told Andrea as long as she doesn't try to suck him dry on alimony, he'll fade quietly into the sunset. Andrea would probably have gotten the house in the divorce settlement anyhow, so she's asked me to move in with her."

"Any fears you're going too fast?"

"Are you kidding me? I've got at least thirty-five years of catching up to do. Andrea feels the same way. I've finally found someone who makes me feel the way I've always wished for. Why would I consider wasting a minute apart when I could spend it with her? Who knows what's around the next corner?" Penny's observation brought back Marilyn's similar comment when telling about how she and Evan had teamed up.

"Good point."

"What about you and Connie?"

Gail was all set to tell Penny about Connie's apparent illness, but then reconsidered. It really wasn't the important news anyhow.

"Remember what you said a minute ago about you and Andrea? Change the names to Gail and Connie, delete the part about jerk of a husband and palatial abode, and you've got the picture."

"I guess that explains your remark about not having been home much lately."

"Right."

"Where will you guys live? Up in the woods or down in the city?"

"We're still deciding. Let me give you the number at Connie's house. I'll probably be splitting my time between here and there for at least the next couple of months. I suppose I should break down and get a cell phone so people can find me wherever I am."

"Good idea. Call me when you do. Oh, that reminds me. I was calling you to tell you my new number at Andrea's. Of all the things I've lost, I miss my mind the most."

They exchanged information about new addresses and phone numbers.

"I really am happy for you, Penny."

"Ditto for you, old friend. We might get to dance at one another's weddings after all."

After she got off the phone with her friend of longest standing, Gail slipped the Judy Collins CD in the player. For old time's sake, she took the photo from the mantle and gazed into Marissa's face. One last time, she felt the thrill of holding Marissa in her arms while music filled the room — filled her heart — as the dance of life continued.

"NICE TO SEE both of you again." Doctor Wentworth came around his desk and shook hands with Gail and Connie as they were shown into his personal office at the Center for Neurological Disorders Tuesday morning. "Let's sit over here and talk." He led the way to a grouping of chairs to the left. "Do you have any questions for me before I tell you what your tests have shown?"

Connie looked at Gail and shook her head.

Gail answered for both of them. "No, but we'll probably have plenty before we leave."

"All right, then. I'll use some big words to start — you know how we doctors try to prove we were paying attention in class — but if there's anything you want me to go over again, stop me, and we won't go any further until you're comfortable." Doctor Wentworth opened his laptop computer and pulled up Connie's record.

"First, the analysis of your cerebrospinal fluid is showing elevated immunoglobulin counts and oligoclonal bands. Your levels are about three times higher than what a normal reading would be. Both of those are indicators of MS. In combination with the shadow on your brain MRI, the outcome of your evoked response tests, and my evaluation of you last week, I am ninety-nine percent certain you have the disease." He clipped the lid of his laptop shut.

"MS is a disorder of the autoimmune system. What happened to you a few weeks ago is called an MS exacerbation. In other words, the illness attacked you. It caused an inflammation, and then left a plaque deposit in your brain. Plaque is nothing more than scar tissue from the inflammation. That's what you see on the MRI film. The process is called demyelination. Nerve impulses traveling along your spinal cord and brain are interrupted because the plaque gets in the way. Do you understand so far?" He looked at both women.

"I think so. How often will I have these exacerbations?" Connie asked.

"God alone knows, and he's not telling. It's different for every MS patient. For some, they come in clusters, and they have several in a short period of time. For others, they have one, and then don't notice another one for years."

"You said 'don't notice.' You mean I might have them and not know it?"

"Yes, in fact, as I looked more carefully at your MRI, I'd say you've probably had MS for as long as five years, but obviously, weren't aware of it."

"How bad is Connie's MS?"

Doctor Wentworth tipped his head from side to side. "On a ten-point scale, ten being the worst I've ever seen, she's about a three."

"So not too bad?" Gail asked expectantly.

The doctor directed his reply to Connie, although Gail had asked the question. "Not bad at all. In fact, because this is a late onset, I don't think you will have a particularly aggressive form of MS. The disease usually shows up when someone is in her late twenties or thirties. With you being in your early fifties, I'm hopeful this will be more of an annoyance than a true life-changing illness."

Gail and Connie looked at one another, relief written all over their faces.

"That's not to say we can ignore it," Doctor Wentworth said, "but, with luck, you can manage it very successfully with little alteration in your day-to-day life."

Gail placed her hand on Connie's forearm. "When we were here the other day you said something about treatments for Connie – "

"Yes, I'd recommend starting a beta interferon drug right away. It's administered weekly, and according to the clinical trials, it significantly reduces both the number of exacerbations and the severity of those that do occur."

"So I'll have to take a pill every week?"

Doctor Wentworth laid his hand on Connie's knee. "Sorry, dear. It's only available as an injection."

"I'll need to come here and get a shot once a week?" The dismay in Connie's voice was plain.

"Worse still – you give them to yourself."

"Oh, I couldn't! Not ever." Gail feared Connie might pass out on the spot.

"Or have Gail give them to you."

It was Gail's turn to consider falling out of her chair and onto the floor in a dead faint.

"We'll arrange for a home health care nurse to visit you and teach you how to do it. A month from now, you'll be surprised at how easily it's become part of your routine."

Neither Gail nor Connie gave voice to their substantial doubts about the accuracy of his statement. They spent another forty minutes with the doctor, going over everything from how often Connie should have MRI's done to what to do if they suspected a new exacerbation. He assured them Connie could keep writing for as long as the muses visited, but he cautioned them about the likelihood for increased fatigue, inability to tolerate heat, and the probability depression would become evident, to some greater or lesser extent. He told them a high percentage of all MS patients suffer from clinical depression, but the medical experts hadn't determined if it was part of the illness or a secondary condition brought on by the life changes and uncertainties of having MS. He explained what they should watch for and how to manage it if it appeared. He stood to indicate their meeting was drawing to a close.

"We have racks and racks of information out in the lobby. I suggest you take copies of most everything with you, but don't—I repeat do not—read it all tonight. And don't go on-line and overwhelm yourselves with everything there, either. You'll do better to assimilate this in small doses. Read enough to answer your immediate questions. You've got the rest of your long, happy lives to learn what you need to know about various nuances of multiple sclerosis."

"Thanks for everything, doctor." Gail offered him her hand.

"You're welcome, Gail. You take good care of our patient."

"I'll try."

"Will I see you again, or will you hand me off to another doctor?" Connie asked.

"No, you're stuck with me, Connie. I want to see you every three months for the next year. We'll see how you're doing by then, and probably cut back to twice a year." He wrapped his arm around Connie's shoulder and gave her a half-hug. "And call me if anything disconcerting comes up. I always return calls on the same day they come in, but it may take me a couple of hours to call you back, so don't panic if you don't hear from me right away."

They stopped at the desk and arranged for Connie's next appointment with Doctor Wentworth in early February. The receptionist handed Connie a plastic bag with handles and said, "This is a copy of each of the brochures on MS. Since you're a new patient here, I was sure you'd want to have them."

Connie took the bag with one hand, then clasped Gail's hand with the other. With a great deal more confidence than they felt, they turned from the desk and took their first steps toward whatever might lie ahead.

"I'M SORRY ABOUT all this." Connie waved her hand in the general direction of the stack of MS educational materials strewn on the coffee table in her living room. She and Gail were snuggled up close to each other on the love seat, where they'd been since getting back from Doctor Wentworth's office two hours earlier. Cubbie and Annette had curled up with their people and were sleeping blissfully. Whatever allergies to the cats Connie might have had early on seemed to have faded into a non-issue.

"Why should you apologize? It's not like you went out and intentionally contracted MS."

"But we didn't get to have any free and easy time together."

"Don't go borrowing trouble. You heard the doctor. This is only as significant as we make it. MS doesn't have to be the central part of our lives."

"But it might be, one day."

"If that day comes, we'll deal with it."

"I wouldn't blame you if you took Cubbie and Annette and went back to Sweetwater as fast as you could get there." Connie tickled the tabby draped over her lower legs.

Maybe sometime down the road—say on their tenth anniversary—Gail would tell Connie that very thought had passed her mind more than once in recent days. On the love seat, though, Gail let discretion be the better part of valor and refrained from so much as a passing reference to any such possibility. Thank goodness Doctor Wilburn and Penny Skramstaad had helped her see it would have been a lousy choice for a course of action. Even Garth Brooks, through the lyrics of a song, had contributed to the cause.

"People who love each other stand up in front of God and everybody and speak vows with notions such as 'better or worse, richer or poorer, in sickness and in health.' We haven't had a chance to say those things to each other, but we don't need to. As far as I'm concerned, it ought to be understood."

Connie caught a tear as it slipped down her cheek. "I don't know if I'd have been able to be as supportive for you as you've been for me."

"You would've been. I don't doubt it for a minute." Gail stroked Connie's hair. "We never have talked about where we're going to live, you know." Gail let her hand linger on the back of Connie's head. "Have you thought about it?"

"I don't really care as long as it's with you."

"Good answer, but we still need to decide."

"Do we need to decide today?"

"If you can put up with the fur flingers and me a while longer, I'm happy to stay right here for the time being. It's nice Lydia has been so understanding about giving me time off from editing to go to with you to your doctors' appointments, but I need to plug in my computer and get back to work one of these days."

"That makes two of us. I want to get started on my series of books with Hispanic lesbians. And maybe do some about some differently-abled women, too."

Gail smiled to herself. She had a hunch Connie would want to capture some of her experiences in a book plot.

"I've been thinking about something else, too," Connie said.

"Tell me what."

"I want to donate the royalties from my books with Hispanic characters to Agnes Scott College—maybe set up a scholarship fund for Hispanic women."

"I'm sure your books will be blockbusters," Gail replied. "And I'll put my editing stipends in the pot, too. The Connie Martin Scholarship Fund. What a great idea."

"I'll ask that it be called the 'Consuelo Martinez' fund."

"Better yet."

They sat quietly for a few moments.

Connie leaned forward and reached for one of the pamphlets, disrupting the cats' slumber as she did so. "I suppose we should read some of these."

Gail took it from Connie's hand and tossed it back on the table. "I vote for let's not. We took in a lot of information from the doctor today. I'd say we're off the hook 'til at least tomorrow." Gail pulled Connie back next to her on the love seat and the cats rearranged themselves again.

"Hey, remember my friend Penny in Minnesota?"

"Uh huh. I called you while you were at her dad's house in Plainfield in September. Gosh, that seems like such a long time ago."

"I know what you mean. We've been through two years' worth of worry in the past two months. Anyway, I heard from Penny while I was at the cabin in Sweetwater."

"Yeah?"

"She called to tell me she and Andrea have moved in together."

"Was she the woman at work Penny had the hots for?"

"The very one."

"Is she happy?"

"Ecstatic."

"What about you, Gail?"

"I'm ecstatic for her and beyond ecstatic for me." She hugged Connie extra hard.

Connie stirred slightly to reposition herself. "If we're not going to read up on MS, what should we do with the rest of the day?" She wrapped her arms around Gail's waist.

"Let's talk about all of the happy things the future holds for us."

"Some of it might not be so happy." Connie's voice caught. "I mean because of the MS and everything."

"The first night we were together up at Sweetwater and I told you about Marissa, you said I might need to consider the possibility she was trying to help me make the most of the rest of my life, even if she had to reach from beyond the grave to do it."

"I remember saying so." Connie sat up a little straighter.

"I think you were right. What could be more perfect than you and me, Connie? With some help from you and Doctor Wilburn, I've figured out I fell in love with Marissa — Marissa the person. I loved her for being her, neither because of nor in spite of her polio. And it's the same with you. I was already counting on spending the rest of my life with you. So what if the doctor says you've got MS? We've got something to trump it every time."

"What's that?"

"Each other."

Connie let the tears slide down her cheeks unchecked. Gail was content to hold her, silently, until the tears abated.

"Ready to talk about some happy prospects for our future?" Gail asked.

"Such as?"

"How about what songs we want to dance to at the reception for our commitment ceremony?"

"Okay. What's your favorite song to dance to?"

"What an easy question," Gail answered. "It's whatever's playing when I'm dancing with you, especially the second verse."

Other Jane Vollbrecht titles to look for:

Heart Trouble

Jackie Frackman is a consultant for a human resources firm based in Washington, D.C. Her job keeps her on the road much of the time delivering seminars, but she's grateful for the diversion. Her mother's death a few years earlier threw her family life into chaos. Her distress was further compounded when the only woman she'd ever loved backed out on their relationship. If it weren't for her job, Jackie would have little with which to fill her days.

Beth Novatny, rising managerial star in an office supply company in Atlanta, Georgia, is drowning in her deeply unsatisfying relationship with Sharon Chisholm. When Beth and Jackie meet in a seminar Jackie teaches, the mutual attraction is undeniable. Jackie and Beth acknowledge their love, but their happy life together is blocked by Beth's difficulties in extracting herself from her union with Sharon. As time goes by, there is one problem after another, though Jackie does her best to believe in a future with Beth.

Can Beth break free from Sharon? And can Jackie maintain the conviction in her heart to wait until Beth is finally hers alone? Or will they only succeed in generating the worst trouble of all - Heart Trouble.

ISBN 978-1-932300-58-1
1-932300-58-9

In Broad Daylight

Colleen McCrady, an aspiring writer, is on the verge of having her first novel accepted for publication. Elizabeth Albright, owner and managing editor of Standing in Sappho's Shadow Publishing — Triple S, as it's known in the lesbian publishing industry — gives Colleen a helping hand, and in the process, the two discover that a love for lesbian literature isn't the only thing they have in common.

Despite their romantic chemistry, Colleen and Elizabeth are at odds over other aspects of their relationship. Try as she might, Elizabeth can't get Colleen to reveal many details of her childhood and family life. Colleen is likewise stymied in her attempts to get Elizabeth to bring their relationship out into the open. The situation comes to a head when Colleen offers Elizabeth a new manuscript — one which will either take their relationship in a new direction or destroy the bonds between them.

Elizabeth is drawn into Colleen's tragic past as she discovers the long-buried secret that Colleen reveals in her new book. A mystery that is nearly a half century old is reopened when Elizabeth helps Colleen unravel the puzzle of what really happened to a lone, deaf black man who worked on Colleen's father's farm in northern Minnesota all those years ago. The story that unfolds is a multilayered tale of love and hate, bigotry and acceptance, heartbreak and triumph.

Once the mystery is solved, only one question lingers: can Elizabeth and Colleen step out of the shadows and stand together In Broad Daylight?

ISBN 978-1-932300-76-5
1-932300-76-7

Close Enough

It's 1942, and nineteen-year-old Hilda Stenkiewicz has a secret: she's given birth to an illegitimate child. Ashamed and overwhelmed, Hilda turns to her older brother, Martin, for help. On his advice, she gives the baby to Martin's Army buddy and his wife, who are strangers to her. Hilda, heartbroken and devastated, leaves her hometown in northern Pennsylvania to start anew. She forges a bond with Elaine Huebner, the landlady of her boarding house, and soon, their friendship blossoms into a much deeper relationship. With Elaine's help, Hilda tries to put her past behind her but she can never forget the baby she surrendered.

Frannie Brewster knows she's adopted but believes her birth mother abandoned her in an Alabama truck stop. Though gifted in academics and athletics, Frannie struggles with her identity — including her attraction to women at college and in the Women's Army Corps. After a long separation, Frannie is reunited with the lover she thought was lost to her forever. They discover that they share a similar heartache — one that will shape the rest of their days.

In the mid-1980s, before the convenience of cell phones and the Internet and with few clues to guide then, Hilda and Frannie go searching for the missing pieces in their respective lives. They draw ever closer to finding one another, but can they get Close Enough?

ISBN 987-1-932300-85-7
1-932300-85-6

FORTHCOMING TITLES
published by Yellow Rose Books

To Hold Forever
by Carrie Carr

In the seventh book of the Lex and Amanda series, three years have passed since Lexington Walters and her partner, Amanda, have taken over care of Lorrie, their rambunctious niece. Amanda's sister, Jeannie, has fully recovered from her debilitating stroke and returns with her fiance, ready to start a family. Adding to the volatile situation are Amanda's unsuccessful attempts to become pregnant.

Meanwhile, a hostile new relative arrives. He resents everything about Lex, including Amanda's love. Lex's brother, Hubert, recently paroled from prison, returns to Somerville with his own special surprise. And, an old adversary returns with more than a simple reunion in mind. Through it all, Lex begins to have doubts about continuing to run the ranch she's worked so hard to build.

Will Lex and Amanda finally have the family they have longed for? Or will the people and circumstances surrounding them destroy their chances?

Available April 2008

Blue Collar Lesbian Erotica
Edited by
Pat Cronin and Verda Foster

We don't all live in million dollar homes and drive fancy sports cars. We don't all live the life portrayed on television or in some of our books. Most of us live average lives in average homes and average circumstances. So why not have stories about us?

Blue Collar Lesbian Erotica is a collection of stories about the average lesbian in hot, steamy encounters in not-so-average places. Okay, sometimes the women are lawyers or actresses, but the sex doesn't always take place where you would expect: taxi cabs, convents, back yard tents.

This anthology goes outside the norm and provides a collection of stories you won't see anywhere else.

Available July 2008

Family Affairs
by Vicki Stevenson

Assigned to work undercover in a small-town nursing home, insurance investigator Stacey Gardner sets out to find fraudulent medical claims. When she meets local resident Liz Schroeder, romance begins to bloom. But then she discovers widespread elder abuse of which the entire nursing home staff is aware, and she fears that the whole town may be participating in a cover up.

Liz persuades Stacey to trust her to accept help from her LGBT family in exposing the abuse. The family discovers an elaborate scheme that seems to defy exposure. Many of the nursing home staff members are dedicated to stopping Stacey at any cost, and the rest are too intimidated to reveal any information.

The family presses on, determined to bring justice to the perpetrators and relief to the suffering patients. While the bond of love between Stacey and Liz grows ever stronger, they face the agonizing reailty that success will spell the end of the chance at happiness that both women desperately crave.

ISBN 978-1-932300-97-0

Download
by J. Y. Morgan

Cory Williams's settled and predictable life as a young, successful teacher in a small town in the middle of England is upended when she discovers the Internet and the joy of emailing friends all over the world. Her comfortable existence is thrown into total turmoil when she begins exchanging emails with an on-line American friend, Dylan Matthews, a computer technician who's having problems with her partner, Sarah.

The intensity of her friendship with Dylan forces Cory to examine choices she's made and secrets she's chosen to hide. The relationship between Cory and Dylan escalates, and both women realize that despite enormous obstacles impeding their hopes to be together, their feelings for one another are too powerful to deny.

Ultimately, Cory must choose between her true love and what she believes is her duty to her job, her country, and her family and friends. Cory's journey of self-discovery is complicated by the re-emergence of all her inner demons, the death of her beloved grandfather, and the pressures exerted on her by well-intentioned associates.

What course will Cory choose? What will be the upshot of that message from Dylan she opted to *Download*?

ISBN 978-1-932300-88-8

OTHER YELLOW ROSE PUBLICATIONS

Sandra Barret	Lavender Secrets	978-1-932300-73-4
Georgia Beers	Thy Neighbor's Wife	1-932300-15-5
Georgia Beers	Turning the Page	978-1-932300-71-0
Carrie Brennan	Curve	1-932300-41-4
Carrie Carr	Destiny's Bridge	1-932300-11-2
Carrie Carr	Faith's Crossing	1-932300-12-0
Carrie Carr	Hope's Path	1-932300-40-6
Carrie Carr	Love's Journey	978-1-932300-65-9
Carrie Carr	Strength of the Heart	978-1-932300-81-9
Carrie Carr	The Way Things Should Be	978-1-932300-39-0
Carrie Carr	Something to Be Thankful For	1-932300-04-X
Carrie Carr	Diving Into the Turn	978-1-932300-54-3
Linda Crist	Borderline	978-1-932300-62-8
Jennifer Fulton	Passion Bay	1-932300-25-2
Jennifer Fulton	Saving Grace	1-932300-26-0
Jennifer Fulton	The Sacred Shore	1-932300-35-X
Jennifer Fulton	A Guarded Heart	1-932300-37-6
Anna Furtado	The Heart's Desire	1-932300-32-5
Anna Furtado	The Heart's Strength	978-1-932300-93-2
Lois Glenn	Scarlet E	978-1-932300-75-8
Melissa Good	Eye of the Storm	1-932300-13-9
Melissa Good	Red Sky At Morning	978-1-932300-80-2
Melissa Good	Thicker Than Water	1-932300-24-4
Melissa Good	Terrors of the High Seas	1-932300-45-7
Melissa Good	Tropical Storm	978-1-932300-60-4
Maya Indigal	Until Soon	1-932300-31-7
Lori L. Lake	Different Dress	1-932300-08-2
Lori L. Lake	Ricochet In Time	1-932300-17-1
K. E. Lane	And, Playing the Role of Herself	978-1-932300-72-7
J. Y Morgan	Learning To Trust	978-1-932300-59-8
J. Y. Morgan	Download	978-1-932300-88-8
A. K. Naten	Turning Tides	978-1-932300-47-5
Lynne Norris	One Promise	978-1-932300-92-5
Meghan O'Brien	Infinite Loop	1-932300-42-2
Paula Offutt	Butch Girls Can Fix Anything	978-1-932300-74-1
Sharon Smith	Into The Dark	1-932300-38-4
Surtees and Dunne	True Colours	978-1-932300-52-9
Surtees and Dunne	Many Roads to Travel	978-1-932300-55-0
Vicki Stevenson	Family Values	978-1-932300-89-5
Cate Swannell	Heart's Passage	1-932300-09-0
Cate Swannell	No Ocean Deep	1-932300-36-8

About the Author

Jane was born and raised in a farming community in northwestern Minnesota, where she received her elementary education in a one-room country schoolhouse. She holds a Bachelors' degree from St. Cloud (Minnesota) State University and is a member of Lambda Iota Tau, an international literature honors society. In late 2004, she retired from Federal civil service after more than thirty years with the same agency. She is now pursuing her new career as an author and editor.

Second Verse is Jane's fifth novel. Her first two books, *Picture Perfect* and *Heart Trouble,* were finalists for Golden Crown Literary Society awards. Her third novel, *In Broad Daylight,* was published in January 2007, and her fourth book, *Close Enough,* was released in July 2007. She also has had several short stories included in anthologies.

Jane lives in the foothills of the north Georgia mountains with her partner of twelve years and their many cats. In addition to spending time at the computer writing and editing books, Jane enjoys tending her gardens, feeding the wildlife on her property, and playing the piano.

VISIT US ONLINE AT
www.regalcrest.biz

At the Regal Crest Website You'll Find

- The latest news about forthcoming titles and new releases

- Our complete backlist of romance, mystery, thriller and adventure titles

- Information about your favorite authors

- Current bestsellers

Regal Crest titles are available from all progressive booksellers and online at StarCrossed Productions, (www.scp-inc.biz) and also at www.amazon.com, www.bamm.com, www.barnesandnoble.com, and many others.